"DO YOU KNOW WHAT YOU DO TO ME, NORA?"

Sliding his hands into her tumbled hair, Paul turned Nora's face up to his and kissed her mouth until she was almost breathless, then pulled her down to the bed. Nora slipped her arms invitingly around his neck.

"I'll race you," Paul challenged her, grinning. "Last one undressed has to make love to the winner."

They scrambled up to throw their clothing aside. Nora slid under the covers first, laughing as Paul struggled with his riding boots.

"Damn it," he muttered, finally dislodging the stubborn boots and dispensing with the rest of his clothes.

"You lose," Nora cried, clapping her hands in delight.

"Oh, no, you're wrong, my love," Paul said as he joined her beneath the covers, his hands moving over her rounded hips and down her thighs. "I win."

ABOUT THE AUTHOR

Twenty-five years as an accounting manager might seem an unlikely background for a romance writer, but Sally Garrett has made the transition successfully. Sally always knew she wanted to be a writer, but it wasn't until her four sons were on their own that she had the chance to try–and she hasn't stopped since. *Northern Fires* is her third Superromance. After the acceptance of *Until Forever,* her first, Sally resigned from her accounting position in her native Arizona and headed north for Montana, where she now lives with her husband, Montie.

Books by Sally Garrett

HARLEQUIN SUPERROMANCE

90–UNTIL FOREVER
139–MOUNTAIN SKIES
173–NORTHERN FIRES

These books may be available at your local bookseller.

Don't miss any of our special offers. Write to us at the following address for information on our newest releases.

Harlequin Reader Service
P.O. Box 52040, Phoenix, AZ 85072-2040
Canadian address: P.O. Box 2800, Postal Station A, 5170 Yonge St., Willowdale, Ont. M2N 6J3

Sally Garrett

NORTHERN FIRES

Harlequin Books

TORONTO • NEW YORK • LONDON
AMSTERDAM • PARIS • SYDNEY • HAMBURG
STOCKHOLM • ATHENS • TOKYO • MILAN

My appreciation to Harve Wolfe, D.D.S.,
who gave me his time and knowledge
on the subject of
oral and maxillofacial surgery.

My special thanks
to all the ranch women in the area
who shared their experiences and feelings
as I gathered background material
for *Northern Fires*.

Published July 1985

First printing May 1985

ISBN 0-373-70173-X

Printed in Canada

To my husband, Montrose Everett Dingley.
He brings love, joy, happiness and companionship
to my life after so many years alone.

CHAPTER ONE

NORA LANE awoke with a start, alarmed to find herself in a strange motel room.

"Where am I?" she gasped, clutching her throat in a futile attempt to calm herself. She glanced down at her pink tricot nightgown, half expecting to see the erratic palpitations of her heart through the shiny material.

She dropped back to the pillow and waited for her pulse to slow down. The dream! It had become an almost nightly occurrence since the deaths of her husband and son.

"Oh, Jerry, why?" she murmured aloud to the empty room. Her psychiatrist, Dr. Daniel Taylor, had assured her that eventually the dreams would cease. *But when*, she wondered.

Salt Lake City! Now she remembered where she was. Salt Lake City, a city she knew only by the twinkling lights she'd seen as she had approached it through the darkness the previous night. She was here at her own insistence, along with Dr. Taylor's encouragement. As she lay in the bed she thought back to the day, several weeks earlier, when she'd made her decision.

She had gone to the psychiatrist's office for her regular appointment. Dr. Taylor had rubbed his chin thoughtfully as he studied her, then abruptly turned away and stared out the window of his fifth-floor office at the ships in the San Diego harbor.

"Nora," he said, returning his attention to her, "are you sure you want to do this? I know this has been a very trying time for you. Until now you've let your grief slowly engulf you. I've said many times that you must stop dwelling on the past, but this is a pretty drastic step, my dear. Are you sure?"

"Yes," she said, and her shoulders stiffened.

She was sitting on the sofa, her hands fidgeting in her lap. Her blond hair hung limply around her shoulders, its lack of sheen the result of the extreme weight loss she'd suffered since the tragedy.

"Did you bring the photo?" Dr. Taylor asked.

She nodded her head.

"May I see it?"

She shrugged, then opened her purse and withdrew a five-by-seven color portrait still in its gold frame.

"When was this taken?" he asked, reaching for the photograph.

"About a year ago," she replied.

The woman in the photo was strikingly attractive. Wavy hair the color of newly spun gold cascaded around her oval face. Her sparkling turquoise eyes declared her love for the dark-haired young man in the uniform of a U.S. Navy ensign and the smiling toddler in his arms.

"You were a handsome family," he murmured as he handed the photo back to Nora. "But they're gone. You have a lifetime ahead of you." He frowned down at her as he leaned against the corner of his desk. "How old are you, Nora?"

She stared at him for several seconds. "Twenty. . . I'll be twenty-one the first of October. Why?"

"My dear," Dr. Taylor said, smiling sympathetically, "you've done too much living in too short a time. Most people won't have your experiences in a lifetime. I know you're strong, or you wouldn't have been able to withstand what's been handed you. You can draw on that inner strength."

Nora's eyes avoided his.

"Tell me about your family," he suggested.

"My husband?"

"No, you've told me all about him. I mean your parents or your sisters or brothers."

"Oh," she sighed. "My father died several years ago. I was sixteen when my mother remarried. I didn't like my stepfather. I was seventeen and had just graduated from high school here in San Diego when I married Jerry. My mother and her new husband moved away. She promised to write, but she never did. I think she lives in Georgia somewhere, but I've lost touch with her."

Nora hesitated, then went on. "I have an older sister who's in the air force. She's stationed in Korea, and I used to hear from her once in a while. We're not very close anymore. She sent me a gift and note when Jeremy was born, but I haven't heard from her since then. She said she might be transferred to the Orient or to Guam. She's a linguist. I...I didn't want to burden her with my problems, so I didn't write when...when it...happened." Her eyes glistened, and her thoughts drifted.

"Nora?" Dr. Taylor called softly.

She didn't respond.

"Nora!" The sharpness in his tone brought a mild reaction from her. "Nora, please look at me. I want to help you."

She shifted her position on the sofa, tugging on the skirt of her beige dress and covering her knees. She was five foot seven and long-legged, but much too thin for her medium frame. The dull color of the dress detracted from her delicate features. Creamy skin stretched tautly over her cheekbones, accenting the slight slant to her eyes and the dark hollows beneath. There was a haunting beauty about her face, almost hidden beneath her sad expression.

"Nora!" Dr. Taylor said firmly, forcing her to look up at him.

"Yes, Dr. Taylor. I'm sorry, I was just thinking about...I'm sorry. I know I shouldn't..." She wiped her sweaty palms on the skirt of her dress. "You see, that's why I must move away."

"I understand. Still having the dream?"

She nodded. "Four times this week." The dreams were always the same. Her husband, Jerry, and her infant son were lying on a satin couch. Jeremy would giggle and smile at his father, and Jerry would pat his son's shoulder reassuringly. Nora would enter the room carrying a hammer and nails and with a stack of wooden planks under her arm. She would drop the pieces of lumber nearby and start to build a wall around the couch.

"No," Jerry would plead, but Nora would continue to hammer with an intense rhythm until finally the walls were completed. Immediately she would start on the top. "Please don't," Jerry would whisper as she finished nailing down all the boards but one. A tiny boy's fist would appear through the narrow slot. Nora would reach for the last board and, without another glance at the child's clutching fingers, take a full swing. She woke up just before the terrible impact of hammer, nail, board and hand.

"Sometimes it changes a little and it's me on the couch. I wish I could take a pill or drink something to keep it away, but you said..."

"That's right, my dear," the doctor replied. "Only time will make it disappear."

She nodded. "I bought a map of western United States. I've been studying it all week. I have it with me." She pulled the folded brochure from her purse. "Will you help me find somewhere different?"

"Of course, Nora." Dr. Taylor reached for her hand and helped her up from the sofa. Together they went to his desk. She spread the travel map across the desk top. He reached for a box of bulletin-board pins with large colorful plastic heads and selected one with a bright green head.

"I don't want to forget them, but I. . ." She pushed a section of hair away from her face. "Sometimes I feel as though I'm going crazy. I think I need to find a new life."

"You'll always remember your husband and son, but there might be a new husband and more children in your future. You have probably fifty years of living ahead of you."

He laughed good-heartedly at her surprised expression. "Actually I'm being conservative. Women have a life expectancy of seventy-eight years, young lady. You've used up only twenty of them. Do you want to spend fifty-eight years productively or despondently?"

"Oh, Dr. Taylor, I'm so tired of being depressed. I'll do anything to change, even move someplace new. My medical leave expires in two weeks." A tremor shook her slender form. "I can't bear the thought of going back to the bank."

"I understand," the doctor said. "You've been in treatment for six months and we've gone in circles. You should get away from the ocean, the sailors that constantly remind you of Jerry and your former life. You must, Nora, if you want to make a new life for yourself. You're young. You're very pretty when you don't bury yourself in these drab dresses. I know you're intelligent. The tests I've given you prove that. You can make the change if you set your mind to it. I'm glad this is your idea. Otherwise I would be forcing the change on you, and that wouldn't be right of me professionally."

She stepped closer. "May I have a pin?" Dr. Taylor dropped the bright green pin into her cupped palm.

"I don't know anywhere else," she murmured. "I was born here. I have my home, my job...but I did call a realtor about the house yesterday."

"Most towns have a bank. An experienced teller can get a job anywhere."

"I hope so."

He took a black felt marker and made a bold stroke about an inch inside the coastal boundary along the Pacific Ocean. "Away from the ocean," he cautioned.

Her thick lashes swept up to challenge his restriction, and Dr. Taylor's gray eyebrow arched in response.

"I do want to get better," she murmured.

Her eyes changed to a deep sea green mixed with blue as she glanced at the map. She closed her eyes and moved her hand in a circular motion several times before stabbing the pin through the map. "There!" she cried. Her eyes slowly opened. "Where is it?"

Their heads came together as they tried to read the names near the small pinprick in the map.

"Nowhere," she said as her fingers brushed the stiff crinkly paper.

"You're right," Dr. Taylor agreed. The pin had pierced a mountain range in the northern Rockies without a town or city nearby.

"It's not much like Southern California," she observed.

"I took my family to that part of the country once on vacation," Dr. Taylor said. "Marvelous country! Lots of wide open spaces and clean air...rivers and creeks, mountains and valleys." He chuckled. "More cattle and sheep than people. There must be some cities around." He ran his finger along the crest of the mountain range separating Idaho from Montana. "I believe this is part of the continental divide," he said, then followed the red line of the interstate highway up and down the map. "This is I-15. Here's Idaho Falls...and Helena...and Great Falls."

"I think I would prefer a smaller city than those," Nora said, surprising them both with her assertiveness.

"Why?"

"Sometimes I feel closed in here," she explained. "The freeways and all the cars, so many people around when I go to a shopping center. It never bothered me before, but sometimes I feel as though I'm going to suffocate if I don't get away."

The doctor began to retrace the red line. "Well, there's Monida, Dubois..." His finger moved north again. "I remember Lima and Dell. Dell has a wonderful little restaurant. It's a converted one-room schoolhouse. The food is served family style at harvest tables, and you sit with strangers who become your friends before the meal is over. The roast beef is unbelievable, better than any world-class chef could prepare."

Nora smiled. "You sound like the president of the local chamber of commerce. Maybe those places are too small to have a bank. I *do* need to find a job."

"You're right, my dear," he replied, and returned his attention to the map. "We'll try county seats. Let's see now. Here's one I know." His finger settled on a final selection. "Dillon, county seat of Beaverhead County. We spent a night there. How does that sound?"

He turned to Nora, who was standing tall and erect, the first true sign of confidence she'd displayed since she had become his patient. "It sounds like a good start," she said.

Impulsively the doctor hugged her. "Congratulations, Nora. You may have just found a new home. Now, when you come next week, I want you to tell me what you've learned about the area."

"But how?" she asked.

"The library, bookstores. You'll find a way."

She nodded. "I will. Dr. Taylor, do you think a person can get to like any place she finds herself in?"

"If she sets her mind to it," he replied. "Nora, you've had some almost unbearable problems to shoulder, but I have a good feeling about you. Call it my professional training or good old-fashioned human intuition, but I have a positive feeling about your future."

Now, as Nora left the bed and hurried to the motel room's small bathroom, she recalled what she had uncovered about the area of southwestern Montana that would be her new home. The community was a study in contradictions. It was a college town, but had a financial base in agriculture; the population numbered only a few thousand, but was outnumbered by tens of thousands of cattle and sheep; the people were conservative in their politics, but fiercely independent in their thinking. Living in this part of the country would be very different from her life in San Diego.

She would never forget Jerry or Jeremy, but they had been gone for fifteen months. In spite of her attempts to suppress it, a strangling sensation gripped Nora's throat.

Hurriedly she dressed in a comfortable pair of slacks and a knit top, a coordinated outfit in navy blue with a splash of red and white stars across the front. It had been the first outfit she'd purchased after making her decision to relocate. No more lifeless beige for her. She had thrown the ugly dress away, wondering why she had ever thought it attractive.

A short time later she left the motel and spotted a restaurant that belonged to a chain she was familiar with in San Diego. The summer air was already warming to the eighties, and vacationing families with children milled around the waiting area of the busy restaurant. Nora gave her name to the hostess and found a seat.

As she waited she spied a dark-haired preschooler who was holding his mother's hand. Restless, he began to tug for his freedom.

"No, Joseph, you must stay with me," his mother said in a stern voice as she gave a yank on his arm.

A fleeting image of her own lost son, his eyes sparkling with life, surfaced in Nora, but in the same moment the hostess appeared and called her name. Nora tore her eyes away from the precocious little boy and followed the woman to her table.

When her breakfast arrived, she concentrated on the scrambled eggs and toast, trying to calm her thoughts about what lay ahead. She had called a realty firm in Dillon, and a woman in the office had agreed to find her a small house or apartment to rent. A furnished two-bedroom older home was awaiting her arrival. Two months' rent and a cleaning deposit had already been made.

Nora took a final sip of coffee, slid a few coins under the saucer and left the booth. After paying the bill, she hurried outside to her car. As she studied the map lying in the passenger bucket seat, she thought of all she had left behind.

Her house in San Diego had sold in a surprisingly short time. The closing funds, along with the insurance settlement from the deaths of her loved ones, gave her a certain amount of financial independence, but she had invested most of the money in savings certificates. She'd kept only a few thousand dollars in traveler's checks to carry her until she found employment.

She had sold her furniture and packed her remaining possessions in a few cardboard boxes, which were neatly stored in the back of her car. There was nothing left in San Diego but memories.

With a grimace Nora turned the key in the ignition and was soon merging with the other cars along Interstate 15 on her way north.

DR. TAYLOR'S VOICE warmed Nora's spirit as she sat in her house on a cold November evening and gave him a detailed progress report since her arrival in town.

"I assume you're working," he said.

"Yes," she assured him. "Three days after I got here I found a job at the Stockmen's Bank. It's one of only two commercial banks in town. They'd just converted to an automated-teller system and needed someone with computer-terminal experience. That's the only kind of tellering I know!"

"I told you so," he said with a laugh. "And the people you work with?"

"They're very friendly, but..."

"Are you finding it difficult to mix with them?"

"Yes."

"Do they know about your background?"

"Just that I'm from San Diego."

"That's enough for now," he agreed. "You'll find a friend to confide in soon. That helps, Nora. Don't underestimate the value of new friends. Have you dated at all?"

"Twice."

"Have a good time?"

"No," she admitted. "The first was okay, but the second guy tried to...he seemed to think that buying me dinner entitled him to..."

"That's unfortunate," Dr. Taylor said, "but remember, there are lots of friendly people out in the world who want to be just that—friendly. I have a suggestion."

"What is it?"

"The Bible says in order to have friends, you must show yourself friendly, or something to that effect."

"I know," she said, mulling over his words.

"At least try."

"Perhaps...but it won't be easy."

"Do it anyway," he encouraged her. "This move was your idea and a damned good one, too. Now make the most of it and extend your own hand in friendship. The first time is the hardest."

Such an opportunity presented itself a month later. Most of the unmarried employees at the bank had fallen into the routine of arriving early and sharing a cup of coffee in the employees' lounge before starting to work. The weather outside was cold and blustery as Nora shed her coat and hurried to the large coffee urn to fill her mug.

"Good morning, Nora," a vivacious sandy-haired woman called, patting the empty chair beside her.

"Good morning, Leslie," Nora replied.

Leslie Coleman had gradually become Nora's friend.

They had met when Nora had first applied for employment at the bank. Leslie had taken her under her wing and shown her around the departments, introduced her to everyone and then insisted they have dinner together after Nora's first day of work. Leslie had bulldozed her way through Nora's reluctance to socialize and had coaxed her into movies, dinners and once to a play at the local college, but when she had suggested they visit the saloons in town, Nora had balked.

"We were discussing what to do about Christmas," Leslie explained, drawing Nora into the conversation. "You know how families can be. They ask why you haven't married, when you're going to make them grandparents and aunts and uncles." She tossed her shoulder-length permed hair. "They'd better be glad I haven't presented them with a bouncing bambino. I have no intention of tying myself down. The single life is too much fun. I swing to the beat of a steel guitar and shuffling cowboy boots." She stood up and gyrated her shapely hips to prove her point.

The others around the circular table laughed as Leslie dropped to her chair again.

"Seriously," a lean young man said, "we want to do something on Christmas Eve, but no one has the space."

"You're right, Jay," Leslie agreed. "And don't forget the noise. My straitlaced landlady would have a fit if I had a party. I can sneak in one guy at a time, but she watches me like a hawk. She knows mom and dad, and I think she gives them weekly reports on my conduct." Leslie arched an eyebrow at Jay and winked.

"So who's got the place?" Jay asked.

Several men and women shrugged, one by one eliminating their own places as possibilities.

Nora surveyed the faces around the table. "I guess that leaves me."

"Well, I'll be darned," Leslie cried. "Miss Cool and Reserved?"

Nora blushed. "You've been after me, Leslie. If you'll help me with the food and drinks, we can have it at my house."

Two young women from the loan department volunteered to coordinate a pot-luck dinner.

"I'll bring some booze," Jay offered, "and Luke and Emery owe me some favors. They'll help."

Soon the arrangements were made and the time agreed upon.

The operations officer stuck her head through the doorway. "The doors open in five minutes. Will there by any employees to service our customers?"

"Of course," Leslie assured her with a dazzling smile that brought a softening to the older woman's features. "You know you can always count on us," she added as the others scurried to their places.

THE PARTY WAS A SUCCESS. While Leslie coordinated a work detail for cleaning and tidying the house, Nora stood aside and watched. Some guests had brought dates, but most had come alone. Yet as they gathered their coats, a definite pairing revealed itself.

The courthouse clock several blocks away struck the midnight hour, and Christmas day was ushered in with kisses and embraces.

"This was fun," Leslie said. "Let's do something for New Year's. Not a party at someone's house, but out! The Matador and the Crystal are having live bands."

"Those are cowboy bars, Leslie," Jay said. "Do you think they would welcome us commercial types?"

"Of course." Leslie smiled. "Especially if we dress right. I know that none of us are from the ranches, but maybe if we wear high-crowned Western hats and the girls wear tight jeans, they'll forget our daytime professions and treat us like equals. Don't forget, I went to school with these boys."

"Who are the bands and where are they from?" someone lost in the crowd asked.

"The Balers from the Big Hole Basin and some new group from Butte," Leslie replied.

"How do you know so much about the saloon scene in town?" Jay asked.

"Sometimes I go there and pretend I'm one of them," Leslie explained as the men and women milled around sorting out hats, scarves and gloves. "I know quite a few of the guys from way back. They're really okay, not nearly as macho as their four-by-fours make them look. They're just country boys looking for fun and games."

"Do you give them fun and games?" Jay teased.

"That depends on what games they want to play," she replied. "So what if I do? The guys from the college are too intellectual for me. We're caught in the middle between the ivory towers and the cowboys. I happen to prefer the cowboys. They're so earthy!"

The sexual innuendos of the conversation sent a chill up Nora's spine as she observed the people gathered in the hallway. She knew very little about their life-styles and preferred to stay out of their plans. Most of them agreed to meet at the Matador no earlier than 9:00 P.M. on New Year's Eve. No one would miss her if she wasn't there.

Leslie lingered after the others left the house. Nora turned to her, curious about her reason for staying behind.

"Nora," Leslie said, "I want you to go with me to the Matador next week. You're too much of a loner. I think I have just the cure for your blues. I know some of the guys who hang out at the Matador. They're from the ranches south of town and some of them are real dolls."

Nora laughed. "The ranchers and cowboys I've seen around here have never impressed me as dolls, Leslie."

"Poor choice of words perhaps," Leslie conceded, smiling, "but this one particular guy is tall, dark and handsome. His name is—"

"Leslie, please," Nora interrupted. "I know you mean well, but I don't care about meeting men. I don't care if this mysterious cowboy is tall, dark and handsome. I'm not interested."

"But he's not just a cowboy, Nora. He's rich! He's in partnership with his father, and they own three big places. He's cute, too."

"I'm not interested in a cute guy or any other type," Nora replied.

"But this one is special. When he looks at you with those big brown eyes of his and smiles, you'll just flip!"

"Leslie, we're not teenagers. I'm twenty-one and you're twenty-four. Isn't it time we both acted like women and not girls? And just because you enjoy the bar scene doesn't make it right for me."

Leslie placed her small fists firmly on her hips. "Well, my dear Miss Lane, I'm going to change your mind. I've decided that your period of mourning, for whatever your problems might have been, is about to end. Seriously, will you give it a chance and come with me?"

"I'll think about it," Nora hedged.

"I won't leave until you promise me you'll at least give it a try. If you don't have fun after an hour, I'll excuse you for the night, but for heaven's sake, Nora, no one should spend New Year's Eve alone. That's a night for kissing and hugging, drinking and dancing. . ." She gave a sigh of anticipation.

"Oh, okay, Leslie," Nora agreed with a smile. "I'll give it a try—anything to get you out of here. But just for an hour."

"Good! Now I'll leave you and tramp through the snow to my cold lonely apartment and let my landlady know I'm home. See ya," she called, waving her fingers before disappearing into the snowy darkness.

CHAPTER TWO

NORA STARED AT THE CLOTHING scattered across her bed. Most of the items were unnecessary, impractical and, worst of all, terribly expensive.

She couldn't really blame Leslie for pressuring her. In the end it had been her own decision to spend most of her paycheck on this pile of clothing to be worn for her big night at the Matador.

She had peeked into a few of the saloons in town during the Labor Day weekend and still remembered her amazement at seeing every bar packed with cowboys and tourists, in town for the rodeo and county fair. The crowds were so large that they spilled past the sidewalks and into the streets. Country-Western music had blared from several of the saloons in a battle to capture the attention and money of the passing men and women, most of whom had a beer can clutched in one hand.

She wondered if the New Year's Eve celebration would be similar. Of course the several inches of snow that had fallen since Christmas might keep some of the cowboys snowbound if they lived in the more remote areas.

After finishing her shower and wrapping her shoulder-length hair in a turban, she splashed on a fragrant body cologne and followed with a liberal dusting of talc. She wondered if she was letting herself become caught up in the excitement. It had been a long time since she had taken any pleasure in her own appearance.

Since her arrival in the small town, she had regained some of her lost weight, and her body was rounded yet slender. Although her legs were long and shapely, there was no hint of coltishness in her movements. She smiled to herself, almost glad to be a woman tonight.

She slipped into new lacy blue panties and a matching bra, then reached for her Levi's. She had shied away from the more expensive designer jeans, thinking they would only confirm her urban-cowgirl status, and had washed the jeans she'd bought several times in an attempt to give them a worn look. Her Western-cut shirt had shades of turquoise and gold in an attractive plaid, and tapered seams accented her breasts. She grinned as she snapped the last pearl fastener and tucked the tails into her snug jeans.

She reached for the belt with the letters N-O-R-A stamped into the leather. A silver-dollar belt buckle shone up at her. "I've really gone off the deep end," she murmured, a wave of foolishness sweeping over her. "But why not?"

Guilt crept in as she buckled the belt. What right did she have to be enjoying herself after all the sadness her foolish actions in the past had brought? Dr. Taylor had tried to convince her that the fault had not been hers, but there must have been something she could have done to stop the sequence of events that had led to the loss of her loved ones.

She shook her head. Dr. Taylor was right, and it was good for her to have a night of fun, she thought. What could possibly happen? Shrugging, she reached for the new boots with fancy scroll stitching across the toes. They would probably leave her feet numb and blistered by the end of the evening.

She removed the towel and shook out her hair. Its

sheen was returning as her appetite improved. Using the blow dryer, she coaxed forth the natural curl, and soon her oval face was framed with cascading feathery waves. Her improved health had brought a glow to her complexion, and she decided to skip all makeup except for a touch of soft rose lip gloss.

She cast a critical eye toward her image in the full-length mirror. She had refused to buy a hat to complete her ensemble, and now she regretted that she had. Thinking of the cost of the hat she had admired plus the other clothing she had purchased, she wondered how cowboys could afford their outfits.

She quickened her movements. Leslie would be knocking on her door any moment. She reached for her new cranberry-colored quilted car coat and her purse. After removing a ten-dollar bill from her purse, she slid the purse into the top drawer of her dresser. She didn't intend to drink much, so the ten should be adequate for the night.

Leslie's knock sounded at the front door. Nora grabbed her key ring and flipped off the bedroom light, then detoured to the kitchen and turned on the light over the sink. The thought of coming home to a dark house was unsettling. She hated the darkness. The recurring dream, which had gradually diminished since her move to Dillon, had always been filled with darkness. She refused to let darkness or bad dreams spoil the evening ahead.

Leslie's knock sounded again as Nora raced through the living room and opened the door.

"Hello," she said breathlessly, pulling the door shut behind her.

"Well, it's about time." Leslie tossed her curly head. "I thought maybe you'd chickened out on me."

"I wouldn't do that," Nora replied. She quickly surveyed Leslie from the tip of her high-crowned black hat to the pointed toes of her black-and-silver snakeskin boots. "You look like a rodeo queen."

Leslie's short ski jacket hid none of her feminine charms. Although she was less than five feet two inches tall, her body was full breasted and rounded at the hips, and her tiny waist accented the curves.

"I always wanted to be a rodeo-queen contestant," Leslie said with a laugh, "but I never learned how to stay on a horse for more than a few minutes. Tonight," she announced, linking Nora's arm through hers, "I'm going to be the queen of the Matador."

Doubts and misgivings began to grow in Nora as she and Leslie approached the street in town famous for its drinking establishments. Bright neon signs fought with one another in a blatant attempt to lure potential customers.

"Leslie," Nora whispered near her friend's ear, "I don't think this is really my style of entertainment."

A middle-aged man lurched out of a nearby saloon door, smiled at the two unescorted women and tipped his hat.

"Howdy, ladies. Buy you a beer?"

"No thanks, honey," Leslie replied. "We're meeting our boyfriends at the Matador. Maybe next time. Bye now, darlin'." She winked at the man and waved him away with a flick of her hand, then tugged at Nora's coat sleeve and hurried her up the street.

"Now I *know* I don't belong here," Nora said. "What if that man had pushed himself on us? What if—"

"Don't be such a worrywart, Nora," Leslie admonished. "These guys usually don't get pushy. They know if you're not interested, the next woman they meet might be. Cowboys are born optimists."

She turned to look closely at Nora. "You're really frightened, aren't you?" she said, and grabbing the quilted sleeve of Nora's coat, she changed directions.

They entered the door of a corner café, empty except for a lone customer sipping a cup of coffee.

As Nora and Leslie slid into a booth, Nora glanced at the clock behind the coffee urn. It read nine forty-five. The blackness of the night lay like a coat of paint on the window of the café, reflecting the women's images and making them a foursome.

The waitress arrived carrying a coffee carafe and menus.

"Coffee, girls?" she asked.

"Yes," Leslie replied. "Just coffee."

The waitress poured their cups. "What are two pretty girls like you doing drinking coffee? You should be celebrating. Can't you hear the crowd down the street? Must be those cowboys at the Matador."

Nora's eyes narrowed with misgivings while Leslie's brightened with excitement.

"They really know how to liven up a place, don't they?" Leslie commented.

The waitress threw her head back and laughed. "They're a fine bunch of boys—hard workers and hard players. Just don't believe everything they say. They've worked around that bull manure so long they don't know when to stop slinging it themselves. I'll say one thing for them, though. They're the real things, not Hollywood film dudes who don't know one end of a horse from the other. When you need someone you can really depend on, they're the finest." She shook her bleached curls emphatically as she walked away.

"See?" Leslie said. "I told you they'd be lots of fun."

"I don't know," Nora replied.

"Don't you ever party?" Leslie asked.

"I don't think so."

"You don't think so? Don't you know? You come from San Diego and you're twenty-one and you don't know if you've partied before?"

Nora shook her head. "I married right out of high school."

"Married? You have a husband? I didn't know you were married." Leslie stirred the black coffee in her cup as she studied Nora's bowed head. "Divorced?"

"No."

"Still married?"

"No."

"Well, if you're not divorced and you're not still married, what happened to him? Was it annulled?"

"He...he was killed." Nora glanced up at her friend.

"Oh, God, Nora. I'm sorry. You never talk much about personal things. I just assumed at your age that you were single...not married...oh, Nora, I never thought about you being a widow. Widow—that sounds ancient. No one's a widow anymore unless she's old. If she's young, she's always divorced. I've just never known a twenty-one-year-old widow."

Leslie fidgeted in her seat.

"It's okay," Nora murmured. "It happened over a year and a half ago."

Suddenly Leslie plunked her elbows on the table and rested her chin in her cupped palms. "Geez, Nora, how did he get killed?"

A veil fell over Nora's features. "I...I don't want to talk about it."

"I understand," Leslie said. "I didn't mean to pry. Did you have kids? I guess not, you being so young and all."

"I had a son."

"A little boy? How neat! Where does he live? In San Diego...with relatives, I'll bet."

"He'd dead, too. He was killed with his...father." Nora looked up at her friend. "I think I should go home now. I tried, Leslie, really tried, but I wouldn't be much fun at a New Year's Eve party." She began to pull on her coat.

"No!"

Nora was surprised to see Leslie pulling on her own coat.

"That's right, I said, no way. What's done is done, the past is the past. This is New Year's Eve and that means a whole new year ahead of us. New hopes, new dreams. A chance to begin again. Oh, Nora, let's have some fun tonight. You've lost your family, but maybe you'll find someone new tonight who will..." Leslie waved her hand in the air. "I know, my friend, you've lost the most precious people in your life. I can't do anything to undo that. I'm not a magician. But please come to the Matador and try to enjoy yourself for a few hours. Look at the clock. It's almost ten already."

Nora's slender shoulders rose and fell without a word.

"Listen, do you want to ruin my reputation in this town?"

Nora's brows furrowed.

"I gave up several hot proposals in order to drag you to this place," Leslie explained. "I'll find me a man when we get there, but I certainly don't want them to think I couldn't get a date and had to come alone. You're holding my reputation in your hands."

Leslie's plea brought a slight smile from Nora. "Okay," she agreed, but she knew her heart wasn't in her decision.

"OH, GOOD GRIEF," Nora groaned as Leslie led her into the crowded bar. "Is there really room for two more people?"

"Of course," Leslie assured her.

"Over here," a male voice called to them from the smoke-filled recesses of the saloon.

They weaved their way through the crowd and slid into chairs that appeared from nowhere at a crowded table with two other women and three men, all dressed in Western clothing.

"Hey, Nora, glad to see you out," Jay Sloan said. Jay had asked Nora for a date once, but she had declined.

Nora nodded as he motioned her into a chair next to his.

Jay bought drinks for everyone at the table. When the band returned from its break, it began to play a country swing medley, and several couples moved to the dance floor. He glanced at Nora. "Want to dance?"

"No, thanks, I don't..."

He turned to Leslie, who accepted, and they disappeared into the crowd.

Nora wished desperately that she'd stayed at home. She searched and found an exit, but reaching it would involve running a gauntlet of undulating bodies, so she remained at the table.

The hands of the lighted wall clock passed slowly, over the painted can of Olympia beer. Leslie was seldom in her chair, accepting each new dance partner's offer with a smile and a wink. Jay and the others at the table rarely left the dance floor, leaving Nora alone.

She saw a man in the crowd who reminded her faintly of Jerry, but she refused to let memories of her husband and son influence her tonight. She straightened slightly as she walled herself away from the past. Something touched her elbow and she jumped.

"Dance?" a husky voice sounded through the smoky darkness.

She tried to ignore the man towering over her. "No thanks," she replied, reaching for her drink.

"You haven't danced once all evening," the hoarse voice challenged.

"That's my business," she said curtly, shrugging his hand from her elbow.

"Do you know how?"

She bristled. "That's no concern of yours." She moved her chair slightly and blocked his tall form from her view.

"I'll bet you don't," he said with a chuckle.

She felt an angry surge of tears, but banked them. He was right. Dancing was one of the social skills she had never taken time to learn. Jerry wasn't a dancer and... "How do you know I haven't danced all night?" The moment the words were uttered, she regretted them. He would probably take it as a suggestion that he join her.

A muscular arm covered in a black-and-rust plaid Western shirt appeared near her face. She froze. His hand moved to the closest chair, and she held her breath as he turned the chair to face her. She stared at his well-shaped fingers and noticed the veins on the back of his hand.

"Relax, pretty lady. You're more skittish than a young filly about to be halter broke," he said, lowering himself into the chair.

"That's a chauvinistic thing to say," she retorted indignantly. "I'm not some horse to be tamed!"

"Oh," he replied with a nod, then rubbed his chin thoughtfully. He grinned. "What are you?"

"A woman," she said, and the anger that had caused the outburst began to evaporate.

"I can tell that. I may be a chauvinist, but I can recognize someone special. You're probably the best-looking woman at the Matador tonight."

"Please, I don't. . ." She felt trapped against the wall, hemmed in by the large circular table and the man. Slowly she turned to confront this persistent intruder.

His eyes were hidden beneath the wide brim of his Western hat, but her breath caught in her throat when he smiled at her. His lips were full and sensual, yet his smile was not at all arrogant in spite of his determination to talk to her. The firm line of his jaw angled to a chin that she sensed could be stubborn. She knew he had shaved that evening, and she could detect a pine-scented aftershave lotion. Her lips softened into a smile as she unconsciously inhaled the man's scent. It had been such a long time since. . .

"You *do* know how to smile." He grinned. "I was wondering."

"Please go away," she said. "I've danced enough this evening."

"You're fibbing, pretty lady," he said, his smile replaced with a seriousness that alarmed her. "I know you haven't danced because I saw you come in the door with your friend, and I've been keeping an eye on you ever since. I like what I see." Reaching for her chin, he tilted her face toward the small light on the wall nearby. "You're beautiful. I've never seen you in here before. Are you new in town?"

Nora turned her head away from him. "Don't touch me," she said. She reached for her drink, her hand shaking a little, and found the glass empty.

He motioned for the bartender to bring them two more drinks. "It's on me," he said when she reached in her jeans pocket and withdrew the folded currency.

"But I. . ." She stopped when his closed mouth twisted into another grin. In the dim light his features were hard to see beneath the brim of his hat, but what she saw was very handsome. His dark hair was moderately curly and brushed the back of his shirt collar, and his cheeks were deeply tanned.

She hadn't intended to voice the question, and was surprised to hear herself ask, "Are you a cowboy?"

"Yup," he replied, and his dark eyes twinkled as he pushed back the brim of his hat, exposing a paler forehead. "Can you smile again?"

"When I choose to." She frowned back at him, feeling the heat of a blush on her cheeks.

"Prove it," he challenged.

"I. . .I don't feel. . ." She stammered for an excuse, but his persistent manner and his handsome grin melted her resolve. "I'm sorry," she said, a genuine smile lighting her face.

"That's better," he replied, studying her. "Your lips are the same color as the roses my mother babies each winter on the home place."

"Your mother?" she asked.

"Didn't you think I had one?"

"Yes, but. . ."

"Did you think I was hatched on a rock out in the sagebrush with only the coyotes and magpies for company?" he suggested, a devilish expression on his face.

"Of course not," she said, frowning. "You just don't strike me as the type who would talk about his mother, especially in a bar like this."

"Do you have a name, pretty lady?" he asked, then started to cough, covering his mouth with his hand.

"Are you sick?"

He shook his head. "No, just a trace of a flu bug. I won't give it to you if you're worried about your health. So, do you have a name?"

Nora grew more determined to keep the conversation brief. "Lane," she replied abruptly.

"Lane," he murmured, rolling the word around. "Sounds like a last name or a man's name. Lane... Lane. You don't look like a Lane, but I can get used to it."

Her skin tingled as he caressed a tiny scar on the back of her hand where it lay near their glasses. She stared at his manicured hand. She had expected dirty fingernails and... She pulled her hand away. "Please don't touch me."

The alcohol was beginning to dull her ability to think clearly. His eyes were dark and brown, but his features blurred as she tried to study them.

"I'd still like to dance with you," he said, shifting his chair and blocking the light behind him so that his face was thrown into shadows again.

"Don't you have other girlfriends to bother?" she asked.

"I left them at the other bars tonight. I must have known you'd be here." He reached for her hand again.

"I don't know how," she confessed.

"I'll teach you."

"I'm a very slow learner."

"I'm a good teacher. I taught my sisters how to dance." He pulled her from her chair, adjusted his hat back over his forehead and led her to the dance floor.

The music changed to a two-step. Nora trembled slightly as his arm slid around her waist, and she stepped on his boot toe.

"I told you I didn't know how."

"Like this, see?" he instructed, spinning her away but never releasing her completely. He tried to explain the foot movements to the dance step, then said, "Oh, hell, let's just do it close. I like it better that way." He pulled her closer in his arms as the beat of the music grew stronger.

Nora relaxed in his embrace, inhaling the pine scent once again. The first two snaps of his shirt were unfastened, allowing her to see a few inches of dark curling hair in the narrow V.

"Put your head on my shoulder," he coaxed, and she complied.

The mood of the guitars and drums blended with the euphoric warmth of his closeness. The drinks had relaxed her to the point of throwing her usual restraints away, and she began to move her feet in a coordinated pattern with his.

"Hook your thumb in my belt loop," he said, and she followed his suggestion.

She drew closer and was pleased when his arms tightened slightly. As her head lay on his shoulder, his mouth brushed her cheek. She felt his hip bone beneath her hand, and the sensation created brought forth feelings she had thought buried long ago. She tilted her head back and smiled, knowing that the effect of the alcohol was loosening her tongue. "I don't know why, but I like you, cowboy."

His face drew nearer, and his lips teased hers lightly as they continued to dance.

"I like you, too, pretty lady."

The endearment pleased her, and she forgot her earlier resolve to avoid any contact with the local cowboys.

Several drinks and dances later, he led her back to the abandoned table.

"Can I take you home?" he asked. "Or are you with anyone?"

"I walked. I live only a few blocks away from here." She tried to focus her attention on his dark features. "I came with a friend, but she's. . . disappeared," she told him as she scanned the crowd for Leslie.

"I'll walk you home and protect you from things that go bump in the night," he said. Nora nodded and they gathered their coats. "I came with my brother, but he's down the street. I'll leave a message with the bartender. Don't move. I'll be right back."

As he disappeared in the crowd, Leslie returned to the table. "Do you know who that is?" she asked breathlessly, clinging to Jay Sloan's arm.

"Just a cowboy," Nora replied. "He's walking me home."

"But he's the one who. . . oh, please don't leave yet. It's not midnight. Jay and I are going to the Bull Pen later and. . . oh, you know."

"You go ahead, Leslie," Nora said. "I'm tired and I think I've had too much to drink. My cowboy will walk me home. I'll be safe with him."

The tall man was at her side again with two more drinks. He nodded to Leslie and Jay as he handed one of the plastic glasses to Nora. We'll take them with us," he said as he steered her to the door, covering his mouth as he coughed again.

The night was moonless as they sipped their drinks and began to walk the few blocks to her house.

The cowboy was wearing a fleece-lined, thigh-length sheepskin coat with large patch pockets. When they had finished the drinks he tossed the ice cubes out and put the nested plastic glasses in one of the pockets, then reached for her gloved hand.

"Feeling fine?" his husky voice sounded through the darkness.

Nora laughed. "Maybe too fine. I think I'm drunk."

"Too drunk to walk? Maybe I'll carry you." Teasingly he pulled her against him.

She came willingly into his arms as they stopped by a tall silver spruce tree. "I can't see you," she said, and without thinking she pulled her gloves off and jammed them into his other pocket. She touched his cheek and firm chin, then traced his beard line and cheekbones up to the corners of his dark brows. "You have a nice face."

"Thank you," he whispered, allowing her fingers to have their way.

Her hands slid up to the curly hair at his temples, and she felt him exhale deeply. She pushed the hat back a few inches and admired the strength in his features. "You must work in the sun," she commented as her fingertips traced the fine creases that ran across his forehead. A few curly locks of hair had fallen down toward his brows, but his hat blocked her way when she tried to push them back into place. "I don't usually do things like this," she murmured.

The courthouse clock struck midnight, ushering in the new year as he drew her closer. "Happy New Year, lovely lady," he whispered near her ear. "I'm going to kiss you."

Her arms tightened around his neck as she submitted to the warm feelings welling up inside her. His arms held her safely, and his lips descended to hers, exploring every hidden crevice of her mouth.

"Oh, cowboy," she murmured between his kisses, "I like the way you kiss."

He groaned softly and cut off any further words. A fire began to smolder between them, and their breath made tiny clouds in the frigid night air.

She shivered. "It must be very cold."

"Well below freezing. If we keep kissing out here, our lips are apt to freeze together and they'll have to get the rescue squad to pull us apart." He laughed, pulling her closer again. "Is your place nearby?"

"Yes, just next door."

"Let's go inside and warm up. Okay?"

"Maybe, for a little while. . . I don't fool around."

"I understand," he said. "You're safe with me."

"Why is it so dark around here?" she asked herself aloud. "There's usually a streetlight down at the corner. It's off." She shivered. "I hope we haven't had another power failure. I don't like the dark." She moved into his embrace again.

"I'll stay with you if you want," he suggested.

"Oh, no, I didn't mean anything like that," she replied quickly.

"I'll just stay long enough to check the electricity for you."

"Okay, cowboy, I live here," she said as she turned in to a small yard and walked toward a white house with a screened-in porch.

A wave of dizzy contentment hit her as she searched for her key in her jeans pocket. When she had finally pulled out the ring she tried to find the keyhole in the darkness.

He offered to help, and she gratefully handed the key ring to him. After unlocking the door, he pushed it open, and they stepped inside. The warmth of the gas furnace brought a rush of heat to her flushed face. Reaching for the living-room light switch, she flicked it up and down several times, but nothing happened.

Panic struck as she stepped farther into the dark room and lost her bearings. Reaching out, she touched a solid wall, and immediately the terrifying sensation of being trapped in a closed coffin seized her.

A sudden memory filled her fuzzy mind, and she imagined that her husband, Jerry, and their infant son were standing within a few feet of her. She held out her hand to them, and in a rain of exploding bullets and a blinding flash of light she saw them fall and disappear. Then the room was dark again.

She saw a dark shadow move nearby and exhaled a sigh of relief. Only the friendly cowboy was with her now. He cared. She reached out to him.

"Help me," she called. "I can't be alone."

"Here I am," his voice sounded through the darkness. "Just stand still. I can see you."

"Where are you?" Her voice quavered with near panic.

"I'm coming for you, honey."

"I don't want to be alone," she cried. Her trembling changed to longing when he touched her. She threw herself in his arms and felt her panic and loneliness wash away. "Stay with me for a while," she pleaded.

"Of course," he said. His hands caressed her cheeks, then slid into her feathered hair. "I'll stay until you're all right." His mouth came down and captured her parted lips. As his kiss deepened, it fueled the fire in her.

"I'm still drunk," she murmured.

"You're beautiful," he whispered.

Her knees buckled. Lifting her in his arms, he carried her through the dark hallway and found the bedroom. When he had felt his way to the bed, he set her down.

Her thumb caught one of his belt loops before he could leave. "Stay with me," she pleaded again. "I don't want to be alone, not tonight. Don't leave me alone."

He joined her on the bed, his long legs brushing against hers. "I'll stay," he promised, and as his lips found hers, she clung to him.

CHAPTER THREE

THE MAN LAY MOTIONLESS, troubled about the young woman asleep beside him. He had taken unfair advantage of her, and that knowledge plagued him as he lay awake, staring into the darkness of her bedroom.

The electricity was working again. She must have left a lamp on somewhere in the house, he decided, because a soft beam of light now drifted down the hallway.

Cautiously he slid from the comfortable double bed, gathered his clothing, which had been strewn around the room, and dressed.

The woman turned in her sleep, curled her body a little, and slid a hand to the pillow where his head had made a deep impression. Her golden hair fell over her cheek as she nestled deeper beneath the warm blankets. Watching her, he felt torn. One part of him wanted to rejoin her and watch her wake up, yet he knew he would be wise to leave her without strings or other encumbrances. He had no idea how she would react if she awoke and found him still there.

He had been attracted to her when she had first entered the Matador. She was different from most of the young women he had seen there. As he had continued to observe her, he sensed a vulnerable quality about her that had drawn him closer to her as the minutes ticked away. Finally he had approached her as she sat alone at the table. She had insisted that she did not fool around, and in spite of what had happened, he believed her.

When he had undressed her and they had embraced, her warm naked body had arched against him, responding with a desperate need to be loved. He frowned as he recalled that once she had called him Jerry. Who was Jerry? Probably some former lover who had jilted her. Yet afterward she had lain in his arms and cried bitter torment, and he had consoled her, reassuring her that she would be all right, and later he had made love to her again. The bedroom had been dark and he had been unable to see the expressions on her face, but once he had sensed a smile on her lips just before he kissed her. He could still remember the plum fragrance of her hair when he had buried his face in its luxuriant thickness.

But he had his own responsibilities, and involvement with a woman was not part of his plans—not now, anyway. Perhaps later in the spring he could find time. Leslie Coleman had been with the group at her table. Maybe Leslie could tell him more about her. He had known Leslie for years. No, the timing was not right. He didn't need complications in his life at the moment.

He grabbed his heavy coat and left the bedroom, scanning the layout of the rest of the house as he headed toward the front door. Too bad he would probably never be back, he thought. It might be enjoyable to come again for dinner or drinks or... *Forget it,* he thought. She would be too much trouble. He had enough problems of his own with his father and the three ranches they operated in the area. Still, he would call Leslie when he had a break in his heavy schedule.

He buttoned his long coat against the freezing weather and slipped quietly out the front door, being careful to lock it as he left. He didn't want anyone else walking in on her.

He hurried back toward the street in town with all the saloons, now quiet in the predawn, and entered the all-night café on the corner.

A tall, thin older man ambled to his table, poured him a cup of coffee without asking and plopped a stained menu in front of him.

"Hello, Paul," the waiter said. "It's all of 6:00 A.M. How come you aren't having breakfast at home? Recovering from a big night?"

"Sort of," Paul mumbled.

The waiter chuckled. "All's well that ends well," he said, slapping the young man on his broad shoulders.

"Yeah," Paul replied, but things had not ended well. A heavy frown settled on his lean features. An image of the blond woman named Lane intruded as he reached for the mug. He took a sip of hot coffee and burned his tongue. "Damn it!" he muttered, then pushed thoughts of the woman from his mind and ordered breakfast.

His throat was still sore from the influenza he had had the past week. Perhaps he should avoid the town's night life and get over the lingering effects of the infection. Maybe he would volunteer to check the more remote areas of the family property. His father had been complaining that some of the stock was missing. He said the fall roundup had been conducted in a sloppy manner, and if the cattle were lost during the cold weather, profits would be cut. Paul had argued that the missing stock was probably an error in the books, but his father had remained convinced. Besides, if he stayed away for a while, maybe Lane would be more receptive when he returned.

He grimaced. He was taking a lot for granted, thinking she would ever want to see him again after what he had done.

As he finished the steak and eggs placed before him, he couldn't stop thinking of the sleeping woman he had left behind. He had known her for only a few hours, yet already she had become an obsession. He had to get himself under control. He tossed down a generous tip, paid his bill and went to the pay telephone outside the café.

He dialed the home ranch and waited impatiently for someone to answer. He hoped it wasn't his ill-tempered father. Paul was the eldest of four sons, and his father was constantly making unreasonable demands of him. Their often-stormy relationship threatened to disrupt the family's harmony. Paul had vowed months before that his mother would never have to choose between her husband and her firstborn son. He had made the decision after a heated argument with his father, during which his mother had tried to separate them. Paul had spun her away just as his father had taken a swing at him. His father's fist had missed his mother by inches. The scuffle had sobered them all.

The phone was picked up at the ranch.

"Hello," a woman's voice said.

"Hi, mom."

"Oh, Paul, where are you? Are you all right? I was so worried."

"Easy, mom. Of course I'm okay. I'm a big guy now, remember?" he teased.

"I know, but you're still my son, Paul. I reserve the right to worry." Several seconds passed, and he heard a deep sigh on the other end of the line. "Paul, where are you? I was afraid this call might be from the sheriff. Are you okay? Did you have a good time last night?"

"Sure, mom, a fine time. But now I'm stuck in town without transportation. Steven drove my truck home, so I need a ride. Is he there? Can you get him?"

"He came in early this morning," his mother said. "Your dad was furious, but Steven was too tired to argue and went to his room. I'll get him. Do you want me to come?"

"No, mom. Dad would be more of a tyrant than usual if you did that. Just get Steven, please. I love you, mom."

He waited, feeling a little manipulative. His mother was one of the sweetest, most generous women he had ever known, but she was not very objective where her sons and daughters were concerned.

A few moments later his mother returned to the phone. "Steven says he will be there just as soon as he can. He said he would meet you in front of the Matador. Oh, Paul, you and Steven should stop going to the Matador. It's not the kind of place my sons should patronize."

"No lectures, mom. Not this morning. I have enough to think about. . . I'm sorry, mom. Listen, I'll see you in a few hours. Bye now."

An hour later Paul sat slumped in the passenger side of his own late-model, gold-and-brown, four-wheel-drive pickup.

"Damn it, I'm tired," he groaned.

His younger brother chuckled. "I saw you walking away from the Matador with some sexy-looking blonde and figured you were set for the night. Hey, thanks for loaning me your truck."

"It was a big mistake," Paul said.

"The blonde or loaning me your truck?"

"Both," Paul replied as he stretched his long legs and

settled deeper into the seat. "Steven, you're my favorite brother, you know that, but you're always bumming vehicles, especially my truck. Why don't you get your own?"

Steven laughed. "For one thing, I don't have the money. For another, I'm always running errands for you. And for a third, I didn't bum your truck last night. You gave me the keys early in the evening and told me to keep an eye on it. The bartender told me you were busy for the night and for me to do whatever I wanted to. All the good-looking girls were spoken for, so I went home. Don't tell anyone. Mary and Tim both think I'm the Casanova of the bar scene and I wouldn't want to disillusion them. Mary expects me to kill myself some night coming home." Suddenly he looked very serious. "I keep expecting her to snitch on me about some of the things she's heard, but she hasn't."

"Maybe she just cares about you," Paul mumbled.

"That shrimp of a sister? Doubtful, very doubtful," he muttered, and concentrated on his driving.

Paul rubbed his temples, trying to relieve the headache that had started after he had returned to the café to wait for his brother. He didn't want to hear about sibling rivalry. He had other matters to think about. With each refill of coffee, the image of the woman with hair like fresh honey grew stronger. Was she awake? Would she want to see him again? Or would she twist their night together and accuse him of forcing her? What the hell was a man to do in these confusing days of liberated women? Just when he thought he had them all figured out, he ran into one like Lane, who didn't fit the mold. Ranch girls and women were supposed to be treated with respect, but women who frequented places like the Matador were fair game for cowboys out on the town.

"What's the matter, big brother? Wouldn't she cooperate?" Steven asked.

Paul frowned at his brother. "It wasn't like that. She was willing...only..."

"What do you mean by 'willing...only'? Did she start out willing and then change her mind? Losing your touch, Paul? I thought you prided yourself on sweet-talking any girl."

"Watch it, Steven," Paul cautioned. "She's no girl, she's a woman. She's different...just different." He straightened his legs and flexed his shoulders. "I think Leslie Coleman knows her. She said her name was Lane, but I don't think that matched the name on her belt." He sneezed, and a fit of coughing shook him.

"Having a relapse?" Steven asked.

"I think I'll stay at the home place for a few weeks," Paul said, closing his burning eyes as the sun spilled its rays over the mountains to the east.

The truck left the pavement and bounced onto a gravel road that wound around the foothills south of town. "I feel lousy," Paul mumbled. "Maybe I need a shot."

"Didn't you have enough of those last night?" Steven asked with a chuckle.

"I mean medicine. I really feel rotten...like I've got the flu again," Paul grumbled. "I thought we Russells were invincible, but I sure don't feel that way this morning. If it weren't a holiday, I'd stop by Dr. Morrison's office and talk that cute receptionist into letting me see good old Doc M." He slid back down in the seat and pulled his fleecy collar up around his neck. "When I get over this damned flu, I'll call Leslie and find out more about her. I'll bet you a drink at the Matador her name isn't Lane."

"You sound too confident," his brother replied. "She must have made an impression on you. Don't forget your motto of loving and leaving."

"A guy can always change," Paul said, then coughed again. "I'm going to catch a few winks. Wake me when we get home."

Within minutes he was asleep, his lightly cleft chin bouncing occasionally against his chest.

The maroon finger of a woman's knitted glove dangled from Paul's coat pocket, and Steven couldn't resist the urge to ease the entire glove out. "The latest style in cowboy hand gear, big brother? Not your type at all." He glanced at Paul as the rising sun brought out the bronze highlights in his brother's hair. "Paul, where's your hat?" Steven asked, but his query fell on sleeping ears.

NORA AWOKE shortly after noon. She felt drugged, and every muscle in her body was stiff. Cautiously she opened her eyes, squinting as she surveyed her bedroom. She suspected she was about to learn first-hand what a hangover felt like. Other than an occasional glass of wine with Jerry, she had consumed very little alcohol and never hard liquor. . . until last night.

Last night. For a few moments she couldn't remember anything about the evening from the time she arrived at the Matador with Leslie. Her eyes fell on her flannel pajamas still hanging on the hook near her closet, and her hand slid to the soft skin of her stomach. She'd never slept naked, not even when she'd been with Jerry. She rolled onto her stomach and propped herself up on her elbows, holding her pounding head in her hands. An unfamiliar scent wafted through the air. Drawn to the pillow beside her, she leaned down to sniff the pillowcase. A man's after-shave cologne or... She fell back onto her pillow as fleeting scenes of the previous night materialized. Had she allowed a man to come home with her? Who was he? Surely she had not been so wanton as to invite a total stranger into her bed. She had been with one man in her life, only one, her husband. Had she been disloyal to his memory in a night of passion she couldn't even remember?

Blurry images of a dark stranger filled her mind. Who was he? Had he touched her intimately? Had she responded? A moan of disbelief sounded in the quiet bedroom. Surely it was all a bad dream.

She hurried to her closet to get her worn blue robe, a gift from Jerry when she had given birth to their son. She wrapped the soft material around her and tied the frayed belt, then wilted into a nearby chair. If her suspicions were true, she had made a mockery not only of her marriage but of every rule of personal conduct she had ever lived by.

Her bare foot touched something on the floor, and she bent to retrieve it. It was a plastic cocktail glass, lying on its side near her chair. She dropped the glass as though it were molten rock, and as it hit the bare floor, it bounced. Her knees were wobbly as she tiptoed past the glass, then ran back to her bed.

Perhaps she had brought the glass home herself, but in a flash she recalled a tall man dropping two glasses into his coat pocket seconds before she stepped into his embrace.

All her fears came crashing down on her, and she began to tremble. When her body finally stopped its convulsive shaking and she sank into slumber, only one question remained. Who was he?

NORA AWOKE with troubled thoughts of Jerry. If she hadn't called to him, the evil men would never have noticed him. But why had Jerry come for her that fateful day? Why had he brought their son? Any other moment in time and they would both be with her now. All this while she had thought the fault was hers, but no, Jerry should not have been there at all. His unexpected appearance had changed everything. She could no longer blame herself.

Now she lay there alone, with only the dim memories of a handsome man in the night who had shown her she could still feel and touch and respond. But he had left her without a word.

Again she caught a lingering trace of after-shave. Her fingers touched the pillow where he had left his mark.

Had she finally made a break with her past by allowing this stranger into her life? As she accepted his existence, a certain peace came to her in the shadowy bedroom. She thought of her husband and son, and after twenty-one months of denial and guilt, she accepted the reality of their loss. The edges of their images softened, slipping slightly out of focus.

It was midafternoon by the time Nora left her bed and dressed. She peeked out the living-room window and decided on a walk, but when she searched for her gloves, she couldn't find them. She was determined to go, anyway. Snow flurries were dancing across the sidewalk as she set out, her fleece-lined hood pulled snugly around her face and her hands jammed deep in her pockets.

Rumblings in her stomach reminded her of how long it had been since her last meal. She couldn't stop in the corner café near the Matador. What if *he* was there? She had to pass the Matador on her way north to a fast-food restaurant, but she crossed to the opposite side of the street. Still, she couldn't resist an urge to glance inside as a man walked out of the saloon. No music came from the interior, and she saw only a few lone men sitting on the high bar stools.

The new year was quiet, the town deserted, as though the previous night's celebration had taken place aeons ago.

WHEN THE BANK REOPENED after the holiday, business was brisk. Leslie had been called into duty as a secretary for the loan department, so Nora was spared questions about the Matador.

That afternoon, she began to cough, and by nightfall she felt feverish. The following morning she called in sick and was unable to return to work until four days later.

She had been back at work several days when she realized she had been scrutinizing each man who entered the bank. She knew her mysterious cowboy was dark, so she quickly eliminated the blond and redheaded men. He was rather young, so dark-haired men with traces of gray were discounted. As she studied the taller than average male customers currently conducting their banking business at other teller windows, she realized she wasn't sure if she would even recognize him. One possible subject shifted position to her window, and her heart quickened when he smiled at her.

"Are you all right, miss?" he asked as she continued to stare at him.

"Oh, I'm sorry, I..." she stammered. "May I help you?" She regained her composure when she saw that he was depositing a payroll check from the local college. Her man was from a ranch. He had talked about calving and fillies and made a comment about being hatched on a rock amid the sagebrush.

Smiling absently, she counted the customer's cash back to him from his deposit. If only she had met the man under different circumstances... But considering what had happened between them, she knew she could never face him again.

A few weeks later, Nora was surprised by a small year-end bonus check given to each employee by the bank's board of directors.

"For all your long hours and hard work during our recent computer conversion," the bank president explained to the staff. "Enjoy it. Buy yourselves something special."

During her lunch hour Nora visited the nearest department store. She knew what she'd been searching for when she spotted a navy blue brushed velvet robe. Fleece-lined, ankle-high white slippers and a pair of white satin pajamas trimmed with navy piping completed her purchases. The frigid nights had chilled her since New Year's, yet wearing the tattered blue robe from her past had depressed her.

That evening after work she removed the old blue robe from its hanger, folded and put it in a box, then placed the box on a high shelf in her closet. Her eyes burned as she closed the closet door; she was saying goodbye to a special part of her life. Pushing the momentary depression aside, she plunged into some much-needed housecleaning.

The bedroom floor was covered in harsh black-and-white vinyl tile in a checkerboard design Nora disliked. She had purchased several small throw rugs, placing them strategically so she could maneuver from her bed to the bathroom down the hall without touching the cold floor when she was barefoot.

Gathering up the rugs, she dropped them near her kitchen door, planning to take them to the all-night Laundromat later in the evening. If she hurried, she could mop and wax the bedroom floor, then let it dry while she did the laundry. She hadn't given the room a good cleaning since that fateful night at year's end.

She vacuumed the uncluttered half of the room, then reached for the bedpost to pull the bed away from the wall into the clean part of the room. The bed was heavy, and she pulled and tugged on the posts until it finally moved.

"What a terrible housekeeper I've become," she groaned, seeing the lint and dust beneath the bed. Picking up a collection of lint with her index finger, she playfully blew it into the air. Thank goodness no one shared the house with her, she thought, then frowned. She had always taken special pride in keeping the home she shared with Jerry meticulously clean, but housekeeping didn't seem so important anymore.

She shoved the bed farther into the middle of the room, and in the process her toe touched something hidden underneath. She wondered what it could be. She wasn't in the habit of kicking things under the bed.

Lowering herself to her knees, she reached her arm out and touched a. . .hat? As it came into full view, she gasped. It was a man's Western hat, chocolate brown in color, with two quail feathers stuck in its snakeskin band.

"Oh, no, please, Lord, no. . .it can't be," she whispered as she stood up and dropped to the bed, the hat in her lap. She touched the two feathers, and his handsome face flashed momentarily in her mind.

"My cowboy," she murmured. A collection of tiny hat pins decorated the front of the hat. A bucking horse, a bull's head with the inscription First Place beneath the animal's jowl, a pin with the letters FFA, another with PRCA, and a bucking horse and rider. Several other pins with animals, cowboys and basketballs were neatly attached to the brown felt in a straight line above the snakeskin band. Care had been taken in the arrangement of the pins, and she sensed that each had its own story. This man was no ordinary field hand, no itinerant cowboy satisfied with seasonal work.

She recalled the fleece-lined coat he had worn and, pulling together all her mental resources, tried to form his picture. His eyes had been shielded by the brim of his hat until he had pushed the hat back, and the wall light in the saloon had shown them to be a vibrant brown.

She had put her head on his shoulder, so he must be more than six feet, but with the hat and boots adding several inches she could not be sure. She knew he was slim hipped, because she had held on to his jeans when they had danced, and later she had felt his bare skin when... her thoughts reeled with the vividness of her recollection.

She fell back onto the bed, pulling the hat to her stomach. His shoulders were broad and muscular, of that she had no doubt, but it was the contours of his face that burned strongest in her memory. She would never forget the shape of his chin, the creases on his forehead, his strong jawline....

What if he came looking for his hat? No, she would never see him again. A forlorn smile drifted across her lips. He had left her two reminders of his stay: the flu and his hat.

Pushing him out of her thoughts, she got up from the bed and prepared to do her laundry, but later, as she sat in the Laundromat and tried to concentrate on the magazine in her lap, she thought of him again.

As she stared at the window of the machine directly in front of her, she began tapping her foot in time to the splashing suds, until she realized that in her mind she was dancing with him again.

CHAPTER FOUR

NORA GLANCED UP from her teller's window and saw one of her regular customers enter the bank. Mary Russell was a high-school senior who came every Friday afternoon to make deposits to a savings account. The petite teenager stopped at the customer-service desk and prepared a deposit slip, then approached Nora's window.

"Hello, Mary," Nora said.

The girl pushed her transaction slip toward Nora. "How are you today, Nora?"

"So-so," Nora replied. Ordinarily she kept her feelings to herself, but over the past few weeks an unusual weariness had sapped her strength, and the sincerity in Mary's voice touched her.

"You look a little tired," Mary said.

Nora processed the transaction through her terminal and returned the receipt to Mary. "Just a little down. I guess I'm tired of eating alone and doing nothing but read and watch television week after week."

"Don't you ever date?" Mary asked.

"Not much," Nora murmured. "I'm not very sociable. Most guys don't ask a second time."

"But you're so attractive. I would think you would have lots of offers. No special person among the men you've met since you moved here?"

Nora thought of her cowboy. "One might have been if things had been different," she replied, tilting her head thoughtfully. "No, I can truthfully say there's no one special." She sighed. "I wish there were at times like this."

Mary smiled, her brown eyes sparkling as Nora handed her back her bankbook and she admired the growing balance in her savings account. She dropped the book into her blue-and-gold athletic bag but didn't move away from the window. "When do you get off?" she asked.

Nora told her the bank's closing time. "If we balance," she added, crossing her fingers.

"I have a solution for you, Nora. Have dinner at the Beaver Slide with my sister and me and my four brothers," Mary said. "The Beaver has the best hamburgers in town. Then go with us to the basketball play-off game at the high school."

"I've never been there before," Nora said, recalling the fast-food restaurant on the north edge of town, which was the favorite hangout of teenagers in the area. "Your sister and brothers?"

"Yes," Mary said. "My sister is baby-sitting for a friend in town. I have to cheer and Tim plays guard, but you could sit with my other brothers. Would you join us?"

"Your brothers? I don't know," Nora said. "I'm a little old for high-school sports."

"Oh, no! Only Tim is still in high school," Mary explained. "The others are all older. Tonight during halftime the school honors all the former players, and that includes my three older brothers. How old are you?"

"Twenty-one," Nora replied.

"There, you see? Two of my brothers are older than you, so you won't feel like you're with a group of little boys." She laughed. "Although at times they act like little boys. Please join us. It'll be fun," she persisted.

"Are you sure I wouldn't be an intrusion?"

"Of course not. You'll make the evening more enjoyable for all of us," Mary assured her. "The girls are always flocking around my brothers. I guess they're actually pretty good-looking, even if they are my brothers. The older they get, the nicer they become, except for Steven. He's two years older than I am, and we've never gotten along very well. Personality clash, I guess."

Nora shrugged. "Oh, why not. It does sound better than what I had planned... watching a movie on TV."

"Great," Mary exclaimed. "I think they'll really like you. Girls are always calling them, but they're becoming confirmed bachelors. I guess they have too much fun to get serious. You'll like them."

"Where shall I meet you?" Nora asked.

"We're meeting at a friend's house where Lisa is babysitting. My oldest brother is bringing everyone in from the ranch after work is done. We're meeting about six." She jotted the address down on a piece of paper and handed it to Nora. "See you later."

The next customer, a disgruntled white-haired man, mumbled about the bank's poor service as he stepped up to Nora's window, but Nora only smiled.

After he left, she looked up to see the bank's doors being locked by one of the vice-presidents. She began to count her cash drawer, breathing a sigh of relief when it tallied to her control total. After taking her drawer to the vault and signing it in, she left, calling good-night to the other employees.

The town was so small that Nora seldom drove her car anymore. The evening sky was clear. Only a few patches of ice and snow remained from the storm earlier that week. Pulling the fleecy collar of her coat up around her neck, she quickly walked the few blocks to her small green-and-white house.

A strange sense of anticipation stirred her as she unlocked the front door. This social engagement could hardly be considered a date, yet she wanted to look her best. What did people wear to a basketball game? She couldn't remember, so she selected a pair of jeans and a violet bulky-knit turtleneck that would highlight her blond hair.

As she brushed her hair, she leaned closer to the mirror. The dark circles that had become pronounced during her bout with the flu had disappeared. She still looked a little pale, but it was probably from the upset stomach she had had with the flu. She needed to touch base with the medical clinic in town soon.

She frowned and picked up her curling iron. Dr. Taylor had suggested she get to know a physician in town and tell him or her of her former psychiatric treatment, just in case she had a problem with depression that might be more than she could handle alone.

She was still a little too thin, and at times she resented the tendency of others to express concern for her. She knew she looked younger than she was, and though she would no doubt appreciate this in years to come, she found the innocence people naturally assumed about her could be a burden. One of her boyfriends in high school had nicknamed her Angel, a name that had stuck throughout her junior year until she had met Jerry.

"Jerry," she murmured. Her life with him had ended so long ago. She glanced at a wall calendar. It would be two years next month, two years of hell. But no more. She had mourned enough.

Tonight she planned to have fun, an innocent good time with new friends from the area; no bars, no drinking, no dark handsome cowboy to lure her with suggestive hints of seduction and hot kisses of desire. Not tonight!

She touched her lips with the slender tube of pink lipstick, drawing it back and forth across her lower lip. Thoughts of his mouth on hers intruded, and she quickly slid the cover on the tube and tossed it down on her dresser. Not tonight!

She cut through the alley toward the address, which was only a few blocks away. Darkness had fallen, and the rapidly cooling air made her shiver in her lightweight ski jacket.

As she approached her destination, a brown-and-gold pickup pulled to the curb a few houses ahead of her, its tires squealing slightly. Three dark-haired young men bounded from the back. A tall, slender, fair-haired girl alighted from the passenger side of the cab at the same time another man sauntered from the driver's side. Something about the swing of his denim-clad hips pricked Nora's recall.

A door banged, and Mary Russell hurried down the steps of the porch to meet them. She waved to Nora as Nora reached the gate. Three of the brothers turned to her, but the driver of the truck remained with his back to Nora as he chatted with the tall blond man who had also come from the house.

Nora knew she was being scrutinized. She was taller than average, but suddenly she felt dwarfed as Mary's brothers surrounded her and Mary began the introductions.

"This is Nora Lane," Mary said. "She moved here last summer and works at the bank, so be nice to her. Nora, this is my younger sister, Lisa. She's an eighth grader. This is Tim. He's a sophomore and on the varsity team."

Nora focused her attention on a slender, dark-haired teenager who was mostly long arms and legs. He smiled bashfully as he shook her hand.

"This is Steven," Mary continued. "You'd better watch him. He thinks he's a real lady killer. . . and some of my friends agree. He and I don't get along very well, but you might find him entertaining." The man she introduced was a hazel-eyed, huskier version of his younger brother. Steven gave Nora a charming smile, holding her hand overly long as he shook it.

"This is Russ, Jr. He probably won't say a word all evening, but he's the only true gentleman in the lot." Mary smiled with affection as she motioned to a stocky young man a few inches shorter than the others.

The blond man approached, carrying a little girl in his arms. As he drew near, Nora noticed the prosthesis he wore on his left arm.

Mary continued her introductions. "This is D. A. McCormack and his daughter, Annie. Lisa is baby-sitting Annie later this evening." Although she had finished speaking, Mary's eyes lingered on the man and child until Steven gave her a nudge and she blushed.

"And this is my oldest brother, Paul," she said hurriedly. "Paul, please turn around and meet my friend from town. You promised."

Slowly, as though she was reliving a nightmare, Nora recognized him. His dark curly hair had been trimmed short at his nape in a conservative cut worn by most of the men in the area, and on his head he wore a baseball cap with the letters MSU on the front. As he caught her gaze, Nora felt herself melt.

He opened his mouth to speak, then abruptly changed his mind.

"Paul, don't look so serious," Mary scolded as she

completed the introductions. "He's the old man in the group," she told Nora.

Paul's eyes pierced Nora's, and his brows came down in a heavy scowl. Any doubt as to his identity dissolved as she stared into his brown eyes, and she fought to maintain control, not knowing if he recognized her.

As she extended her hand, his frown eased slightly. "Hello, Paul," she whispered. She wanted to turn and race back to her house, but his hand gripped hers tightly.

"What did Mary say your name was?" he asked as he stared at her. He was several inches taller than she was, and Nora had to tilt her head as he stepped closer, still holding her hand.

"Nora Lane," she replied almost inaudibly.

"That's a pretty name...it fits." His voice softened. "I knew it couldn't be just Lane."

Memories of the night they had shared returned in minute detail. Nora's heart pounded as he studied her in recognition. She recalled his laryngitis, the darkness, the electrical failure, the drinks he'd kept giving her.

"I...you..." Nora stuttered.

His left hand reached out as though to touch her hair, but he quickly changed his mind and shoved it into his jeans pocket.

"Yes," he said.

"But..."

"Let's go eat," Paul announced abruptly. "Steven, you drive. I'll sit in the back with Nora and the girls."

He gave each of the girls a hand up into the back of the truck, then he took a seat near the tailgate. Nora felt his eyes on her as they rode the short distance to the restaurant. Unconsciously she glanced at him and found him frowning at her. The wind blew her hair across her face, and when she tried to control it, the wind whipped it out of her hand.

She saw a flash of blue as his long legs scooted toward her. Sitting beside her, he plopped his baseball cap onto her tangled hair.

"You're not used to riding in the back of a pickup, are you?"

Nora shook her head, and he pointed to his sisters, who had both tied colorful scarves around their heads.

"You'll learn," he said. The implication of his words brought her head whirling around to face him. Before she could recover her composure, he slid his hand to her neck and pulled her head against his ear.

"I told you once that I'd protect you from things that go bump in the night," he whispered in her ear.

His reference to New Year's Eve alarmed her, and she tried to pull away, but he tightened his hold, tangling his fingers in her hair. His face was inches from hers as she stared at him and more memories of the night she'd tried so hard to forget flooded back.

"I didn't include myself," he added as he slowly loosened his fingers in her hair.

"Please don't," she murmured. "Your sisters. . ." Together they turned to his two sisters and found them wide-eyed with curiosity. Paul cleared his throat nervously and released her, but he remained next to her, his arms folded across his chest. Each bump in the street brought his fist into contact with her side, but she couldn't move, wedged between Paul and his youngest sister.

He leaned closer, and to Nora's sensitized ears, his words were as much a threat as a promise. "We have to talk later."

DINNER WAS A STEADY STREAM of flirtatious banter from Tim and Steven until at last Paul cut in.

"Listen, little brothers, I'm asserting my rights as the eldest in this family. You guys can find your own women for the game." A stormy protest came from Steven, but Paul squelched it. "Nora and I met once before." He stared long and hard at his younger brother. "We have things to talk about." Enlightenment shone in Steven's eyes, and he dropped his challenge.

Paul turned to Nora. "I'll protect you from these lecherous brothers of mine," he said, and everyone laughed.

Nora avoided looking at him.

"Fair enough?" he asked.

"Yes," she murmured. If she stayed with him, would he think there might be a repeat of their first encounter? Her fists tightened in her lap. She'd made a mockery of herself the last time, but not again.

Tim and Mary excused themselves and left for the high school, and a half hour later Paul reached for the check. "We should hurry if we're going to make the start of the game."

He draped his arm protectively around her shoulders. "This game is an annual event in town," he explained as they left the restaurant. He tossed his keys to Steven. "Drop Lisa off at D.A.'s apartment, will you, little brother? Nora and I will walk to the school."

The few blocks to the gymnasium passed quickly. Nora listened to his pleasant voice as he told her about the town and the ranch where he lived, then they talked about the bank where she worked.

His next words startled her. "I didn't think I'd ever find you again."

"Did you try to find me?" Nora asked, stopping near a barren lilac bush.

"I'm out on the range a lot without phone access, so I could only try when I'd get back home. I went to school with Leslie Coleman. I saw you come in with her that night, so I knew she could help me find you, but her phone was always busy when I tried to call." He laughed. "Les is always playing matchmaker with me. I wonder why she never told me about you?"

Nora recalled Leslie's words that night. "Are you from a ranch south of town?"

"Yes. Why?"

"Leslie has been true to form," she replied. "She tried to tell me about a tall, dark. . ." A snicker escaped before she could cover her mouth. "I wouldn't let her finish. It could have been you." She turned away. "I don't know what to say. That night was all wrong for me."

"Not for me," he said behind her back.

She whirled around, confronting him. "But you don't understand. I've never done anything like that before. It took me weeks to remember that night. Some of it is still a blank." She dropped her gaze to the sidewalk.

"I remember it all," he said softly.

"I tried to forget it. . .everything," she cried.

He grabbed her shoulders. "I don't want to forget that night. I wanted to find you again, but I didn't know how you'd react. I even thought you might have called the cops. I just didn't know. And I've been busy working with my father. He can be demanding at times, but he holds my future in his hands. I have no choice but to follow his orders. . .for now."

He released his hold on her and stepped back. "Sorry for burdening you with my personal problems. I'm glad I've found you again. I know you didn't want to get involved with me that night and I know I talked you into it, but I have no regrets. You shouldn't have any, either. It was. . .unforgettable."

"I know," she murmured, more to herself than to

him. She stared at him, trying to decide how sincere he was. "How old are you?" she asked, wanting to know more about him.

"How old do you think?" he hedged.

"Late twenties. . . early thirties?" she guessed.

"Damn, do I look that old? My mother says I'm burning the candle at both ends. Maybe she's right." A tight grin curled the corners of his mouth. He reached out and touched a wavy curl near her shoulder. "I was twenty-four last November."

"Oh, my," she remarked. "You seem older."

"Am I too young to be your hero?" he asked, tilting her face up toward the street light.

"My hero?"

"Yes. I think I'd like that."

Nora's heart fluttered, but she didn't pull away. "Why do you want to be my hero?"

"To keep other potential candidates away from your door."

"There's hardly a lineup."

"There should be."

"You don't know me. . ." Immediately she regretted her words; he knew her all too well. "First impressions can be wrong."

He leaned back against a sturdy fence post and folded his arms across his chest, hiding the college emblem on his Windbreaker.

She grew uncomfortable under his continued perusal. "I still want to forget that night," she said.

He nodded. "I know I took advantage of you, but I'm not ashamed of what we shared. Yes, Nora, what we shared. . . it wasn't one-sided."

"I don't want to talk about it anymore," she exclaimed, whirling away. "Just. . . just leave it be. If you think I make a practice of visiting bars and inviting strange men home with me, you're wrong."

"I know."

"But you don't. I let you in my house and my bed. I don't even remember who undressed who. . ."

"I undressed you," he told her.

"No," she said, "I didn't want to know."

"I'm sorry," he apologized. "Do you want me to take you home?"

"Oh, my God, no!"

"I'm sorry. I didn't mean it that way."

She glanced at him. He was still leaning against the fence, staring at her.

"Let's go to the basketball game before it's over," he said and she accepted the hand he offered.

They arrived a few moments before halftime and found his brothers in the crowd with three young women and the blond man at whose apartment they had met. His brothers introduced two of the women.

"You met D.A. earlier," Paul said. "His father runs a ranch up the road from our place. D.A.'s a professor at the college."

Nora nodded to D.A., then was introduced to the red-headed woman who was D.A.'s date. Her name was Rose Marie, and her bright blue eyes smoldered as she stared at Nora.

Paul's arm went around Nora's shoulders protectively, and the fire in Rose Marie's eyes cooled as she claimed D.A.'s arm.

During the halftime break Mary joined them, catching her breath from her cheerleading session.

"Having a good time?" Mary whispered to Nora.

"Very."

"How's Paul?"

"He's fine."

"I mean...how do you like him?" Mary clarified.

Nora smiled. "I like him fine."

"Good."

The announcer's voice came over the public-address system, honoring the former varsity players. Nora smiled with pleasure when Paul and his two brothers stood. She was surprised to see their friend D.A. stand with them and wondered how he had managed to play varsity ball with his handicap.

After the introductions of the alumni, Paul asked, "D.A., could I spend the night at your place?"

"Sure, but why?"

"If Steven or Russ, Jr., will drive all these Russell kids home in my truck, I can take Nora home." He turned to Nora. "I can plainly see the time has come for us Russells to travel in separate vehicles." He glanced at the redheaded woman. "That is, if you're not...if you'll be alone," he amended, noticing the glare in Rose Marie's blue eyes.

D.A. laughed. "Sure, that's fine. Lisa is sleeping in Annie's room, but the sofa is yours if you want."

Rose Marie glared at Paul, turned a pouting red mouth toward D.A., and plopped down into her seat. Mary Russell grinned from ear to ear, clearly pleased at D.A.'s response, then returned to her cheering station.

Paul pulled Nora down beside him, and the second half of the game began. "Now you know I'm spending the night on McCormack's sofa and that my intentions are honorable. I want to walk you home so we can get to know each other better."

"All right," she replied, but she still felt uneasy.

After the game, Nora and Paul meandered through town in the general direction of her house.

"Do you like beer?" he asked.

"Sometimes."

He detoured into the Matador and returned with four cans. He slid one in each pocket of his jacket, opened one and handed it to Nora, then opened the last for himself. They headed in the direction of a small neighborhood park.

"I found a pair of maroon gloves in my coat pocket," Paul said. "They don't fit. If I had known we would meet tonight, I would have brought them."

"I bought another pair," she said. "I didn't think I would ever get them back." She smiled. "Frankly, I couldn't remember what I had done with them. I have your hat, you know."

"I didn't mean to leave it, but when I realized where it was, it was to be my excuse for looking you up again," he told her. "You called me your cowboy. I liked the way you said it."

"You look very different tonight."

He glanced down at his attire. "I'm not always a cowboy."

"I wish we could undo it all," she said, strolling to a swing and dropping into the rigid seat.

He followed her and began to push the swing. "Just accept what happened."

"It's no way to start a relationship," she countered.

"Do you want to start a relationship?"

"No. . . yes. . . I mean. . ." A wave of nausea suddenly hit her, and she asked him to stop pushing.

"We could never tell anyone how we first met, could we?" she said, looking up at him as he moved to the front of the swing.

He ran his hand lightly across her cheek. "It would be our secret."

He offered Nora another beer, but she refused. Alcohol had been her undoing with this man a few months earlier. But tonight the moon was shining brightly, the streetlights were illuminating the area, and he wasn't pressuring her to be close and intimate.

"Tell me about the ranch where you and your family live," she said. "I've never been to a ranch. I'm from San Diego, where there are hundreds of thousands of people." She glanced up at him. "I like it here, though. The pace is slower. I was ill before I came here. This is a good place to heal."

"What was wrong?"

"I had a problem." Troubled thoughts of Jerry and her son came to haunt her. "I'd rather not talk about it." She was quiet for several minutes, then Paul slipped his arm around her and guided her to a nearby bench.

As they sat down, Paul's arm was still around her, and Nora felt an unexpected wave of warmth and a longing to nestle against him. She reached up and touched his hand, and he tightened his fingers around hers.

She turned to him in the moonlight. "This is crazy, but I'm glad we've met again. I had so many questions, but now I can't ask them."

Paul pulled her closer, and she rested her head against his shoulder.

"I know," he murmured against her hair, inhaling its fragrance. "When the time is right, I'll answer your questions."

As they stood, he laced his fingers through her curls.

"Can I see you again?" he asked.

"Are you sure you want to get involved with a woman you picked up in a bar?"

"Don't put it that way," he said, his mouth tightening.

"I want to try again. This time we'll take it slow and do it right."

"I'd like that," she replied, sliding her arms up around his neck.

He drew her closer and kissed her lightly several times, then his mouth hardened on hers. When she stiffened, he eased away. "Sorry," he mumbled.

Nora pulled back. "You'd better walk me home."

"I'm not sure I remember the way," he admitted. "I was busy concentrating on you the last time."

She glanced warily at him as he slid his arm protectively around her and they made their way to her house.

When she reached the front door she unlocked it, but Paul stopped her entry. Her heart quickened. Instinctively she realized she wouldn't refuse him if he insisted on coming inside with her. A sixth sense told her she'd be willing to make a second mistake.

"I meant it back in the park. I want to see you again," he said, looking down at her as she leaned against the doorjamb.

"Okay," she agreed.

"We're calving. . ."

"Really?" she asked, unable to hide the twinkle in her eyes.

He grinned. "Actually, the cows are calving. Technicalities aside, my city-bred lady," he explained, brushing her lips with his, "calving happens to be a very busy time at the home place. I've drawn night duty for the next ten days."

"I don't understand."

"Cows seem to plot against a man's getting a good night's sleep. They prefer to drop their calves during the wee hours of a freezing night, in the middle of a blizzard if they can possibly arrange it." He laughed. "Someone has to be in the cow barns to handle complications. We take turns working nights and sleeping days. The next ten nights belong to Steven and me. Then dad and Russ relieve us. Tim's excused because of school. Mom and the girls are excused because of school and cooking and all those things that make us male chauvinists enjoy having a woman around."

"Are you a chauvinist?" she asked.

"At times," he admitted. "It has its advantages. Are you a liberated woman?"

"I've had to make decisions for myself," she replied. "Does that frighten a male chauvinist away?"

"Not when she's as pretty as you."

"Are you only interested in my beauty and body..." She groaned. "I'm sorry. I can't seem to forget what happened. How can I expect you to forget if I keep bringing it up?"

"Forget it, Nora. It's the total you, all of you, I'm interested in. I just happen to know more about you than usual after one evening. Let it rest."

"I'll try."

"Calving only lasts for about five or six weeks," he said, studying her response.

"Go on," she urged him.

"I won't be back in town until the first part of April. Dad has a raging temper most of the time, and I know through experience that taking trips to town during calving is not the way to keep peace at our place. And he's right. It's our livelihood and we all share in it. He's very generous in our draws and distribution of the profits, but damn it, he makes sure we give our blood and guts in order to earn it. I'm the oldest son, but sometimes I wonder if the price he extracts is worth the problems. If it weren't for my mom and my sisters and brothers, I probably would have split long ago." He stared over the top of her head into the night. "But I love it, really. It's the only thing I want to do." His voice sounded far away.

Nora stepped closer to the door.

"Come back here a minute," he said.

She turned to him expectantly.

Without a word he enfolded her in his arms, and she rejoiced in the feeling of her womanly body pressed against his.

"Goodbye for a few weeks, pretty lady," he said, and he covered her lips with his, savoring their sweetness. "I'm glad Mary invited you tonight. It sure saves me a lot of time searching for you."

He released her gently and turned away, and reluctantly Nora entered the house.

Inside, she listened to his footsteps as he left her porch, half expecting him to knock again, and wondering how she would respond. What was the matter with her? Had she become the wanton woman she feared? She shook the feeling of disappointment away when no knock sounded, and chastised herself for allowing herself to be tempted by a man who was still virtually a stranger.

CHAPTER FIVE

NORA LIFTED HER TANGLED HAIR away from her face, raised her head to squint at the alarm clock, then fell back to the pillow. A wave of nausea rolled from the pit of her stomach and she raced to the bathroom, making her destination with only seconds to spare.

Afterward she gargled and stumbled back to bed. Surely one beer consumed hours before couldn't have done this to her. Only when she kept her eyes closed did her stomach behave normally. She lay in bed, trying to unravel her muddled thoughts, until images of Paul Russell and Leslie Coleman began to merge together, and she fell asleep again.

When she awoke a few hours later, she gave in to an impulsive urge to call Leslie.

"Hello," she said when Leslie answered the phone. "It's me, Nora. I wondered if you would like to have lunch today." She listened for a few moments, then laughed. "I know, but you're always busy, and I've been. . . working out some problems. . . Okay, noon at the Beaver Slide. Bye."

Later that morning as she approached the Beaver Slide for her luncheon date with Leslie, Nora noticed the restaurant's distinctive facade. She couldn't resist smiling. She had been there just last night with Paul, but in her emotional state, such mundane things as restaurant fronts hadn't registered. The building had been constructed in the shape of an oversize beaver slide, a structure for stacking hay that was unique to the locale. The wide entryway made the customers feel they were walking directly into a giant haystack. Nora half expected to see a few head of cattle grazing in the parking lot.

Leslie was waiting in a booth when Nora arrived. During lunch Leslie chattered about the men she'd been dating. "I've been out with Jay Sloan so many times I've lost track. There's an older guy named George. He's a cowboy, and you know I take to cowboys. And there's always Paul Russell."

The color drained from Nora's face. "You've been dating Paul? I thought he was working...away from phones." She stared at her hands, which were tightly clenched in her lap.

Leslie took a long sip of her chocolate shake, then waved her hand at Nora. "Don't worry, my friend. Paul is yours for the taking if you really want him. Paul and I are just friends. We talked on the phone just this morning. Lordy, he woke me up at the crack of dawn. Frankly I thought he'd forgotten who I was." She looked up at the revolving fan overhead. "Once upon a time it looked as though we might become more, and I'll admit we did dally around a bit a few years ago, but no, we're just friends."

"Dally around?" Nora asked, trying to keep her voice disinterested.

Leslie shrugged. "You know...make out...but just a few times. He's great in the sack."

Nora paled.

"Forget I said that," Leslie amended quickly, squinting at Nora. "We're just good friends. Have you been seeing him? I never have had a chance to discuss New Year's with you. What happened?"

"Nothing," Nora replied. "He just walked me home. . . and left after a while."

"That doesn't sound much like the Paul Russell I know," Leslie said with a laugh. "You haven't seen him since?"

"Last night," Nora admitted. "We spent a few hours together. He said he's busy with calving and other things."

Leslie gave a low whistle. "Mostly other things, I'll wager. Better keep your guard up, Nora. Paul's been known to love them and leave them."

Nora took a bite of a long thin French fry and tried to ignore the throbbing in her temple.

"You don't look so good, Nora," Leslie said. "Are you sick again? You said once that you'd been sick. . . ill. . . whatever. Maybe you should see a doctor. I go to Dr. Peters at the clinic. She's in her late thirties and single. . . and is very understanding. She keeps her mouth shut." She rolled her eyes heavenward. "I guess all docs do, but Dr. Peters puts out the right vibes and she's very good, too. Call her. She can help you, no matter what's wrong. Now about Paulie Russell. Ask away. We go way back. I can tell you're interested and just too shy to ask."

"Paulie?" Nora said, unable to suppress a smile.

"Paul was my first love. . . in the seventh grade," Leslie told her. "He taught me how to ride a little, then in high school I was a cheerleader when he played on the varsity football team. He rode in the rodeo circuit off and on during the summers when he was in college. The year he graduated we became a really hot number around these parts, but neither of us wanted to become tied down. We were both having too much fun. I guess there's not much interest in a monogamous relationship for Paul or myself. Who wants to be tied to just one person at our ages? Not me! And not Paul! Now what else would you like to know?"

Nora frowned. "I guess you've told me enough. I agreed to have another date with him when calving is done. I thought he was really nice, but you're right. At our ages, none of us should be tied down. . . or become a burden to each other."

SEVERAL NIGHTS LATER, Nora was sitting in her kitchen having a late-night snack. As she sat sipping a cup of hot chocolate, her eyes were drawn to the Western hat with its multitude of tiny pins which was now perched on top of her microwave oven.

"Oh, Paul," she sighed. "Have you left me a third reminder of your visit that I hadn't counted on?" Her period had ceased during her severe weight loss in San Diego and had only resumed once in the fall since her move to Montana. She had read that irregular menses often indicated infertility. She glanced at the calendar on the wall. Two months had passed since New Year's. Paul had promised to get in touch with her before he returned to town, but that was still a month away. She would have to consider her options and make a decision before then.

She set the empty mug down. Her hand was unsteady as it slid to her lower abdomen. Thoughts of a baby brought back memories of Jeremy. He had been a sweet-natured baby, full of giggles and smiles. She could recall only one short bout with a mild cold when he'd become fussy. The attendants at the children's nursery where he stayed when she worked at the San Diego bank had greeted him with open arms each morning, saying he was the delight of the nursery.

Even in the last few seconds of his life he had been happy. He had waved his chubby fist at her and smiled as his father held him in his arms. She had called to them... and then a bloodbath had taken place before her eyes.

Nora's jaw tightened. She had no tears to shed; most had been wrenched from her long before she'd met Paul Russell. She wondered how Paul would feel if he knew she were pregnant. If he reacted true to the picture Leslie had painted, he'd drop her for sure. She wasn't sure how to take his comments about that night together. Perhaps he saw her only as an easy conquest. A man from a family with property, wealth and standing in the community didn't have to marry a woman who had given herself to him in a reckless moment of indiscretion and found herself caught with the consequences.

She knew that in a small town when private misconduct became public knowledge, the scandal often raced through the entire community like a windblown grass fire. The media publicity when Jerry and Jeremy had died had been a major factor in her withdrawal and the depression for which Dr. Taylor had treated her.

A cool logical decision came to her as she returned to her bedroom; it was distasteful, but the only sensible course of action available.

On Thursday, a visit to Dr. Peters confirmed Nora's suspicion, but the physician wanted to conduct a laboratory test, as well. The office nurse would call Nora when the results were received from the hospital.

Several days passed. Nora was balancing her cash drawer at the end of the day when the secretary for new accounts beckoned to her. "The clinic called. The nurse said she didn't need to talk to you, that I should just tell you yes. What did she mean, Nora?" the inquisitive woman asked.

"Nothing," Nora replied, and her heart formed a hard lump in her chest. "Just some routine tests."

Another week passed. Some of her skirts and slacks began to tighten around her waist, but still she stalled.

On Friday during the last week in March, she received a letter from Paul, hand delivered at the bank by Mary Russell.

"He tried to call but couldn't reach you," Mary said before leaving the window. "He's been at the upper place most of the time. It's pretty remote up there."

Nora quickly put the Closed sign at her station and turned away, ripping the envelope and cutting her finger on the sharp edge. As she sucked on the cut, she read his note. Paul was being detained at Pinto's Meadow. There was no phone, and the only time he'd been back to the home place and tried to call, he'd received no answer. They were still tagging new calves, he explained, and would have to postpone their date until the second Friday in April. His father kept finding things to do that kept Paul "away from civilization." He asked that she please forgive him and that he was looking forward to seeing her again. He closed by saying he missed her, but the letter was signed simply "Paul."

She reread the letter every day for the next week, still unable to make her decision. Time was running out. Paul would be with her in less than a week. She grimaced as she imagined herself greeting him with this surprise and what his probable reaction would be. She made her decision the Monday of the week he was to return. During her morning break at the bank she placed a long-distance call to a gynecologist in Missoula and made an appointment for the following day.

Through the rest of the day she concentrated on attending to her customers and ignoring a questioning look from Leslie, whom she had avoided for several days.

Late in the day she notified her supervisor that she had

scheduled some outpatient surgery and needed to be off for several days. The woman didn't ask for details, and Nora didn't elaborate.

That night she lay awake for several lonely hours, sickened by the thought of what she was about to do. She thought of all that Leslie had told her about Paul and then reread his letter, but found no solace. Early the next morning she drove to Missoula.

WHEN PAUL ARRIVED at Nora's house the following Friday, her small white automobile was gone, the house was dark, and a note was tucked into the crack between the storm door and jamb. The note was dated earlier in the week.

> Paul, I've changed my mind. I don't think we should see each other again. I have a problem I must solve alone.
>
> Sorry, Nora.

What the hell, he thought, puzzled. He stared at the door and knocked on it in spite of the note, stopping only when the next-door neighbor stepped out onto her porch.

"She's been gone most of the week," the woman called.

He waved an acknowledgment to get rid of the curious woman, jammed his weathered beige Western hat down on his head, then shoved the note into his pocket. As he returned to his truck, he glanced at the neighbor's house and saw the curtain drop abruptly.

"Busybody," he grumbled, then frowned. Where was she? Had he done something? He pulled the note from his jeans pocket and reread it. After all the effort he'd made to get away. . . and now this.

"Damn it," he muttered as he shoved the note deep into his pocket again and headed for the Matador.

He bought a glass of beer, and when he was half finished nursing the drink, he felt someone brush against his side. He turned to find a tall, dark-haired, very attractive young woman from his high-school years.

"Hi, Paul," she said, smiling coyly. "I haven't seen you around for ages. Been busy, fella?"

The woman had a reputation for being easy. Maybe that was what he needed tonight to get his mind off Nora Lane. But he had no desire to forget Nora. She had been in his thoughts daily. Never before had he felt trapped at the ranch. Several times he had wanted to head into town, but his sense of responsibility had prevailed, and he'd stayed. He thought of the note and shook his head.

The young woman shrugged and sauntered off, her tight-fitting jeans flaunting her shapely buttocks as she walked away. The beer had gone flat by the time he ambled to the poker tables, where two games were in progress.

"The buy-in twenty?" he asked as he slid into an empty chair vacated by an acquaintance.

"Yup," the dealer replied, keeping his teeth clenched on a long cigarillo and nodding to the sign posted on the wall. "You've played before, Russell. Is your memory failing you tonight?" The others at the table laughed good-naturedly.

"Too steep for me tonight," Paul said, and slid out of the chair again. He looked around and found nothing to hold his interest. As he shoved his fist into his jeans pocket he felt Nora's note, made up his mind and left the saloon.

Two cowboys called to him as he climbed into the cab of his truck and invited him back to do some serious drinking with them at another saloon up the street, but he waved them on.

He drove to Nora's house, but she was still gone. He'd hoped... He studied the note again, then turned it over and decided to write a response.

"Damn it," he growled, searching the cab for something to write with. Finally he found a pencil stub on the floorboard under the seat.

Pretty Lady,

I'm sorry about your problem. Let me help you. I've got to see you again.

I have to go check the summer pasture for the grazing association we belong to before we move the pairs. I won't be back in town until the end of May.

I'll be here to pick you up at 10:00 A.M. on Memorial Day. I plan to take you on a Russell family picnic. It's an annual tradition. This is an order!

I'll have a bucket of chicken and two fishing rods. No excuses.

Cowboy

He found a used envelope, scratched out the names and addresses already on it and penciled his and hers in the appropriate places. He tried to lick the flap shut, but it wouldn't stick. "Damn it," he mumbled under his breath, and dropped it into her mailbox.

When he returned to his truck, he was plagued by the possibility that she didn't live there anymore.

Early the next morning, before heading out to the upper place again, he called Leslie and asked about Nora.

"She's acting kinda funny, Paul," Leslie told him. "She's been gone since Tuesday. She won't talk to me anymore. We used to be rather close, but lately...I'm a little worried. Something is definitely wrong."

"Try to find out what's bothering her, Les," Paul said. "I'll be out of touch for several weeks, but I'm worried, too."

"Is she getting under your skin?" Leslie asked.

"Don't joke," Paul cautioned.

"Who's joking? I think it's great. It's about time you settled for one woman. But take it easy with Nora. She's been hurt. I don't know the details, but I know she's still getting over it. Treat her with tender..."

"Loving care," he finished. "Just keep an eye on her while I'm gone."

"Agreed," Leslie said, and he hung up the phone.

A nagging sense of frustration gnawed at him as he led the two horses up the ramp and into the horse trailer hitched to his truck. He loaded the truck with gear, tack and food. She might be avoiding him, he thought, but at least she hadn't quit her job or left town.

PAUL RUSSELL knocked on Nora's door at ten sharp on a bright sunny Memorial Day.

Nora's hand trembled as she turned the doorknob and greeted him. His hair was rumpled from the breeze, and he wore a short-sleeved, beige-and-white striped sports shirt tucked neatly into his faded blue jeans.

"Hello," she murmured.

"You're here," he declared.

"Yes."

"Why?"

"Your note was so threatening that I feared for my life if I wasn't. Besides...I missed you," she said as she stared at his face, thinking how handsome he was.

"Good," he replied. "You were sick?"

"I'm okay now."

"What was wrong?"

"Nothing."

"Oh." He looked around the room, noting a few scattered boxes. "Moving?" he asked, his eyes narrowing.

"Possibly."

"To a larger place?"

"Maybe smaller to save money. I'm incurring some unexpected expenses. I need the money. I'm not sure yet."

"Keep me posted. . . I'll try to get away and help you," he offered. "May is branding and castrating, et cetera, and in June we move the cattle to summer pasture. Can you wait until July?"

"I don't know," she hedged.

He took a step closer and put his hands on her shoulders. "May I kiss you?"

"No," she cried, then changed her mind. "I mean, yes." She lifted her face in acquiescence. He tried to draw her closer, but she laid her forearms against his chest, preventing any body contact.

"Sorry," he murmured, lightly caressing her lips. "Ready?"

She nodded.

"Here, you won't need this," he said, reaching to unsnap the turquoise Windbreaker she was wearing. "It's going to be warm today."

"No!" she cried, clutching the light jacket and pulling away from his inquiring hands. "I. . . I. . . I get chilled easily. . . since I've been sick."

"Sorry, Nora," he apologized. "Do you still want to go with me? You don't have to if you really don't want to."

"Yes, I still want to go. Just. . . don't nag me," she said, moving to the door.

As he helped her into the truck cab, he tugged her blond ponytail. "You look like an innocent teenager with your hair like that," he teased.

"I assure you, I'm neither."

He frowned again and mumbled, "I'm sorry," then closed her door and went around to the driver's side. When he gunned the engine, she knew he was venting some of his frustration.

"*I'm* sorry," she said, trying to smile. "I'm just a little tense today."

As they drove away from town, Paul's frown eased. Nora lost track of the miles as they drove over the spillway of a dam and around a large man-made lake, then followed a winding dirt road. Once he reached for her hand, squeezed it and refused to release it until he needed to shift gears.

"Where are we going?" she asked to break the silence.

"A place called Trail Creek. It's not far." The silence returned, until Paul pointed to a shady area near a cluster of trees just across a narrow stream. "There they are," he said. "Through the willows and across that wooden bridge and you'll get to meet my mother and father. Mom's the greatest. Don't be intimidated by my father. His growl can be frightening and sometimes he actually bites, but seldom when he's fishing." The truck thudded across the narrow bridge, and within minutes they were parked. Paul helped Nora down, and she tugged at her Windbreaker, making certain it covered her hips.

Paul's sisters and brothers greeted her warmly, then Paul took her hand and led her to meet his parents. His mother fulfilled Nora's image of a ranch woman—middle-aged, slightly overweight, a touch of gray in her caramel-brown hair and hazel eyes filled with affection for the children surrounding her.

"This is our little mother," Paul said, hugging the woman and kissing her cheek.

"Call me Julie," his mother said as she accepted Nora's outstretched hand and squeezed it. "Paul's talked a lot about you. I'm glad we get to meet at last."

Paul's father returned from the creek carrying a fishing rod and tackle box, along with several pan-size trout on a stringer.

"Dad," Paul called to the short husky man. "This is the woman I've told you about, Nora Lane. Nora works at the bank in town. She's from San Diego."

A very dark pair of eyes beneath a black, high-crowned Western hat drilled into Nora as Paul's father grumbled a greeting she couldn't understand.

"Welcome to our little gathering, Nellie," he growled.

"No, dad, it's Nora," Paul said.

"Yes..." Paul's father scrutinized her from head to toe and back again. "Norma it is," he announced, and accepted the hand she had been extending the entire time he had been standing near her. He shook it up and down twice, then dropped it quickly before turning away and disappearing into the willows again.

"Damn him," Paul muttered under his breath.

"It's okay." Nora touched his arm gently, reminding herself that when she followed through with her plans and moved away, she would not see any of them again... including Paul. She tried not to think of her growing affection for him. Their relationship had been topsy-turvy from the beginning, founded on lust and desire. She wanted to shield herself from the possibility of loving him, but now she wondered if it might already be too late.

Paul stirred emotions in her that she wanted to keep alive, to nourish and allow to grow. She wanted to be in his arms and feel his touch when he kissed her and made love to her and—

Her reverie was broken by the touch of his hand on her cheek.

"You're far away," he said, frowning down at her.

"Yes," she admitted, lowering her eyes.

"Lunch is ready." He draped his arm around her shoulders, kissed her cheek, and led her to the food-laden table where the family had gathered.

When the meal was over, Paul leaned toward Nora and whispered in her ear, "Let's go fishing."

"Okay," she replied, tugging the Windbreaker down past her hips. Beads of perspiration dotted her forehead, and she wiped them off with her napkin.

Paul frowned at her actions but said nothing.

They wandered along the winding creek for more than half a mile, fishing, talking, crisscrossing the stream. The water was icy cold from its source high in the mountains above them, and Nora deliberately allowed her canvas shoes to get soaked, hoping the cold would somehow reach her cheeks.

They left the creek and made their way to an outcropping of rocks. The undergrowth was just leafing out, bringing a lush, pungent fragrance to the warm air.

"Want to stop and rest?" Paul asked. "Your face is flushed."

"Okay," she agreed, tugging the jacket down past her hips once again. "It's warmer than I had expected."

"For God's sake, Nora, take that damn jacket off before you faint from the heat!" He reached forward and grabbed the lapels. Nora stumbled backward and fell, momentarily knocking the wind from her as the jacket unsnapped and spread open.

"Oh, my God!" he exclaimed as he stared down at her.

CHAPTER SIX

NORA WAS WEARING JEANS, but not the kind Paul had expected. What he had assumed was a T-shirt was actually a knitted maternity top.

Nora fought to bring the jacket sides together again, but her mounting hysteria made the effort impossible. She gave up and covered her eyes with her forearm.

Paul dropped to his knees. "Are you all right?"

His eyes raced over her, and as the full impact of her condition registered, he laid a hand on her abdomen. "Is this your problem?" he asked, continuing to study her. "You're pregnant." With his other hand he reached for her wrist and pulled it away from her face. "By me," he added, cynicism twisting his mouth.

"Yes," she hissed, rolling away from his inquiring hands and eyes. She scrambled up again, clutching the jacket sides together. She was panting heavily, and suddenly the rage she felt at her predicament was overwhelming. "I'm pregnant, and if your sister hadn't reintroduced us, I wouldn't even know who the father was. I let you get me drunk...and you...forced me, but I'm not sure. Sometimes I feel like I let you rape me. Is such a thing possible?" she asked, laughing hysterically. "Did I ask for it? I can't remember. Normally I would never have done a thing like that, and certainly not with a stranger!"

She clutched herself, as if perversely relieved that now

he knew. "You danced with me and held me, but your face was shadowy. It was so dark that night...and when the electricity went off, I was frightened and lonely. You must have decided I was a very desperate woman."

She shook her head slowly from side to side. "You weren't satisfied to do it once and leave, were you? I let you stay with me and...and you made love to me again and I liked it! I remember," she groaned. "It was so degrading to wake up the next day and realize what I'd done. I didn't know your name. I knew nothing about you except that you were tall and dark and you had a nice smile. *That's all!* I went to bed with a man because he had a nice smile and he..." Her mouth tightened.

Paul bowed his head, unable to face her directly.

"You left me with three reminders of that night," she continued. "You gave me a terrible case of the flu...you left a brown cowboy hat with lots of special pins on it...and you left me with this." She jerked her jacket open again.

Her breast was heaving. "I didn't do anything about it when I could," she sobbed. "So now this baby is growing inside me." Her voice died with a forlorn moan as she stared past his shoulders to the trees behind them.

When she spoke again, her voice was hoarse. "I wanted to go with you today because it would be the last time I'd see you. This baby wasn't conceived out of love. It was conceived in lust, and there's no reason for you to be bothered. I'm going to move and start over again someplace else, just the two of us. We'll make out okay. I've dealt with worse problems."

She turned her back to him. "I wanted to see you once more, but I couldn't fit into any of my regular clothes except two loose dresses with jackets that I wear to work. So last week I bought two of these tops and this pair of jeans to wear at home. I didn't want anyone to know what a mess I'd gotten myself into." She dropped to her knees, burying her face in her hands, and began to cry again.

The burden of Paul's guilt pressed more and more heavily on him as he listened to Nora. He slumped down onto a fallen tree trunk and watched her crying in torment. He had to help her. Straddling the log, he reached for her and lifted her into his arms, holding her tightly against him.

She clung to him. "I hate you, I hate you... but at the same time I... Help me, Paul," she pleaded. "I don't know what to do."

She buried her face against his chest and he rocked her gently, gradually calming her.

"I realized what had happened the day after I met you again," she said between sobs. "I spent a week in Missoula. That's why I wasn't home when you came that Friday night. I went to have an abortion. Oh, Paul, I was all alone, trying to decide if I wanted to kill this baby inside me."

She moved her head against his chest. "I've been married before and had a child."

"What?" he said, unable to hide his surprise. "But you're so young, and you've never said anything."

"There was no need. I didn't know you. We were like strangers. They were killed in a senseless crime, and I saw it happen. My husband's name was Jerry. He was twenty-four years old, and my baby had just had his first birthday." Her voice grew soft. "His name was Jeremy." Suddenly she pulled out of his embrace and stood a few steps away from him.

"I worked in a bank in San Diego. We had made an appointment to have Jeremy's portrait taken, and I was going to meet them at the studio a few blocks away. Out of the blue, two men entered the bank and pulled guns. They took all the money from my cash drawer and the teller's drawer next to me. We had been instructed never to resist a robbery attempt. The two men were threatening the bank manager with their guns, when suddenly Jerry and Jeremy came through the door."

She turned and stared at Paul, and her trembling began again. "I was so terrified for their safety that I shouted at them to go back. One of the robbers turned on them... and shot them both at point-blank range. They died instantly, and I saw every drop of their blood, shed because of my carelessness."

"Nora, don't torture yourself," Paul said. "You don't need to tell me."

"But I do, Paul, don't you see? We've conceived a child whose mother is a former psychiatric patient because she brought about the deaths of her husband and her own child and whose father is a carefree cowboy who wants to keep his freedom. We were together one night. That's all."

"You're no psychiatric patient," he challenged.

"I felt like one...and the rest of my description is true."

"No, it's not," Paul said. "Where did you get that carefree cowboy and freedom bit?"

"Leslie said..."

"Leslie doesn't speak for me."

"She told me all about you. She said..."

"People change."

"Then what Leslie said is true?"

"I might have been that way once, but I can change."

She came closer and took his hand, stroking it lightly. "Sometimes people have change forced upon them.

You've known about this for only a few minutes. I've lived with it for five months. That makes a difference, Paul. I've had time to think and make decisions."

She lifted his hand to her lips and kissed the tip of his index finger. "I like you, Paul Russell, very, very much," she whispered, more to herself than to him, "but it's not enough." She frowned. "I wouldn't embarrass you by staying around, especially now that I've met your family."

Her voice became bitter. "For six months after their deaths I tried to pretend it hadn't happened. I began to go to a shopping center near our house. I'd sit and stare at the entrance of a toy store and watch the mothers and their little boys come out of the store. It became an obsession with me. The shop was next door to a maternity-dress shop, and I'd watch the pregnant women come out with their unborn babies safely in their wombs and then I'd go home and sleep. If I slept, I wouldn't cry. Jerry was in the navy, and every time I'd see a sailor in uniform I'd break down. You can't live in the San Diego area without seeing those white uniforms. Then I started having dreams. Either I was hammering nails into my family's coffin or I was trapped in one myself. It was so horrible.

"Finally my family physician made me see a psychiatrist. I knew he was concerned about my lack of progress. I was afraid he might recommend commitment to an institution, so I decided to move and start over. I took a map to his office one day, explained my idea to him, and he agreed. I closed my eyes and chose a new home. Dillon was the nearest town to where the pin stuck on that map. I'd never heard of it! I sold my house and moved here last summer.

"I was able to make it through the night without crying and the terrible dream had finally stopped, but I was so lonely. Except for Leslie I had no friends. I didn't want any. Then Leslie talked me into going to the Matador on New Year's Eve. Everything changed when I let you into my house, and my life started to fall apart again." She tipped her head thoughtfully, as if making some private observation.

"I decided to keep this child because I wanted someone in my life to care for and someone to care about me. I'm all alone. You have a family to love and care about you. My father is dead. I've lost track of my mother and my only sister. If I died tomorrow no one would cry for me, because nobody cares." She began to sob again as he pulled her into his arms.

"Oh, Nora, honey, don't cry. There's no need. Someone cares." He tightened his arms around her.

Nora looked up at him through her tears.

"I care," he whispered, his voice husky. "I care. I've seen you only three times, but I knew from the first that you were special, that I could easily... Oh, God, Nora!" He clutched her to him, lost in his grief at hurting her more terribly than he could ever have imagined.

He caressed her cheek, and when she looked up at him, his mouth slowly covered her lips in a kiss more tender than any he had dreamed of during the many times he had thought of her.

Her jacket fell open, and his hand traced the curve of her breasts, lingering a hairbreadth inside the neckline of her T-shirt.

"You're beautiful," he said.

"I'm skinny and pregnant."

"You're slender and radiant," he insisted, continuing to study her. "Marry me."

"No."

"Why not?"

"It wouldn't be right."

"I want to take care of you," he insisted.

"I'll take care of myself."

"You're being stubborn."

"Probably, but I've thought about it a lot and I've made up my mind. My given name on my birth certificate is Honora. Nora is just a nickname. Honora is middle English and comes from a Greek word. Do you know what it means, Paul?"

He shrugged his broad shoulders.

"Honorable," she explained. "Honorable. Can you find the honorable part of this situation, Paul? Don't try, because there isn't any honor in what I've done with you. That's why it can't work for us. You'd be forced into having a wife and child you didn't want. I won't marry you. It would be wrong."

"Then live with me."

"No. People would talk. Your family...I can just imagine what your father would say."

"My father doesn't run my life. He just controls the purse strings. That's one of the prices I pay for being born into one of the largest cattle operations in the valley."

"So you see? I couldn't stay with you. You live at the ranch and your father would never allow it." She shuddered. "What an uproar that would cause."

"Then live with me in town," he persisted.

"Paul!"

"Living together would solve problems," he said, kissing her lightly. "You wouldn't be alone. We could play house until I convince you we can get along, and you'd have someone with you when the baby comes. You can't cut me out of this, Nora. I have a right to determine the future of my...own...child. It's a little awesome, isn't it? And you're right. I need time to adjust to the idea of becoming a father. But we can do that together."

"It's crazy," she said. "Would you commute to the ranch each day? You'd spend all your time on the road."

"I could quit the ranch," he insisted. "A friend in town has offered me a job at his Sweetwater grain elevators anytime I want."

"But you love your work. You said so."

"I know, but my father and I don't get along very well. Maybe it would do us both good to be apart for a while. It would give me some breathing room." He pulled her close again. "Now kiss me, Nora, or Honora, or whatever your name is. I've missed you for months, and now I want to make up for lost time."

Her lips parted and she responded to his ardor as desire swept through them both.

"Shouldn't we go back?" she asked, reluctant to move. "Your family will wonder what happened to us." But instead of leaving his embrace, she turned and studied his face. "I never thought today would end like this, Paul. I thought I'd keep my secret, we'd have a few hours together, and then I'd never see you again. I don't understand why you reacted so differently from what I'd expected."

He kissed her mouth with the warmth of a southern wind. "You've been in my thoughts since that night we first met. You were a burr under my blanket. I couldn't forget you even when I tried." He looked down into her upturned face. "Until you, a lot of my life has been superficial. In school everything came easy for me, good grades, sports, charming the teachers. Dad made it clear to me from the time I was a little boy that I'd be expected to follow in his footsteps on the ranch. It was as though my life had been arranged for me. All I had to do was go through the motions, take the right steps at the right time and everything would work out according to schedule."

He smiled down at her, his dark eyes sparkling. "I went to Montana State University at Bozeman and majored in agriculture with a minor in business. I didn't have to try for a scholarship because dad had already made plans for my going there and had set aside the necessary funds. I concentrated on sports and girls and keeping my grades up enough to keep my father off my back."

He curled a tentacle of her golden hair around his index finger, then let it slowly slide away. Suddenly he frowned. "I work like hell on that place, but dad pays me a cowhand's wage. I participate in the profits at the end of the year, but he makes it clear that I should reinvest most of it into the operation. I have a B.S. in agricultural sciences, but at times my dad acts as if all I can do is shovel manure. I could run one of the places if he would let me." He looked off into the distance and laughed. "It's a good thing my mother had four sons. She gave my father a lot of cheap labor."

"Paul, that's not very nice," she scolded.

"I know," he admitted. "Mom's got a heart of gold." He laughed again. "Dad set up trust funds for each of us kids and made them legally ours when we turn twenty-five. I thought he would have a heart attack one evening at dinner when I announced that I might cash in my fund when I had my birthday. I was just mulling over the idea aloud, but he turned a dozen shades of red."

"I'm sure he wants what's best," Nora said.

"For him or his children?" He kissed the tip of her nose. "Depressing subject. Let's change it."

She shook her head. "Would you really leave home? I wouldn't want you to do it just for me."

"You're worth it," he assured her, "but I'd be doing it for myself, too, and for my mother. She's taken a lot of abuse from dad over the years. At times I've wondered why she's stuck it out. I suspect we kids had a lot to do with her perseverance. Anyway, I'm sure the place would be more peaceful with me gone. It would only be temporary until we worked everything out." He appeared thoughtful for a moment. "Dad and I need to discuss a legal matter that might cause trouble."

"What kind of legal matter?" she asked. "Oh, Paul, are you in trouble with the law?"

He smiled. "No, it's more of a civil legal matter, just between my father and me. I never gave it much thought before I met you, but now... I'll work it out. My father can be reasonable if he sets his mind to it. Forget I mentioned it." He eased her off his lap and brushed off the seat of his pants, then playfully did the same to hers.

"Let me," he said, carefully resnapping the lower portion of her turquoise jacket and leaving the collar open to allow some cooling air to enter. "All of us birds have to leave the nest sometime. I think it's time I built my own nest... with you."

PAUL DELIVERED HER TO HER DOOR a few hours later.

"Please, won't you stay with me for a while?" she asked. "We see so little of each other."

"That's about to change, thank goodness. You're a difficult woman to keep track of, Nora." When he stayed in the truck, she turned to him questioningly.

"Don't worry," he said. "I'll get us something to eat and be right back."

Nora hurried inside, anxious to shed the jacket that had made her miserable most of the day. She stripped off her jeans, T-shirt top and underclothes and ran to the bathroom, impatient to shower before his return. She felt as though she were in a dreamworld, about to be fed and wooed by the man she longed for, when just that morning she'd felt sure he would be gone from her life forever.

As she showered, she wondered if he might change his mind later in her pregnancy when her belly would be conspicuous and questioning looks would be cast their way when they appeared in public.

The odds were against them ever creating a lasting union. At the thought she stopped soaping her body and smiled. Sometimes odds were meant to be beaten. Leisurely she soaped herself again, enjoying the fragrance of the shower gel. She felt as though she were taking a shower with rainwater, or under a cool waterfall on a tropical island, or . . .

Suddenly she heard the door in her living room open, then bang shut. She peeked through the shower curtain to the small clock on the back of the toilet and gasped.

"I'll be right out," she called through the closed bathroom door. She stepped out of the shower and reached for a towel. Frantically she looked around the small room. She'd left her clothes in the bedroom. The only article of clothing available to her was a thigh-length terrycloth bathrobe.

Strands of hair had slipped from the coil she'd made on top of her head, but her comb and brush were also in the bedroom. Clumsily she slipped into the short robe and tied the belt around her thickening waist, combed her loosened hair with her fingers, and opened the bathroom door.

She was a few feet from her bedroom and safety when something alerted him to her presence. Her breath caught in her throat as he turned, dropped the sack of food into a nearby chair and approached her, his long strides covering the distance in seconds. She pressed against the bedroom door and her weight eased it open with a subtle squeak of the old hinges.

"Don't fall," he cautioned, catching her hand as it flailed the air.

She clutched at his fingers while his other arm swung around her waist and brought her securely into his embrace.

"Oh, Paul," she murmured, overcome by his closeness.

"Did you hurt yourself?" he asked, his eyes filling with concern as he guided her into her bedroom.

She realized she was sitting on her bed when he dropped down beside her and the old-fashioned metal springs squeaked.

"Why is it so dark in here?" she asked.

"A storm is brewing in the west. The usual spring rain, but it might turn to snow." His arm stayed around her shoulders as they looked toward the single window in the room.

"Snow? In May?"

"Could happen." He touched the curve of her cheek. "I've seen it snow on every holiday but the Fourth of July."

"Really?" She turned her head, allowing his hand to caress the sensitive skin of her throat and collarbone.

Her hand joined his. She had intended to push his fingers away, but instead pulled the terry cloth away to give him access to her shoulder.

"It rains here when it damn well pleases," he whispered as he eased her back onto the bed.

The front of her skimpy robe loosened, exposing the curve of her breasts. She thought lazily about pulling the robe lapels together, but his dark eyes trapped hers and held her motionless.

"Does it rain a lot? This is my first spring." Her breath came more quickly as she felt his hand completely brush the robe aside.

"It rains every time," he assured her, his eyes roaming over her. "You're so beautiful."

"Thank you," she said, trying to ignore his wandering hand as it explored her hip and traveled down her thigh. Suddenly she frowned. "What does that mean? That it rains every time?" Her arms encircled his body, and she tugged his shirt away from his belted jeans and slid her hands up his back, rejoicing in the masculine warmth of his skin.

"Hell, I don't know," he mumbled, and his hand returned to caress her cheek. "Who wants to talk about the weather?" he said as his mouth covered her soft lips.

She gave herself to his kiss, straining to be closer to him as desire awakened in her.

"I want to make love to you, Nora," he said. His voice was steady, with a hint of stubborn determination. Nora wondered what he would do if she resisted, but the thought of resisting was the furthest thing from her mind.

"I don't usually let a man make love to me on the second date," she said, unable to hide the trembling in her voice.

"It's the third date," he reminded her. "And every time I've been with you, I've wanted to make love to you. No other woman has ever had that effect on me, Nora."

"You'll think less of me..."

"No."

"Yes."

"No, you're wrong," he said. His fingers traced the

curve of her blond brow. "You've become very special to me."

They lay facing each other, their bodies several inches apart. As she touched his lips with her fingertips, he playfully snapped at her. She smiled. Her uncertainty about lying half-naked on the bed with Paul, a man she hardly knew, was buried under a blanket of arousal as his hand again stroked her breasts.

"I still want to make love to you, but I want you willing," he said. "Are you willing?"

"Yes."

He pulled her upright and removed the robe, then rose from the bed to undress. Self-consciously she pulled the robe across her stomach, and he frowned at her actions.

She watched as he removed his shirt. His chest was covered with a scattering of dark curly hair that formed a narrow line running down his stomach and disappearing beneath his silver belt buckle. In seconds the buckle and the rest of his clothing were in a pile on the floor. Her heart thudded as she saw him standing before her, aroused and so masculine.

"This will be like our first time," she said softly.

"Yes."

"I mean, I don't remember much about the first time, so..."

"I know," he said. "It's a new beginning for us."

"We have no guarantees, do we?"

"No, so we'll make our own way. We'll never know if it's right unless we give it a try."

"You mean, making love together?"

"No, Nora. I mean living together, till death do us part." He smiled before coming to her, and rolling onto his back, he pulled her to lie partly across him.

Her fingers trailed down the stripe of dark hair on his chest until it thickened and broadened. She hesitated before touching him, then caressed his stomach with several lingering kisses.

"You've teased enough." He drew her hand away and she found herself on her back again. His tongue flicked across her lips, and her teeth parted to permit his entry.

She arched her neck to allow his mouth to journey inch by inch down her throat, and soon his tongue tasted the valley between her breasts. He nibbled at her ribs, then slowly worked his way to her rounded abdomen. She tensed as he kissed her stomach and laid his ear against her, then he raised his eyes to hers again.

"Let me love you, Nora. Let me take care of you," he whispered as his mouth covered hers. "I don't want to hurt you," he said, holding himself away from her.

"Don't stop," she pleaded, pushing her hips closer to him.

Desire soared in her as he entered and moved inside her, bringing new sensations wherever he touched her. She ran her hand down his thigh and up to his waist, torn between trying to prolong her feelings or throwing all restraint aside and reveling in the splendor of being with him. The decision was made by her own body as she responded to his thrusts and submitted to an uncontrollable spiraling burst of pleasure. As she caught her breath, he groaned and joined her in an explosive tremor.

"Oh, Nora," he said, when his breathing had calmed, "you're my little heating stove in this cold country. We'll be good for each other."

Nora moved her head just enough to see his face. "I've never been called a stove before, but the way you say it, it's quite romantic." She kissed his cheek. "I don't understand how it could have happened when our relationship has been so strange, but I love you." With a sigh of contentment she curled in his arms and drifted happily to sleep.

CHAPTER SEVEN

NORA'S BEDROOM was filled with an unusual brightness when she awoke. She felt a warm arm near her waist, and memories of the previous evening rushed in.

She slid from beneath the bed covers and pattered to the window. A blanket of white covered the lawns and sidewalks, the street and trees, and the lilac bushes just beginning to bloom. The scene before her was breathtakingly beautiful, pure and fresh. She ran back to the bed and shook Paul's shoulder.

"Paul," she called, but he didn't stir.

"Paul," she repeated, shaking his bare shoulder again and sitting down beside him. "It's so beautiful."

His dark eyes opened and he stared up at her, watching her eyes sparkle with excitement.

"You're right, you're very beautiful," he agreed, pulling her closer and trying to kiss her.

She drew back, playfully slapping his hands. "No, no, I mean outside. You were right! It snowed last night..." She stopped, thinking of their lovemaking and the hours they spent talking into the night. Later they had warmed the cold food in the microwave, eating it long after they'd satisfied their other hungers. "Oh, Paul," she sighed, coming into his arms again.

His free hand played with her hair, drawing it to its full length then allowing it to fall free. The flying strands tickled her cheeks and nose, and she giggled.

As reality slowly returned to her, she groaned. "Oh, this is Tuesday." She lifted her head and squinted at the clock, then collapsed against him.

"What's wrong, honey?" he asked.

"I have to be at the bank in an hour and a half," she replied, frowning. "I wanted to stay here with you forever." She reached up to touch his face. "I've felt lost for so long, and now..."

"And now we've found each other." His mouth covered hers, his lips caressing her warmly as his hand found her breast and drew tingling circles around the crest.

She moaned, knowing her nipple had hardened in response to his touch. Then his head lowered to her breast, and his tongue flicked across its taut peak.

Nora moaned as his lips sought her other breast, and any thought of leaving the bed evaporated as she pressed her body against his.

"Oh, Paul, love me again," she cried, tugging at his curly head. Her hands became lost in his thick dark hair, and she was filled with a sensual longing only he could appease.

LATER, WHEN THEY HAD DRESSED, Nora cooked breakfast while Paul called the ranch. She heard his subdued voice and knew he was talking to his mother.

"I'll be there in an hour," he said, then remained silent, listening. "I understand...yes...yes...of course I will. Just tell him...oh, damn it, I'll tell him myself. Thanks, mom." He hung up the receiver and dropped into a chair.

"Something's wrong," Nora said.

A troubled scowl darkened his features. "It's my father. He started moving the cattle to summer pasture this morning. . .a little ahead of schedule. We were going to head out tomorrow. All the arrangements had been made last week, and some seasonal cowboys were hired. When dad got home yesterday from fishing, he moved the time up to early this morning. He rounded up all the hands and my brothers and they worked all evening getting ready. When my mother asked him why, he said it just couldn't wait, that I should have been there to take charge of my men. Damn him! He carried on, saying that if I had been where I belonged, I would have known about the time change."

He pounded the table, spilling his coffee. "Damn it, he did it deliberately. He set me up! He called the McCormack ranch for help. They agreed to put the two crews together, do our cattle first, then move to the other place and move theirs next."

Nora handed him a paper towel, and as he wiped up the spilled coffee, she asked, "How do you get the cattle moved?"

"The place north of town uses trucks. We'll trail the pairs from the home place and Pinto's Meadow, which is our upper place. It will take a few days. I wonder how much snow fell up the Blacktail. It'll be a muddy trail drive when it melts."

He grew quiet. "It's a good idea, but why didn't he discuss it earlier? David McCormack has suggested it several times but dad has always been against it. All that free labor of his, I guess."

"Paul?"

He glanced up.

"Is it my fault?" she asked, fearing his involvement with her had jeopardized his position in the family's ranching operation.

"No."

"But your father said you should have been there."

"It's not you, it's the town, the distance," he explained. "You see, the house is seventeen miles from town, the road is gravel and winding, and the range land is farther still. I'm in charge of one of the summer pastures for the grazing association. The cabin I'll be staying at belongs to David McCormack and—"

His voice cut off and a mix of emotions played across his face. "That's it! The answer to our problem." A broad smile swept away all other expressions, and he reached for her hand. "Yesterday I talked about taking a job at the Sweetwater elevator, but I can't leave the ranch. Dad and I have made all these plans for the season, and the McCormacks have asked us to help them with...oh, damn it all. Do you understand, Nora? It's my life." His eyes pleaded for her support.

"Our days start very early and sometimes run late into the evening. I couldn't live in town and still work out there, and I know I wouldn't really be happy at the elevator. I need to have a horse under me and be out in the open. But look! I'll go to the cabin and get moved in and come get you the middle of June. Give the bank notice that you're quitting in three weeks. You'd have to take a leave pretty soon, anyway. Come spend the summer with me at the cabin. God, Nora, it's beautiful up there."

"Oh, Paul," she cried, imagining a summer alone in the mountains with him.

"Don't worry about money. This is on me." He broke out into lighthearted laughter.

"What about the baby?"

"We'll be back in town by Labor Day. The baby isn't due until the end of the month."

"But I have a medical checkup each month," she reminded him.

"Are you having any problems?"

She shook her head.

"Then talk to the doctor. See if it's okay to skip them if everything's fine. She can give you some signs to watch for."

"Paul, this is crazy," she said, but the idea was beginning to sound irresistible. She had already made arrangements to cash in one of the certificates of deposit, which matured in the summer. She planned to use some of the funds for the hospital and medical expenses for the birth, and after she moved, to pay several months' rent on a new place. *Now everything is changing,* she thought, *but how secure will I be? I can't allow myself to be totally dependent on Paul.*

She brushed the disturbing thoughts away and smiled. Live each day to the fullest. Hadn't she read that bit of philosophy somewhere? If Paul's impulsive scheme backfired and they decided not to stay together, she would be prepared with an alternative, and she would have saved several hundred dollars in living expenses for when she might need it most.

Paul came to her chair and knelt in front of her. "Nora, why not? I'll talk to my father. If he goes along with it, he'll be doing one of the few nice things in his life. Honey, the only person I've ever seen my father do an unselfish thing for other than his family is our neighbor, Mr. McCormack, and more recently McCormack's wife, Sammy. A few years ago she was an outsider. When he gets to know you better, he'll like you. Mom loves everyone, but dad is suspicious of anyone new to the area."

He laughed. "He picked out Leslie Coleman for me once. Can you imagine either of us settling down?"

Nora's eyes widened.

"Sorry, honey," he said. "I meant before I met you. What do you say? Will you spend the summer with me in the mountains?"

She smiled at his eagerness. "It would be nice to get away. And you're right, I do have to quit the bank. I don't want to explain my condition." She gazed into his dark eyes, breathless with love for him. "I'm so glad you're the father of my baby."

He wiped away a few tears running down her cheek. "I have to get back to the ranch. I'll call you tonight and we'll make definite plans. Be ready to leave the second Friday in June. Honey, it'll be great."

He swept her into his arms, and when he released her, she felt a painful loss.

"Hurry back to me," she whispered.

He motioned toward his hat, still sitting on her microwave. "May I? It's my favorite. I've missed it."

"Of course," she replied with a grin. "I'll miss it, though."

He grabbed the hat and his Windbreaker and disappeared through her door. His long strides carried him quickly to his truck, and then he was gone.

NORA WAS VERIFYING the opening funds in her cash drawer when she realized Leslie was standing in front of her customer window.

"Well, Miss Lane," Leslie said. "You've been smiling all the time you've been counting that dirty old money. You must have had a very nice holiday. You're glowing!" Leslie herself was looking very chic in a red-and-black dotted silk blouse and white pantsuit. "Let me guess. It looks like...love?" She tipped her head slightly, peering at Nora. Suddenly she clapped her hands together. "Is it Paul?"

"Maybe," Nora hedged.

"Let's have lunch," Leslie suggested. "We can talk."

"Okay," Nora agreed. "I go at one o'clock."

"I'm scheduled for noon, but I'll change mine," Leslie said. "I wouldn't miss this lunch for the world. Oh, Nora, I'm so happy for you." She turned and saw the manager from the loan department swing around the corner carrying a fresh cup of coffee. "See ya." She waved, and followed the manager, mimicking his lanky gait.

During lunch Nora let Leslie prattle on about her social life. She listened with only half an ear to Leslie's detailed description of her numerous dates and gave a start when Leslie touched her hand.

"Did you hear me?" her friend asked.

"I'm sorry, I was daydreaming a little," Nora replied. "What did you say?"

"I said I'm so glad things have worked out for you and Paul. He's a doll. When I saw you with him at the Matador and realized that out of all those people you two had met...well...I had planned to play matchmaker, but you two lovebirds didn't give me a chance." She smiled, thoroughly satisfied with herself. "Have you been seeing him much?"

"Some," Nora replied. She knew Leslie was a notorious gossip at the bank, though most of the stories were about Leslie herself.

Leslie smiled again. "You look much better. You've put on some weight and it looks good."

Nora picked out the pieces of chicken from her salad while she tried to decide how much she should tell Leslie.

"I'm quitting the bank," she said at last. "I gave my notice this morning." Leslie's mouth dropped open in surprise. "Paul and I are going to spend the summer at his grazing association's cabin in the mountains south of town."

"Are you getting married?"

"No."

Leslie's eyes grew round with curiosity. "Gee, Nora, you're not the type to mess around. Are you sure you're doing the right thing? I mean, Paul's sweet and all, but he's been known to drop girls left and right, and, well, he's never been very serious about anyone, really. I wouldn't want you to get hurt." She frowned, and an expression of genuine concern showed on her pretty face. "Has he gotten you pregnant?" she asked, her voice dropping to a whisper.

Nora blanched. "If I were, it would be between the two of us."

The silence between them became awkward, until Leslie broke it at last. "Right," she said. "Sorry I asked. Well, he's a doll. You're lucky, especially if he sticks with you. You'll be the first." She glanced at her tiny gold wristwatch. "We'd better hurry or we'll be late. You leave the tip, lucky lady. This meal is on me." She grabbed her purse and the check and hurried to the cashier's stand near the door.

That evening Nora waited until midnight for the phone to ring. As the hours passed and Paul failed to call, Leslie's warning began to chip at her confidence. She crawled into bed, longing to feel his body beside her. Just that morning he had made love to her and given his word to call, but he hadn't. As she drifted off to sleep she scolded herself. She wouldn't let Leslie fill her with doubts.

The ringing of the phone early the next morning woke Nora. The sun was peeking through a light cloud cover, and shards of rose and gold were splintering the gray dawn as she raced for the phone in the kitchen.

"Hello," she whispered breathlessly.

"Hello," a cheery woman's voice answered. "Is this Nora?"

"Yes, but..."

"I probably got you out of bed, didn't I?" the pleasant voice continued, and slowly Nora recognized it.

"Is this Paul's...Mrs. Russell?"

"Yes, but please call me Julie. I'm sorry to call so early, but I wanted to be sure and get you before you left for work."

"Is...is Paul all right?" Nora asked.

"Yes, I'm sure he is," his mother said. "When he arrived here yesterday he told me he planned to call you last night, but his father sent him and another of the boys out to find some missing pairs he had spotted earlier in the day. Russ was angry because one of the cattle trucks had broken down a few miles from our place and the cattle had to be unloaded and trailed to one of our pastures and watered and fed. It messed up his timetable. He told Paul and his brother not to return without the stock. They took rain gear and sleeping bags just in case. They didn't come back last night, and I didn't want you or Paul to worry about each other."

"I was concerned," Nora said. "Paul is...special to me. I'm so glad you called."

"I know, my dear," Julie said. "Paul has told me a little about you. I think you've become very special to him, too. You're the first young woman he's ever brought to one of our family picnics."

"Will you see him today?" Nora asked.

"I'm sure I will."

"Please tell him that I..." She tried to think of a

word other than love. "Tell him I miss him...very much."

"I will, my dear. You have a nice day, and bye for now."

Three more weeks without a word from Paul chipped away at the slender underpinnings of Nora's confidence, yet when the phone finally rang, she knew it was Paul.

"Hello, sweetheart."

She tried to speak, but her voice failed to make a sound.

"Nora?" he called. "Are you there, honey?"

"Yes," she replied as a sob of relief swept through her.

"Nora, honey, don't cry. I'm so sorry it's been such a long time, but there are no phones up at the cabin or any of the other places I've been the past few weeks, just me and my horse and hundreds of cows. But now I'm home again. I'm coming for you, love. Are you packed? Speak to me so I know you're there." He laughed, his voice sounding like sweet music to her ears.

"Yes...yes, I'm here, Paul," she replied. "I've missed you so much. Your mother called weeks ago, but since then I've heard nothing, except when I saw your sister Mary. She said you were on the upper range somewhere." She stopped to wipe her eyes. "I'm sorry I cried." She laughed nervously. "Are you really coming for me? When?" She glanced at the wall calendar beside the phone. "Thursday is my last working day."

"Then Friday morning I'll be there. No, make that Thursday evening. Why waste a night when I can have you in my arms again. Do you need clothing? I'll buy you some."

"No, I have maternity jeans and tops. I haven't worn

maternity clothes to work. I've been hoping people would just think I'm getting fat. I don't want to answer questions. I have tennis shoes and a pair of boots and two warm jackets. My personal things are boxed and ready to take to the storage place I rented. I didn't know what else to do."

"Hush, woman, we'll talk about it Thursday night. I want to take you to dinner when I get there, then we'll make plans. How are you feeling? Getting lots of rest? Eating properly?"

She laughed. "I'm fine. And you? Been eating your own cooking, cowboy?"

"Yes, and I've lost weight, so you'd better get up here fast, honey." He whispered several love phrases to her and she felt her cheeks blush. "I'll see you in two days. Take care, and, you know, I've been thinking...the baby's going to be a boy. Bye."

Nora's hands trembled as she returned the receiver to its cradle. Two days loomed like an eternity. Two more long twenty-four-hour days and they'd be together again.

NORA PEEKED OUT THE WINDOW when she heard the pick-up roll to a stop in front of her house. She slipped through the door and watched Paul vault over the low fence and jog up the narrow cement walk. He took the steps two at a time, and suddenly she was crushed against his chest and her face smothered with kisses.

He released her and guided her back through the door, closed it, then drew her close again.

"Hello, sweetheart," he whispered, holding her face in his hands and tipping it up and down slightly, examining every inch. Her lashes fluttered, and a hot tear rolled from the corner of her eye. "You're more beautiful than

I remembered," he said, then his mouth claimed hers again.

She wrapped her arms tightly around his waist, trying to get closer to him. He lifted her up in his arms and strode to the sofa, then dropped into the comfortable seat, cradling her in his arms. "I've missed you so much, Nora. These weeks without you have made me realize how much you mean to me. I love you, pretty lady."

She rested her head against his shoulder as they sat quietly, absorbing each other's presence. Finally Nora straightened up and smiled at him.

"What's this coming between us?" he asked. His face was somber until a boyish grin pulled at the corners of his mouth.

"What?"

"This." He placed his large hand on her abdomen. "You're bigger. I can tell when I hug you."

"Do you mind?"

"Of course not," he murmured, his lips against her hair. "I'm partly to blame."

She grew momentarily perplexed, wondering if he blamed them both for getting into this predicament.

"This summer we'll have time to decide. . . on everything. We'll come in for the rodeo and fair, but the cattle aren't moved back to the winter pasture closer to home until late October, depending on the weather. Steven will relieve me and we'll stay in town until the baby comes. By then I hope you'll be Mrs. Paul Russell. My father is mostly Austrian, though I don't know where Russell comes from. Some Englishman in the woodpile, I guess. My mother is German and English. The combination makes for one hell of a persistent nature, so don't expect me to give up." He pulled her close and buried his chin in her thick hair.

"Let's go eat," he suggested. "I'm taking you to the Eagle's Nest. They have the best prime rib in the county. It's several blocks from here up on the hill. Do you want to ride or walk?"

"Walk," she replied. "I want to be with you, and walking will take longer."

He reached for her hand and held it as they walked through the quiet streets of town. Several times they met people who called out his name and waved.

"You know so many people," Nora commented.

"I've lived near here all my life. I went to school here. There are only a few thousand people in the town and less than ten thousand in the entire county." He laughed. "I would have to be a hermit not to know people."

"They'll notice I'm pregnant. I can't hide it anymore," she persisted, knowing she was forcing the issue.

"Stop it, Nora," he chided, taking both her hands in his. "I'll tell them the baby is mine. As for marriage, that's our own business, no one else's. There's no need to bring it up again."

MUCH TO HER CHAGRIN, Nora awoke the next morning and realized that she had fallen asleep after receiving just one kiss from Paul.

"I'm sorry I fell asleep so soon. I thought we'd—"

He interrupted her with a kiss. "Forget it. Lovemaking wasn't important last night, just loving." He pulled her closer and shut his eyes again.

A few hours later his brother Steven arrived in a Wagoneer and helped them move her boxes of personal possessions into the small storage space she'd rented. Steven didn't appear to be surprised at her condition. He teased her and playfully hugged her, calling her sis more than once, and Nora wondered what Paul had told his brother.

Shorty after lunch Steven climbed back into the station wagon, waved to them and drove away.

Paul carried her suitcases to the back of his truck, along with two boxes of kitchen utensils, books, a portable cassette-tape player with extra batteries and a box of art supplies. "What are these?" he asked, peering into the box.

"I've always wanted to paint," she explained. "I bought a how-to art book and all this stuff at the Country Gallery. This summer I'll find out if I have any creativity in me."

He nodded his approval, then turned to her. "Ready?"

"Yes," she replied, accepting his outstretched hand.

CHAPTER EIGHT

NORA HAD NEVER BEEN to the southern part of the valley.

"The wild flowers are so pretty," she said, admiring the riotous colors scattered across the rolling green fields and meadows.

"They're weeds," Paul told her. "It's a continual fight to keep them under control."

"I think they're lovely. Oh, look at that pretty lavender one," she cried, pointing to a plant near a fence post.

"That's a spotted knapweed." Paul grimaced. "It's the worst of the lot. It would fill the whole valley and make it impossible to grow the hay we need if we didn't constantly keep after it."

"Oh," she replied, forlornly regretting her comment.

He reached over and squeezed her hand. "They're not all bad. Even knapweed has its good points. Sheep love it. I've thought about suggesting we get a few bands of sheep to help control it, but..." He chuckled. "Dad's from the old school about not mixing cattle and sheep, but those days are gone. I know they would be compatible, but still...I hesitate to bring up another controversial idea on the Rocking R. And you're right, some are just pretty flowers. You'll learn the difference. It takes time."

Houses and mobile homes on small acreages were quickly left behind as the road changed from smooth pavement to roughly graded gravel. A creek raced and bounced along an endless line of willows and cottonwood trees on its way to join the river north of town, and the undulating valley floor rolled up to gentle foothills, which ended abruptly against jagged bluish mountains, studded with evergreens and still dotted with snow in their deeper crevices. In the distance Nora could make out the sprawling houses and outbuildings of the various ranches.

A short time later the truck pulled into the yard of what looked to be a rather large and prosperous ranching operation. Barns stood on both sides of the road, with a cluster of houses to Nora's right, and cattle corrals and a long horse barn to her left.

"I just want to stop in and see how things are going here," Paul explained. As he slowed the truck to a rolling stop, a tall brown-haired young man approached him, holding the reins of a saddled horse. A large horse trailer, its goose neck attached to the bed of a pickup truck, was parked near the stable. Several horses were already in the trailer. Two older men waved to Paul as they climbed into the truck in front of the trailer.

"Nora, this is Kevin Ramsey," Paul said, introducing the tall man. "He works here at the Shoestring. The ranch started out years ago on just that, but now it's the biggest spread in the county with more than one hundred forty thousand acres. It makes our home ranch, the Rocking R, look small."

The man nodded to Nora and brushed the brim of his black hat. He and Paul talked for several moments, while Nora surveyed the activity in the ranch yard. She felt like an alien as she listened with half an ear to Paul's talk of cattle, haying, equipment-repair problems and especially the weather.

The truck's horn sounded twice, and Kevin Ramsey waved a friendly goodbye, touched his hat brim again with his forefinger and murmured, "Ma'am," then ambled to the truck.

Nora tilted her head, listening to the sounds of the departing cowboy. "What's that jingling?"

"Spurs."

"You really wear spurs?" she asked, her eyes alight with surprise and amusement.

"Of course, if you want the horse to go."

She grinned. "I thought cowboys only wore spurs in the movies."

"You're in the real West now, honey. You've got a lot of new things to learn." He turned the ignition. "We're stopping at our place for a late lunch. Dad and my brothers will be gone, but mom is expecting us." He sensed Nora's apprehension. "It's okay. Mom knows about... you and me. This lunch is her idea. She insisted. She has some things for the cabin."

"Does she know I'm..."

"Yes."

"She must think I'm terrible."

"I told her we were working on a solution."

"What about your father?"

He shook his head. "He doesn't know. He wouldn't understand, anyway. I'll tell him when the time is right."

THE TRUCK PULLED UP in front of a very large, two-story, rambling white frame house, with a covered porch running completely across the front and around one side. Four steps led up to the porch, and a few feet from the front steps was a hitching rail.

Paul came around to Nora's side and helped her down

from the high cab. As they approached the house the front door opened and Paul's mother greeted them.

"Welcome, Nora," Julie said, reaching out her hand. "It's so nice to see you again. Come in."

"She's so friendly," Nora whispered to Paul.

"She's a friendly person," Paul replied as Julie disappeared into the house.

"But she's your mother."

He smiled. "That she is."

"But she knows I'm carrying... her grandchild. Good grief." Nora looked up at Paul.

"That she does."

"And she knows we're not married."

"Right."

"Oh, she has to think I'm scandalous." She turned away from the door and stared at the distant mountains, trying to build up enough confidence to face Julie Russell again.

"Mom's not the kind of woman to judge others," Paul assured her. "I told her we had some problems and we would work them out. She's a very liberated woman in her own country way. Now let's eat. You wouldn't want to hurt her feelings, would you?"

Nora shook her head, still skeptical of all the saintly qualities Paul attributed to his mother. He led her through the house to a large kitchen. Three patchwork placemats and table settings were already on the large harvest table, and a bouquet of wild flowers adorned the center. Julie added a chicken casserole and tossed green salad, then returned to the counter to get a small plate of fresh biscuits, hand-churned butter and homemade strawberry jam.

"Let's eat," she said, smiling warmly.

Throughout lunch Julie chatted about the town, her

children and rural living. "I love it, and I hope you will, too."

"But—" Nora said.

"I know," Julie broke in, "but you'll work things out. Five or ten years ago I would never have said this, but I've always wondered about the importance of that piece of paper issued at the courthouse. It doesn't guarantee love and happiness, only a legal marriage in the eyes of the government. How did the government get into the act of marriage? It should be between the man and woman and God. I always thought it would be nice to get married in a small meadow surrounded by a forest with just the wind and the wild animals witnessing the vows."

Paul laughed. "Why didn't you and dad do that?"

"Your father thought I was a little crazy when I suggested it," Julie admitted. "So we got married in the Baptist church in town. Ordinary but legal. I guess with six kids, it was best."

Paul excused himself and left the room. Julie turned to Nora, took her hand and squeezed it.

"You've been good for my son," Julie said. "He's changed since he met you. It's amazing what six months can do to a person. You see, Nora, I love all my children, but my oldest son is special, perhaps just a little more than the rest. His father expects unchallenged obedience from all his children. It's an unrealistic way to treat them." She shook her head. "Paul takes the brunt of Russ's demands. If he didn't love this life, I know he would have left long ago. My husband doesn't seem to realize what a gift our children are. They're becoming adults and he thinks they'll never leave home, but I know they will, especially if he refuses to change his attitude. He's so positive they'll all stay home that he enlarged the house about ten years ago so each child could have his own room. We could be worse off. At least Russ is very generous with the house and modern conveniences. A lot of men here still retain the old-world attitude that women don't need appliances to make their work easier. You know, 'If grandmother made do, so can you.'" She smiled sadly. "But his generosity won't win him permanent control of his children in this day and age. This is a seven-bedroom house, but sooner or later it will be empty."

"I think I understand," Nora replied, "but I'm in a very different position. I have no family. I would put up with the problems in order to have a family."

Julie nodded her understanding as she rose and began clearing the table.

A few minutes later Paul returned. "We'd better go, mom. We want to get settled before dark."

Julie motioned to a box containing jars of home-canned food and kitchen supplies. "Take that and the ham radio, Paul. Just in case. Perhaps it's silly, but I hate to see anyone go out unprepared."

"Okay," Paul said, reaching for the boxes. "Bye, mom." He leaned down to kiss her cheek. "We'll see you in a few months."

Nora experienced a surge of warmth when Julie kissed her cheek and hugged her.

"Take care, my dears. Enjoy the peace and privacy." She followed them to the door and waved as they drove away.

THE WEEKS IN THE CABIN passed quickly as life settled into a routine. Nora learned to cook on the wood-burning stove with a bit of help from Paul, and to use the hand pump at the kitchen sink.

Paul was usually gone during the long hours of daylight, leaving on horseback right after an early breakfast, so Nora spent a few hours outdoors with her paint tubes, brushes and paper, using a cardboard box on a chair as an easel and clothespins to hold the paper. Finding herself alone in the forest brought her serenity rather than loneliness, and she knew Paul would return around dusk.

One day on his rounds he came across a calf's mutilated carcass.

"I know it's a bear," he told Nora during dinner. "I spotted his tracks near the carcass."

Early the next morning he saddled his horse, tied a sleeping bag and an all-weather riding duster behind the saddle and returned to the cabin for his rifle. Nora shivered when she saw him shove the gun into its scabbard and drop a box of cartridges into his saddlebag.

"I may be gone overnight, but you'll be safe," he said as he climbed into the saddle. "You have the keys to the truck." He leaned down and Nora stood on tiptoes to touch his lips.

"Bye," she whispered, feeling like a heroine in an old Western movie as he rode away.

He returned the next afternoon, tired and frustrated, but glad to be home. "He's gone—not a sign of him anywhere. I hope he doesn't come back." He slid from the saddle. "I'll take care of my horse and be back. Damn it, I'm sweaty and stink to high heaven. I want to love you, honey, but I wouldn't blame you if you refused to allow me in the house. Heat some water and I'll bathe in our fancy bathroom." Then he disappeared, leading the appaloosa gelding to a small corral behind the cabin.

Nora smiled as she rekindled the fire in the wood stove. Their "fancy" bathroom consisted of a chemical toilet and a dry sink. The tiny kitchen had a sink and a pitcher pump, and though she still had trouble with the pump at times, she was thankful to have a water supply inside the cabin. At times she felt like a pioneer woman living with her husband on a turn-of-the century homestead.

Paul washed while she prepared supper, and after they'd eaten he helped her with the dishes. She had bought several skeins of yarn, an instruction book and three sizes of crochet hooks in a variety store in town, determined to teach herself to crochet during their stay in the mountains. When Paul settled in a chair and began to read a livestock magazine, she got out the book and played with the yarn and hook, feeling very clumsy and dropping the hook several times.

"Oh, darn," she huffed in frustration.

Paul dropped his magazine onto the floor near the stone hearth and came to her chair. "Let me help."

"You?"

"Sure," he said. "One time we were snowed in for a weekend. I was about fourteen and we were driving mom nuts, so she made us all sit down and she taught us each how to crochet, girls and boys alike. My brothers and I all swore an oath never to tell what we did that weekend, but it was lots of fun and I've never forgotten how to do it. Mom made us each do a sample square, then we had to complete something. I made a giant granny-square mat for my dog's house outside. It's still there, kelly green and orange and covered with dog hair. Ugly as hell... why, it's as ugly as old Blue."

"Blue?"

"My dog. He's a blue heeler. He's fifteen years old and can hardly move sometimes, but his descendants are the best working dogs in the valley."

"I don't know whether to believe you or not," Nora said.

He took the hook and quickly chained several inches, turned it and made two rows of double crochet. He handed the hook and yarn back to her, scanned the directions in the book, then instructed her in the stitch. When she made a mistake he tactfully stopped her and corrected her, insisting she do it right.

When he was sure she had mastered the stitch, he moved away and scooped his magazine off the floor, then returned to his chair. Soon he was deeply involved with his reading. Nora sat quietly for a few moments, staring at his bowed head and loving him more than ever.

When she turned back to her book, hook and yarn, she soon had completed a sample square all by herself. She went to Paul and proudly held up her accomplishment.

"See?" she bragged.

He raised his head and scrutinized her handiwork, then nodded. "I see," he said. "I see more than just that square. I see a beautiful woman standing before me." Reaching for her hand, he drew her onto his lap, discarding the magazine on the floor again.

"Oh, pretty lady," he whispered, drawing her closer. His lips molded to hers, and he explored her velvet mouth. His hand shook slightly as he unbuttoned the front of her smock, allowing his fingers to trail over her breasts.

Then abruptly he stopped and eased her off his lap. "Come with me," he said, leading her into the small bedroom and starting to unsnap his Western shirt.

"No," she cried. "Let me." Her fingers slowly worked at his shirt front, the springy dark hairs on his chest enticing her as she caressed them. Her mouth inched to his nipple and daringly she touched it with her tongue.

He groaned. "Do you know what you do to me?" Sliding his hands into her tumbling hair, he moved her head away from his chest. His fingers pressed softly into her cheeks as he turned her face up to his and kissed her mouth until she was breathless, then pulled her down to the bed.

She started to giggle as her arms slid around his neck.

"What's so funny?" he asked.

"We forgot to finish undressing."

He started to laugh. "I'll race you. Last one undressed has to make love to the winner."

They scrambled up to throw their clothing aside. Nora slid under the covers first, laughing as Paul struggled with his riding boots.

"Damn it," he muttered, finally dislodging the stubborn boots and dispensing with the rest of his clothes.

"You lose," she cried, clapping her hands in delight.

"Oh, no, you're wrong, my love," he said as he came to her. His hand moved over her rounded hips and down her thigh. "I win."

PAUL KISSED HER as he left the cabin early the next morning, promising to return for lunch. "What's on the menu?"

"Stew, beef stew, of course," she replied.

"I'll be here at high noon," he said, saluting her as he mounted the gelding and rode away.

She straightened the cabin, swept the bare wood floors, and made the bed, smiling as she thought of last night's lovemaking. She hummed as she worked, and as she gave the pillows a final pat, she hugged them and whirled around, deliriously happy. She started when a loud knock sounded at the cabin door. No one had visited them since their arrival. Apprehensively she twisted the knob and slowly pulled the heavy wooden door open a crack. Steven Russell's handsome face peered back at her.

"Hi, sis," he said, grinning. "Can we come in?"

"We?" she asked, still hesitant to open the door.

"Russ and myself."

Her throat tightened. "Your father?"

He laughed. "No, my brother, Edwin Russell, Jr."

She pulled the door open. "I'm sorry. I'm not used to having callers. Come in." She stood aside as they entered, removing their hats and holding them in their gloved hands. They were dressed in well-worn plaid shirts and jeans, and Steven had a blue neckerchief tied around his throat. Their legs were covered with leather chaps, which showed signs of scratches from the sagebrush that grew on the rugged range land.

"Would you like some coffee?" she asked.

"Yes," they replied in unison.

"It's from breakfast. It might be strong."

"That's fine," Steven said. "It's been a long morning." As they followed her into the kitchen, their spurs jingled. Steven's hazel eyes sparkled. "Do you really think I would bring my father to visit? He doesn't know you're up here."

As she poured the stout coffee into the mugs, Nora invited them to stay for lunch. Steven lifted the lid and sniffed the bubbling stew in the heavy cast-iron dutch oven on the stove, then nodded to his brother, who also accepted.

"Your father doesn't know I'm staying here?" Nora asked. "Paul said he would tell him...to make sure it was all right."

"Well," Steven said, taking a long draw on his coffee, "dad's not very easy to talk to, especially when you know he'll have a fit over what you want to talk about." His eyes flickered toward her abdomen. "Dad is a modern businessman, but he is an old-fashioned hypocrite in other ways. To hear him tell it, in the good old days nobody got pregnant until after the wedding." He chuckled. "God, you should have seen his face when mom said once that there must have been a lot of seven-pound premature babies then."

"What would he do if he knew? What if he comes here?"

Steven patted her hand. "Don't worry, sis. We'll protect you from his wrath. We all promised Paul...Tim, too, and the girls. We've learned to stick together."

"Your mother knows," Nora said.

"But you can trust mom," Russ said in a low soft voice.

"He never comes up this way," Steven assured her. "This is the back of the McCormack property. Dad is busy running from one place to another to check on the managers of the family ranches. He doesn't trust them. He pays them a decent salary, then wastes time checking up on them. That's our father."

Paul returned at noon, and the four of them sat down to lunch. As the brothers talked, Nora watched their animated gestures, enjoying the still-unfamiliar experience of being part of their family. Steven teased and flirted with her, but Russ, Jr., spoke only when she asked him a direct question, and then with a minimum of words.

After lunch, Paul kissed her again, and the three brothers rode off together. She painted for an hour, satisfied with her rendition of two chipmunks perched on a fallen log. She had spent a week on the painting and was pleased that finally she had a piece of art she was willing to show Paul. She had destroyed all her previous pieces, telling him, "They were just for practice."

When she returned to the cabin, she cleaned her brushes and put away the art supplies. After crocheting several rows of the growing afghan, she grew restless and tossed the yarn and hook down. She walked from room to room, trying to expend some of her nervous energy, then went for a long walk in the wooded area behind the house. But thoughts of Paul's father kept intruding, and finally she returned to the cabin and concentrated on her crocheting.

As she began to prepare supper, she found she had trouble reaching items on the top shelf of the small cupboard. She was well into her eighth month of pregnancy, and at times she knew she waddled, though she tried desperately to prevent the awkward gait. At least Paul didn't seem to mind her bulkiness. The unborn baby suddenly gave a resounding kick against her ribs, taking her breath away.

She heard the sound of the horse when Paul returned. She imagined him at work unsaddling the horse and putting the tack away, returning to groom the gelding and probably give him a measure of grain to augment the sweet natural grass in the fenced meadow nearby. The horses had frightened her when she had first arrived at the cabin, and Paul had promised to teach her to ride after the birth of their child. She had never been astride a horse in her life, and he had teased her about being a city girl. She realized she had grown to love Paul Russell more than any other man, even, she painfully admitted, her husband, Jerry.

Using a long fork, she stacked the pieces of chicken fried steak onto a small platter. Another platter of fried potatoes and onions was already on the table, and she had heated a jar of canned green beans his mother had included in the boxes for the cabin. Dinner was ready.

Her heartbeat quickened when Paul entered the cabin and smiled at her. He washed up and joined her at the table, his lips warm as they brushed hers. She watched him serve himself from the platters. His appetite amazed her, yet he stayed slim and rock hard. He was quiet during dinner, his brows furrowing as his face darkened.

"Problems?" Nora asked as they took the dishes to the sink.

He joined her, drying as she washed. "It's that bear again. He brought down another calf yesterday. I found the carcass late this afternoon." He dropped his damp towel on the counter. "Honey, I hate to leave you alone overnight again, but I can't let that bear continue to get the livestock." He pulled her into his arms and held her for several moments, rubbing her tired back muscles. She settled against his chest, enjoying the warm soothing feel of his strong hands.

"Maybe I should take you back to town. Mom told me to keep a close eye on you. She said a baby can come early." He tipped her chin up and peered into her eyes. "I don't want any harm to come to you or the baby," he said, sliding his hands through her hair and holding her head immobile.

"Paul," she moaned as her mouth sought his, her arms circling his neck as she pressed against his hard body. He laughed, and her puzzled expression brought another lighthearted laugh from him.

"I felt the baby kick. He's a strong little fellow. I..." An unreadable expression filled his eyes, then was quickly erased by a sweep of his thick black lashes. "I'm glad you were alone that first night, and that the power failed, and all the rest, too," he said softly, and his mouth caressed hers again.

That night sleep evaded Nora. Her fear of the darkness

had become tolerable when Paul was with her. Once she had tried to describe the dreams but had given up, and he had held her, pushing away the walls of darkness. She shivered.

"Cold?"

"Just a chill."

They lay quietly for several minutes. "I don't want to go back to town, Paul. I would rather stay here with you." He tightened his arm around her. "What must you do about the bear?"

"I've got to find him. . . and probably kill him before he gets any more of our cattle. Steven is contacting the Fish and Game Department, so we won't have trouble with them." He touched her silky hair. "I'll track him. I'm taking my sleeping bag and a mess kit and rain gear. I don't know how long I'll be gone. Are you sure you'll be all right? You know how to use the propane lights and the pump. I hate to leave you alone, but if you have any problem, no matter how minor, drive the truck to mom's or to town. Hear me?"

She nodded, suppressing a rising tide of apprehension. "I'm trying to be a good wife. . . oh!" she cried, realizing her slip.

"You should be my wife," he said. "Marry me. This is stupid of us to live like this. I want you as my wife, in the eyes of God, the townspeople, the government and my family. My father will come around. He's not completely insensitive."

She hesitated for a few seconds. "I will," she said, her heart thudding in her breast.

"You will?" The surprise in his voice made her laugh aloud. He pulled away. "You really will?"

"Yes."

"Why did you change your mind?"

"I think you'll be a very good father. You've had so much practice with your brothers and sisters, and I do want my child to have a legal father. But most of all," she whispered, "I want to marry you because I love you so very much."

CHAPTER NINE

THE BRIGHT MONTANA SUN rolled across the sky as Nora counted the hours since Paul had left the cabin. She had successfully hidden from him her growing apprehension at being left behind. She knew there was no way she could accompany him, and she didn't want to return to Dillon without him.

He was doing the job he had accepted for the association members and was concerned about all the cattle, even if they weren't his own brand. She had teased him about it just that morning when they had gone on a short walk before breakfast. "You treat the cattle like humans," she had said.

He had smiled down at her. "Don't laugh, Nora, but they do have different personalities and temperaments." He pushed back the brim of his hat and scratched his head. "Do you suppose I've been with them too long?"

"Possibly," she said with a laugh. "It's a good thing you have me here to talk to, so you can tell the difference." She rested her hand on her abdomen. "Sometimes I feel as big as those old cows." She turned to him with a frown. "I must look a sight. I wish I were thin again."

He had turned away without a comment, leaving her to wonder if he was beginning to find her size unappealing. Several minutes later they had returned to the cabin. He had seemed preoccupied during breakfast and rode away shortly afterward.

As the morning wore on, she tended to the kerosene and propane lamps. She cleaned the chimneys of the two kerosene lamps, polishing the glass, and replaced the broken mantle on one of the propane lights.

Living without electricity had proven to be more tolerable than she had imagined. The propane lights cast a bright illumination that allowed reading and crocheting. Later each night Paul would light the softer kerosene lamps and turn out the propanes. The mellow golden glow from the lamps brought a romantic mood to the primitive cabin, and modern conveniences were quickly forgotten as his arms went around her and he held her and talked about their life together.

Later that morning she painted for a few hours, fascinated by the shades and shadows of the forest. She ate under a pine tree, enjoying the cool air and sharing her roast-beef sandwich with the friendly chipmunks, who scurried to her feet to steal a crumb of bread, then raced away to nibble on the tidbit. She had been feeding them daily since her arrival at the cabin.

The afternoon slipped into evening, and she hurriedly lit the lamps to push away the darkness. She had three more inches of crocheting to do before her afghan would be finished, but she felt no desire to work on it, so she picked up a novel she'd been reading.

Twice she nodded off, her head jerking and her heart thudding when she awoke seconds later. Tossing down the book, she went to the bedroom to change into her nightclothes, bringing some warm blankets with her when she returned. She put three more small logs onto the fire and curled up on the sofa for the night. The darkness of the bedroom frightened her when Paul was gone. Her bed would be the sofa until he returned.

She had hardly closed her eyes when the bright morning sun woke her. As she stretched she felt the baby move, and she settled back onto the sofa, reluctant to start the day without Paul. She lay quietly, trying to control her thoughts, but the attempt was futile. Paul, their child, her dead husband and baby all fought to gain prominence in her mind.

Paul had taken first place in her life, but she was reluctant to allow his complete dominance. Sometimes she had doubts about his love for her. She sensed he was holding back full commitment. What if he had a change of heart and wanted out? True, he had asked her to marry him, but many engagements were broken before the vows were exchanged. She had to be prepared to live without him. The baby moved again, reminding her of its imminent arrival in their lives. Would it be a wedge between them or have a melding effect on their relationship?

She forced herself from the comfortable sofa and dressed in maternity jeans and a top with gold smocking on the yoke. The top was her favorite. Its yellow-and-white gingham made her feel as though she had wrapped herself in a bundle of sunbeams. She refused to let anything spoil her day. She would enjoy the privacy, paint awhile and experiment with new color combinations, perhaps go for a long walk in the forest and feed her chipmunks, read a little and finish the afghan.

She smiled as she brewed a small pot of coffee on the wood stove. The afghan was only a few inches wider at the end than the starting rows of stitches. She'd decided to give it to Paul for his birthday in November. Normally a man would never notice such a flaw in an afghan, but her Paul would tease her and probably say he could have done better.

He would kiss her and say he loved it, and then he

would hug her and maybe make love to her. She'd be slim again, the baby would be a few months old, and they might be married.... Her thoughts were erased by a noise outside. She peeked out the window in time to see three mule deer disappear into the trees beyond the clearing, heading for the creek several hundred feet from the cabin.

San Diego was a million miles away. Even the new town of Dillon was in a different world. Here only Paul's truck parked in the clearing reminded her of modern times. The rustic cabin, the horses, the wood stove, the hand pump at the sink, the kerosene and propane lights, even the jars of meat, fruit and vegetables that Julie Russell had given her were from a life-style that had been alien to her a few months ago.

As she ate dinner alone, she accepted the fact that Paul would not be home that night. Perhaps tomorrow. She fell asleep on the sofa as the sun disappeared behind the western mountains.

Two days later he still hadn't returned. Nora's growing concern had wound her up until she felt like a bundle of frayed charged wires, ready to spark at any moment.

A LOUD KNOCK on the cabin door jerked Nora awake from an afternoon nap. Dizziness swept through her as she clumsily rose from the sofa. The baby kicked, and her knees wobbled as she grabbed for the small table nearby and tried to steady herself. The knock sounded again, this time a heavy thud.

An unfamiliar male voice boomed through the timbers as the door rattled. Nora ran her hand through her hair, trying to bring some order to its disarray, then rubbed her eyes to erase the sleepiness that lingered. Adjusting her jeans and red smock, she hurried to the door and pulled it open.

A husky middle-aged man of less than average height stood before her. The rounded crown of his black felt hat flowed into a broad brim and shielded part of his face, but Nora could sense the anger in his stance and the firm set of his mouth. His long-sleeved denim shirt was sloppily tucked into his jeans, and his belly shielded the buckle on his leather belt. He wore muddy work boots and scuffed leather gloves, and a greasy cloth hung from his hip pocket.

"Where's my boy?" he demanded.

Recognition struck her. "Mr. Russell!"

"Where's Paul?" he asked, ignoring her greeting.

"He's...he's tracking a...bear." Her voice squeaked with nervousness.

"What the hell are you doing here?"

She stepped back into the room and he followed her.

"Regular little love nest, ain't it?" he commented, turning to her. They were eye level with each other. His face was florid, and his black eyes glared at her. "I knew he was up to something, but I thought he'd have more sense than this!"

He stepped closer, and Nora could smell his sweaty odor. She choked back a gagging sensation and fleetingly wondered how Julie Russell could be his wife. She scolded herself. Any man could smell after a hard day of physical labor, even Paul, but he always bathed before coming close to her. She stepped away from him.

"Paul's not here," she said.

"You've already said that."

"Paul's..." Her shoulders stiffened. "What do you want?"

"I want you out of here."

"You have no right—"

"You're wrong, lady. I happen to know who owns this

cabin. He wouldn't tolerate this type of goings-on any more than I do. I belong to the grazing association. My son is the one authorized to live here, and it had better be alone the next time I stop by. He's a good boy, wild sometimes, but a good boy. I raised him that way. You've done something to him." His gaze ran down her body, lingering on her abdomen, then slowly returning to her ashen face. "You have no right being here." He stepped closer. "I don't cotton to my son shacking up with no stranger."

Fury changed her pale cheeks to pink. "Get out of here!"

"I'll leave when I'm damned good and ready," he snarled. "I knew he was up to something. My wife is gullible, but she didn't fool me. She tried to convince me she needed another cook on the payroll. She already has a girl from town. That's enough. She said something about insurance coverage. I should have checked this out sooner. That damned wife of mine has some explaining to do right along with my boy." His gloved hand touched her shoulder, and she took a few steps backward. "Lady, you're mistaken if you think I'll pay one thin dime in medical insurance for a bastard kid fathered by some bar-hopping cowboy in town. You got that? Not a dime."

"Get out," Nora insisted.

He stomped to the door, leaving clumps of dried mud on her clean floor, then turned and shook his fist at her. "I want you out! Out of this cabin, away from my boy. You're Nellie, aren't you, that blonde he brought to the picnic? I should have been suspicious right then and there. He never brings girls around. He's a good boy." He stepped through the doorway, paused and turned one last time. "Out!" he shouted as Nora slammed the door on him.

She slumped against the closed door. Why hadn't Paul told his father about her? Was he afraid of his wrath, or his control of the family finances? Where was he? "Oh, Paul, please hurry back," she murmured, slumping into a chair.

Her appetite had vanished after the upsetting confrontation. Dusk fell. She lit one of the kerosene lamps and built a small fire in the fireplace, but a chill permeated the room. No fire or lamp could warm her and chase away her concerns.

She tried to read, but the words swam on the page. She dropped the book onto her lap and stared blankly into the flames, knowing her stay with Paul in their honeymoon cottage had ended.

The room darkened as night descended, and she fell asleep, only to awake a few hours later as the kerosene lamp flickered and threatened to plunge the room into darkness.

"The kerosene," she gasped, glancing at the almost-empty glass fount. She had forgotten to refill the lamps. The chore had become a morning ritual, but for some reason it had completely slipped her mind that morning. She ran to get the propane lamp and kitchen matches, but in her haste she fumbled and dropped the box of matches.

"Oh, no!" she cried as the matches scattered across the floor. The flickering rays of dim light cast ghostly shadows on the dark wooden walls and ceiling.

She reached for the kerosene lamp. If she could move it to the table's edge, she could use its dying rays to help her find a few of the fallen matches. Her shin collided with the small table, and the sharp pain brought her to her knees. The table fell on its side, and the lamp smashed to the floor, shattering.

Tiny rivulets of flaming kerosene raced in all directions, following the grooves in the wood floor. The room seemed to burst into flames around her, filling with bright orange light. The cabin was old, its logs, hand hewn decades ago, were now weathered and dry, and it would become a tinderbox of death for her and her unborn child.

"Oh, Paul," she sobbed. She saw the blue-and-brown afghan she'd labored on all summer. Grabbing it, she thew it over the flames. Some of the fingers of fire were snuffed out, and she sighed with relief, then suddenly the acrylic yarn began to melt and the flames leaped up with renewed vigor.

Nora raced to the bedroom for the stack of blankets she'd used the night before on the sofa, raced back to the living room, and threw them over the flames. Paul's rubber overshoes were still by the door and she ran to them. Balancing herself against the wall, she stepped into the oversize boots, shuffled back to the smoldering blankets and stomped out the lingering flames.

The room was plunged into darkness. She backed away from the fire-damaged center of the room until she bumped into a hard wall. Her confidence drained away and her fear of the darkness crept in.

She squeezed her eyes shut, then realized it didn't matter if her eyes were open or closed, the darkness was the same. The stench of kerosene, melted yarn, charred wood and scorched woolen blankets choked the breath from her lungs as she lost her hold on reality and fainted.

WHEN NORA REGAINED CONSCIOUSNESS she was chilled to the bone. She heard the sounds of prowling outside the cabin and tried to stand. Visions of bears, cougars, coyotes or even a rare timber wolf came to her. The sound grew louder as the intruder approached the cabin door.

The door opened and a giant figure filled the entryway. A bright flashlight beam moved around the room, settling on the pile of charred blankets.

"Nora?" Paul called, then shouted, "Nora!" The beam of light finally found her, pressed against the chinked log wall.

She was unable to move. He stepped around the blankets, his spurs jingling in the cold night air, and swept her into his arms. He felt her chilled arms and shoulders and eased her away while he unbuttoned his sheepskin coat, then he pulled her closer to share the warmth of its fleece lining, and he held her until her trembling subsided. Tilting her head up, he used his mouth to warm hers, and she slid her arms around his waist, absorbing the heat of his body through his clothing.

"Paul, I've made such a mess of things," she sobbed.

He shone the flashlight around the room. "Yes," he agreed. "It looks that way. Where's your coat? Why haven't you lit the propane lamps? Did you run out of firewood? I thought I left you with plenty." He squeezed her tight. "Oh, honey, I've missed you. I shot the bear about dusk this evening. He was a good-size male black bear. Strangest thing, I got him near a road. He was standing over another calf carcass. We can go back for him tomorrow. I couldn't stay away another night. I needed you in my arms, my love, and I hoped that you'd need me, too. . . but I didn't expect all this."

In a quavering voice she explained the accident that had led to the fire, trying to recall details of the terrifying evening, but she avoided mentioning his father's visit and threatening words.

Paul slid out of his coat and put it around her shoulders, then quickly built a roaring blaze in the fireplace. "Fancy shoes you're wearing, pretty lady," he remarked, chuckling.

She glanced down at the oversize rubber boots on her feet and smiled for the first time in hours. Paul went to the bedroom and returned carrying her gown, robe and slippers, two sleeping bags and pillows. He prepared a bed for them before the fireplace and soon had her nestled in his embrace in the warm bags.

She listened to his adventure with the elusive bear, feeling very proud of his mountaineering skills and loving him so much she ached with it.

He looked down at her drooping eyelids. "Go to sleep, sweetheart. If you can stand me without a bath, then let me hold you. I've been away too long."

"Yes," she murmured drowsily, inhaling the musky smell of leather and man, savoring the very essence of him as she drifted off to sleep.

WHEN NORA AWOKE the next morning Paul was gone, but as she lay in the sleeping bag, Nora heard a melodious tenor voice coming from the kitchen. He completed a respectable rendition of a passage from the opera *Rigoletto*, then immediately swung into a nasal imitation of Willie Nelson's song about mothers and cowboys.

She reached for her robe and slippers and rose from the makeshift bed, feeling very awkward. She padded to the kitchen door, her breath catching in her throat at the sight of Paul's naked body. Soap glistened on his broad shoulders as he lathered himself, using water from a small white enameled pan that had been placed on the tiny kitchen table. His shaving gear was spread nearby, and he stood on a towel to protect both his bare feet and the wooden floor.

She remained quiet, admiring the powerful contours of his torso and legs, his muscles rippling each time he moved. When he finished his sponge bath he dried himself and dressed, except for his shirt, then lathered his beard and shaved. As he wiped the traces of foam from his face, she moved to his side.

He turned and smiled. "Good morning." Snatching up a red-and-navy-blue plaid Western shirt, he pulled it on, tucked the tails into his jeans and buckled his belt. He turned to her again, this time rather solemn. "I wanted you to sleep."

"I awoke to a concert," she said. "Where did you learn to sing opera?"

"My mother plays records sometimes. I grew up hearing them during the summer whenever I didn't have to work with my father. He hates the stuff. He'd probably question my manhood if he ever heard me sing it. He says it's for city sissies and gays. I like most kinds of music, but—" he grinned down at her "—you can't dance to opera." Still in his bare feet, he playfully danced her around the room.

The unborn child kicked violently in protest to the activity, and Nora gasped.

Paul released her. "Are you okay? I'm sorry, Nora. I got carried away. I'm just so glad to be home again. But you didn't have to literally keep the home fires burning. Now tell me again what happened."

While Paul brewed a pot of coffee and made several pieces of oven toast, Nora fried bacon and eggs and recounted the previous day's events.

As they ate, he reached for another piece of toast, but stopped in the middle of spreading strawberry jam on it and frowned. "But what made you so upset in the first place, honey?"

"Your father!"

"Dad?"

"Yes."

"Dad was here?"

"Yes."

"What the hell did he want?"

"He ordered me out!"

He grabbed her shoulders. "Nora, tell me every word he said."

Nora relayed her conversation with his father, leaving out only her reaction to his physical presence.

"Damn him!" Paul cried. "He has no right! He thinks his children are puppets and he can manipulate them, but he's wrong." He got up and began to pace the kitchen restlessly.

"Why do you let him?" Nora asked.

Paul cast her a piercing look that caused her to shrink back in her chair. Sensing her intimidation, he pulled a chair close to hers and took her hand. "I'm sorry, Nora. Let me explain. My father makes a specialty out of dangling financial carrots in front of our noses. The ranch is incorporated, and each of us owns shares in the operation. Because I'm the oldest son, I have more shares than my brothers and sisters. I'm not sure it's a fair way of doing things, but my father insists. Several years ago he bought a neighbor's ranch, known around these parts as Pinto's Meadow, and hired a man to run it. For some reason my father is very successful in his business dealings."

He rubbed his temples and sighed. "That's not really fair to him. He's successful because he's stayed out of debt with the banks and the Production Credit Association. While other ranchers have been forced into financial ruin by high interest rates, my father has had enough reserves to pull through hard times. Two years ago he bought another ranch north of town, and here's the problem. He promised me that if I stayed with him instead of getting a higher-paying job somewhere else, when I had my twenty-fifth birthday he'd turn the place over to me and let me run it alone. He said that if I ran it for five years and kept it profitable, he'd deed it to me outright. I could have become a county agent, gone into agri-business, livestock marketing... I had an offer right after graduating from MSU to join a commodities firm in Denver. They liked my cattle-ranching background, but I turned them down because I'd promised my father I'd stay with him."

He jumped from his chair. "But he put in a stipulation that I haven't been able to live with." He ran his fingers through his thick wavy hair. "Lord, I should have told you about this before. When I marry, my bride has to be a local girl he approves of. Damn it, Nora, it's in writing and I signed it." His face flushed with anger. "Until I met you I didn't give a damn. I had no desire to marry anyone. The women came and went so fast I've forgotten most of them. They were willing to put out, and marriage never entered the picture."

He stood before her, towering over her. His hand tilted her chin, forcing her to look up into his face. "Until I met you."

He pulled her gently out of her chair and into his arms. "I want you as my wife. I love you." His hand dropped to her swollen abdomen. "I want the world to know this child is mine. I'm going to marry you, but I haven't talked to him yet. He can be ruthless with power when he wants to be. If I don't get that ranch, then I have to find a new occupation or stay here dependent on him until he dies. I don't like the situation, but I haven't found a workable solution yet."

"You have to choose between me and a piece of property?" She buried her head against his chest. "That's not fair!"

"I'll make him change his mind," he said, resting his chin in the cushion of her hair. "I'll convince him. I want that ranch north of town so bad I can taste it. I went with him when he first looked at it and we talked about it being my place someday. Did you ever want something so much it hurt?"

She nodded against his shirt. "My family back."

"Of course," he murmured. "I'm sorry, sweetheart. I didn't think. But I want that place, too, in a different way." He eased her back, kissing her lips lightly. "We'll work it out. He'll come around. But we have work to do today. I'll clean the living room and get rid of the damage if you'll pack our bags."

"We're leaving?" she asked, surprised at his words.

"Yes. Haven't you looked at the calendar? Steven is coming to relieve us. It was decided several weeks ago. You'll think we're all fussing over you, but mom says you belong in town this late in your pregnancy, so we three arranged a trade-off. Steven takes over here, and we spend September in town at my cousin's house. I'll commute to the home ranch for a month."

"Your cousin? We'll be staying with someone?"

"No," he replied. "My cousin and her husband are in Seattle on a month's vacation. They run a fertilizer company in town. This area is full of my relatives. You promised to marry me, remember? This weekend is the fair and rodeo. After the holiday we'll get blood tests and the license and find a justice of the peace..."

and you'll be Mrs. Paul Russell when you have this baby."

"But the ranch your father promised you."

"I'll talk him into changing his mind. Technically I have until the middle of November."

"When is your birthday?" she asked. "You've never told me the exact date."

"November 16. I'll talk to the fellow at the Sweetwater Grain Elevator, too, in case dad isn't receptive to my suggestions. I'll find something. I have enough money in the bank to take care of your medical bills. I was saving it for a little future investment in land and such, but I'll manage both." He laughed softly. "Dad is generous. He just extracts pounds of flesh and blood in the process. When he gets to know you, he'll come around, Nora."

"He still calls me Nellie," she said.

"He'll learn to call you Nora. Under that thick hide of his is a loyal heart. He just has his own code of ethics and he expects us to all follow suit. I think a month in town will do us both a lot of good." He released her. "Now, let's get moving, woman. This place is a mess."

CHAPTER TEN

NORA WATCHED as Paul began to work on the bear carcass hanging in the tree. "I field-dressed it yesterday, so this won't take long," he said, withdrawing a long bowie knife from the scabbard on his belt.

"Ugh." Nora felt squeamish as she looked at the lifeless body of the black bear and watched Paul skin and dress the carcass. He wrapped the meat in canvas, then carefully rolled the head and skin in another tarpaulin.

"We'll drop the meat off at the house for processing."

"How do you do that?" Nora asked.

"It hangs and ages for a few days, then we cut it up," he explained. "We have a butchering room with a power saw and meat grinder. Dad and Russ, Jr., will probably do the work after supper later in the week." He glanced at her and grinned. "We process all our own meat. You didn't think we went to the local supermarket, did you?"

He wiped the blood from the hunting knife on the grass and returned it to its scabbard, then turned to her. "We'll have the skin tanned and made into a rug."

Two hours later they were driving through the gate of the Rocking R.

"I'll stay in the truck," Nora said quickly.

"You have to face him sometime," Paul insisted. "You'll be his daughter-in-law soon. I'll take the bear to the butchering room, then we'll go inside." He got out of the cab.

Nora followed him a few minutes later. She was filled with trepidation as they approached the rambling white house, but only Julie Russell and her youngest daughter, Lisa, greeted them in the living room.

"Where's dad?" Paul asked, surveying the room.

Julie clutched her hands together. "He's gone to town. Oh, Paul, he said he's going to list the ranch north of town with Beaverhead Realty and sell it. He said...he said you'd failed to live up to your part of the agreement. He said...oh, he was terrible. I'm so glad you two weren't here. He can be so cruel and insensitive at times."

Paul clenched his fists. "He doesn't give me a chance. I'm not married yet. I'm not twenty-five yet. What the hell does he expect of me?"

Nora turned to Julie. "Was it me? Am I the cause of this?"

"He doesn't even know you, dear. You're a convenient target right now. I think he's having his own midlife crisis and doesn't know how to deal with it. He only reads his livestock journals and gets irate if I suggest an article on the subject in one of my women's magazines. He thinks he's invincible. Nora, please don't let this upset you. You have enough to be concerned about right now. Come," Julie said, heading toward the kitchen. "Join us for lunch. Russ doesn't know how to let his sons and daughters go free. He'll calm down when he realizes how important Paul is to him. I'm just sorry it happened at this time."

Lunch was delicious, but everyone was somber, and conversation was restricted to the upcoming fair and rodeo.

As they finished slices of apple pie, Paul stood up and tugged Nora's hand. "Let's go before he comes home. I wouldn't want to hurt my own father and I don't trust myself right now. Bye, Lisa. . . mom. . . and thanks."

"Let us know if anything happens with Nora," Julie said.

As they drove away, Nora turned to Paul. "I'm sorry, Paul. It's all my fault. If I hadn't gone to the cabin with you, your father would still. . ." She turned and stared out at the rolling meadows and pastureland.

"It's not your fault, honey. It's the whole situation. I wanted my own place, but in today's economy a guy has four ways to go if he wants to be involved in ranching. This is one thing I agree with my father about. He inherits a place, he comes into a large sum of money and buys a place, he's rich and needs it as a tax shelter, or he goes into debt. With today's interest rates that's a sure loser. Borrowing is too risky."

"Couldn't you save for it?" she asked.

"Sure, but that can take a lifetime. McCormack, our neighbor up the road, didn't get his place debt free until he was forty-five. I'm not waiting that long." His lips tightened into a grim line.

"Maybe you're being impatient," she suggested. "How did your father get his ranch?"

A look of disgust settled on Paul's features. "The Rocking R has been in his family for four generations. Dad was an only child and inherited it free and clear from his father, just like I always thought I would be doing. That's why I've stuck it out all these years. My father is a rich man and he's just reneged on his promise." His eyes darkened as he stared at the dirt road ahead. "I've worked for him since I was old enough to climb on a horse and I learned to ride before I started school."

He fell silent for several minutes. Finally he reached for her hand and squeezed it. "We'll work it out. Don't worry."

She studied his stern profile, wondering if she should free him from his commitment to her.

He glanced at her, and a troubled smile softened his face. Her heart ached at the thought of life without him, but she refused to risk having his love turn to hatred and resentment.

As they drove into town, Nora noticed that the traffic was heavier than usual.

"It's beginning," Paul said. "The population doubles this weekend for the rodeo, and some want to get a head start. I'll drop you off at the clinic, go check out my cousin's house, then come back and get you. Okay, hon?"

Several hours later they had settled into the spacious house on the northern outskirts of town.

"You must be exhausted," Paul said, leading her to the guest bedroom. "Let's call it a day."

Nora reached toward the bedside lamp and playfully switched it on and off several times. "Electricity. . . nice," she murmured, and Paul laughed.

The following day they toured the small county fair. Nora admired the needlecraft exhibits, especially the crocheted afghans. Paul put his arm around her shoulders.

"I'll buy you some more yarn. Maybe this one will be even at both ends," he teased. "Next time, check your gauge."

Nora elbowed his ribs in response. As they strolled through the livestock exhibits, Paul explained the qualities that made an animal a champion. A woman's voice called through the crowd when they stopped at a hamburger stand along the midway.

"Hi, you two," Leslie Coleman greeted them as she sauntered to their stools, dragging a middle-aged man with her. When Nora turned around, Leslie's eyes shot wide open.

"Wow," she declared, her questioning glance flying from Paul to Nora, then back to Paul. Neither offered an explanation, and she awkwardly shuffled the toe of her boot in the dust.

"Hello, Leslie," Nora said, rescuing her friend from the uncomfortable silence. "How are you? Still at the bank?"

"Yes," Leslie said breathlessly. "Well, let me introduce everyone. George Holman, this is Paul and Nora... Russell?" Her brows arched.

"No," Nora corrected her. "Paul Russell and Nora Lane. How are you, George?" She extended her hand and the flustered cowboy accepted it.

"Howdy, ma'am." He turned to Paul, his face breaking into a good-natured smile. "Howdy, Paul."

"Hello, George," Paul replied. "George and I know each other from way back," he explained to Nora. "He worked for my dad several years ago and we've done some weight lifting together... of beers at the Matador."

Nora busied herself at the counter, trying to regain her composure. Slowly she revolved around on the stool and glanced at Paul, but he was concentrating on Leslie. Nora had never seen Paul and Leslie together before. Leslie had told her that she and Paul had dated long before Nora had come into the picture, admitting they had been lovers a few years earlier. As Nora watched them, she wondered if Leslie had understated the relationship.

Nora glanced down at her maternity smock. She knew she'd grown significantly in the past two weeks. Leslie's waist was tiny beneath a bright belt buckle displaying a bucking horse. Her hips were emphasized by her tight jeans, giving her a very sensual appearance. She wasn't beautiful in the classical sense, but her bouncy manner exuded sex appeal and a promise of good times for the man to whom she attached herself for the night. She made no bones about her willingness to enjoy whatever opportunities came her way.

Paul's arm went around Nora's shoulders and he coaxed her off the stool. "What do you think, honey?"

"What?" She hurriedly glanced from one face to another. "I'm sorry. I wasn't listening. What do I think about what?"

"Leslie and George have asked us to join them tonight at some bars in town," Paul said. "It's a tradition during the weekend...bar hopping...but you look a little tired."

"I am, but why don't you go with them?" she suggested, not wanting to be a spoilsport.

"No, we'll stay home tonight. But what about tomorrow night? Do you think you'd feel like it then? Tomorrow night is the big night in town. Tonight is just the preliminary." He laughed and hugged her affectionately.

"Okay," she agreed. "What will it be like?"

"You have to see it to believe it. Thousands of people crowded into half a dozen saloons for one big night on the town. People who never set foot in a bar during the rest of the year come out for just one night. Then the town returns to normal."

They agreed on a rendezvous, then Paul and Nora left the fairgrounds and drove to the house where they were staying.

"George is one of the local riders in the rodeo tomorrow. He's riding bareback broncs and the bulls," Paul said as they rolled into the driveway.

Nora recalled the tiny pins on his hat. "Did you ever ride?"

"Yes. I've competed in saddle-bronc riding and bull

riding, and Steven and I have won money team roping. Lisa likes to do the barrels. That and goat roping are the only regularly scheduled competitive events for girls and women. I belong to the PRCA."

"What's that?"

"Professional Rodeo Cowboys Association. I traveled the circuit for two summers. It was a lot of fun, but I just barely made expenses, so I returned to the ranch. It was during my college years." He chuckled. "Don't bring my rodeo years up in front of my father. That's another one of our differences."

Nora fell asleep that evening curled up in a comfortable overstuffed chair next to the fireplace. She awoke as Paul lifted her in his arms and carried her to their bedroom. She felt drugged as she lay back on the bed and let him undress her.

"I'm ugly," she mumbled.

He slipped her gown over her head and pulled it down. "No, you aren't."

"I'm big and dumpy and I waddle," she said as he pulled the covers up to her shoulders.

"Sometimes," he admitted, grinning. He quickly undressed and joined her, sliding his arm under her neck and pulling her to him. He kissed her forehead and nestled his chin in her hair. "Next week you'll be my wife. . . and I don't care if you do waddle a little. I always did like ducks and geese."

SUNDAY AFTERNOON they attended the outdoor rodeo. It was Nora's first rodeo, and she soon found herself caught up in the excitement of the crowd and the events. The antics of the rodeo clowns with their escape barrel and straw dummies and their reckless daring with the bulls made her laugh. George Holman rode his bucking horse until the buzzer sounded, and he received a round of applause from the locals, who shouted his name.

When the bull-riding event took place, Paul explained the dangers of mounting the unpredictable animals. "I've always shown them a healthy respect whether here or at the ranch. Some may seem gentle at times, but watch out, because they can change very quickly. Dad's got one old Angus cross who's been trying to get me for years."

His opinion was confirmed a few moments later when George came out of the chute on an ugly gray Brahma bull. Three seconds into his ride he was on the ground. When he tried to scramble away, the bull turned and swung its massive head at the downed man, and its horns grazed George's back. One heavy hoof came down on George's right leg, and he yelled in pain while the clowns distracted the angry animal. The ambulance crew dashed to help the injured man and quickly carried him out of the arena on a stretcher. Moments later the siren wailed as the ambulance drove from the fairgrounds to the hospital.

"He'll be okay, he's tough," Paul assured Nora, reaching for her hand. "Are you okay, honey? You've lost your color."

She nodded. "Everyone seems to be having so much fun, but aren't the events all potentially dangerous?"

"I suppose so, but they have a basis in the work we do. It's just our way of life."

"It seems a little violent."

Her attention was distracted from the accident to a wild cow-milking event that had the crowd roaring. Each contestant had to obtain milk in a bottle from an uncooperative range cow and pour it out in front of a judge stationed at one end of the arena. The cow was controlled by another volunteer, who held the cow's head by twisting the horns, forcing the cow to submit tc the stranger's hands on her udder.

On their way home, she thought about George. "Does this change our plans?"

"I doubt it. I think it's a simple fracture of his shinbone. It's not unusual at rodeos." He smiled. "If I know Leslie, and George is not available, she'll find someone else. She's a very resourceful woman."

"Do you know her... very well?" Nora asked.

"Two years ago we were quite involved." He saw her expression and teased, "Jealous?"

She frowned. "Should I be?"

"Don't worry. She's not my type. She's incapable of loyalty to one man."

"Do you have a sense of loyalty?"

"A year ago, no, but now... very much," he said. "You should know that."

Thoughts of loyalty bombarded Nora as she showered. Perhaps Paul's sense of loyalty depended on whatever situation was most important at the moment. His loyalty to his father and the family business; his loyalty to her because of the pregnancy. It had been a few weeks since he had expressed his love for her. Lovemaking had become difficult, so they'd agreed to abstain. Perhaps he equated love with sex. When sex was no longer available, the love was withheld. Jerry had never—

A knock sounded on the bathroom door, bringing a halt to her meandering thoughts. "Almost finished?" Paul called.

A flash of irritation shot through her as she turned off the shower. "Almost," she replied.

He knocked again. "Nora, hurry up."

She dried off, wrapped herself in her robe and jerked

the door open. "I'm through. I told you I was almost finished."

He frowned down at her as she stood ramrod straight in the doorway. "I'm sorry. I guess I didn't hear you. What's the matter?" He touched her shoulder gently. "You're grouchy."

She pulled back. "Nothing," she murmured. As she dressed, she thought about their relationship. Every little thing he did since their return to town had held a double meaning, eroding her confidence. The attention he had showered on Leslie the previous day had added one more bit of evidence to her suspicions about his real reason for consenting to marry her.

They had discussed the wedding and arranged an appointment with the justice of the peace for Saturday morning. Now she suspected he was merely fulfilling his obligation.

Paul joined her in the bedroom, frowning at her as he dressed, then left the room without a word. The sun was setting as they walked to a nearby restaurant.

While Nora picked at her food, Paul ate heartily. He had ordered steak, baked potato and salad, then topped the meal off with a double serving of strawberry pie a la mode. *Glutton,* she thought critically.

He finished the pie and dropped the fork noisily on the empty plate. "What's the matter, Nora? You haven't said a word since we got here." His dark eyes were stormy as he reached for her hand. "Have I done something to anger you?"

"No."

"What?" He squeezed her hand harder. "Damn it all, Nora, speak louder. I can't hear you."

She pulled her hand away, hot tears burning her eyes.

"Let's get out of here," he said, dropping a large bill

on the table and ignoring his change. He led Nora past the crowds beginning to gather near the saloons and on to a secluded doorway leading to upstairs apartments over several retail shops.

When she tried to pull away, he refused to release her arm. Her shoulders began to shake. "Honey, what's the matter?" he asked, gathering her in his arms.

Her voice was muffled against his shirt. "I don't know," she said, raising her head and looking into his eyes. "I don't think this is going to be a good weekend. I wish we were still at the cabin. It was like a honeymoon...to me at least."

His hand cupped her chin. "It was for me, too, my love."

"I don't want to marry you," she said, her voice choking, "if you're only doing it because of what happened."

"I'm not, but it's a pretty good reason." He stroked her cheek with his forefinger. "I'm marrying you because I...love...you," he murmured, kissing her between each word.

She wiped her eyes. "Are you sure? I can get along by myself, you know. It's just that I love you, too...very much." She looked up at him. "We have too many problems—you and your family, me and my past and now the baby. A screwed-up relationship like ours can't last."

Instead of answering her, he held her tightly against him. Finally he released her and glanced at his watch. "It's time to meet Leslie and George. Are you going to be all right?"

"Yes," she replied, but uncertainty sounded in her voice.

Paul pointed down the street. "Look. George made it. I told you he would."

Half a block down the street walked Leslie, wearing a

low-cut blouse tucked inside skintight Western jeans. George hobbled beside her, on crutches, a thigh-length cast on his leg and a smile warming his pleasant face.

When the four of them met, Leslie grabbed Paul by his slim waist and hugged him. "Paulie, baby, I guess it's you and me tonight. Nora and George can hold our table while we warm the dance floor. Is that okay with you, Nora?" Leslie turned to Nora with a smile.

Nora waited for Paul's refusal.

"Sure, Leslie, I'll dance a few dances with you. Nora won't mind. Right, hon?" He turned to Nora as he extricated himself from Leslie's embrace.

"If that's what you want," Nora replied, steeling herself for a night spent watching Leslie snuggle in Paul's arms while she kept smiling George company.

"Let's go," Leslie cried, dragging George through the swinging doors of the Matador.

Nora's heart leaped as she entered the dark saloon. Memories of New Year's Eve intruded. Couples were dancing on the congested wooden dance floor, while others milled around carrying cold cans of beer or plastic glasses containing mixed drinks. As the crowd grew, some of the celebrants drifted out to the sidewalk and into the street. Somehow Leslie found an unoccupied table for the four of them.

As soon as they were seated she reached for Paul's hand, trying to tug him out of his chair. He grinned at her, glanced at Nora, then gave in to Leslie's persistent tugging and followed her to the dance floor. George ordered drinks, and when they arrived, Nora watched the ice slowly melt in Paul's glass.

When Paul dropped into the empty chair next to her, Nora saw a faint imprint of pink lips on Paul's neck. She glanced at Leslie and saw that it matched her lipstick.

"I kissed him," Leslie said, following Nora's glance. "We'll have to share him tonight, Nora, with old George out of commission. Besides, we're old friends, aren't we, Paulie?"

Paul shrugged.

"Your neck has lipstick on it," Nora muttered to him.

Paul rubbed his neck with a paper napkin. "Leslie can get carried away when she's feeling affectionate. Think nothing of it." Soon Leslie had commandeered his attention once again, and his head was close to hers in order to hear in the noisy room. With a little coaxing from Leslie he returned to the dance floor, leaving Nora alone with George.

"Damn it, my leg hurts," George complained, propping his cast up on Leslie's vacant chair. "I'm tired. These pain pills make me sleepy." He tilted his chair against the wall, tipped his hat down over his eyes and within minutes was asleep and snoring softly.

Nora jumped when Paul appeared out of nowhere. "Are you okay?" he asked.

At that moment the baby kicked violently against her ribs. "Of course," she snapped.

"Come on, let's dance!" Leslie called, grabbing Paul's hand.

He frowned down at Nora's averted head before returning to the crowded floor. Nora craned her neck, trying to follow Paul's bobbing dark head. She eased slightly out of her chair to gain a better view of him and immediately wished she hadn't. Leslie's lips were reaching up to meet his when another couple blocked Nora's view.

So he had let Leslie kiss him again! How could he after declaring his love for her just a few hours before? Her heart grew heavy, and when they returned to the table,

Nora sat stiffly, staring into the crowd. Leslie playfully kissed George, and he awoke with a start. She let his injured leg stay on her chair and she sat on his lap instead. His hand slid around her hips and patted her thigh.

Leslie leaned over to kiss Paul, but he avoided her. "Ease off, Les." He turned to Nora's averted blond head. "Tired?"

"Very," she replied. "Could we leave?"

"Okay, honey, but I promised Leslie one last dance. I'll be back in a few minutes." He was gone without a backward glance.

Nora was furious. Paul was acting as though she were some stranger in the crowd, undeserving of any special attention or consideration. He had clearly shown his preference for Leslie's company. Leslie had moved to the area with her family when she was still in grade school, and Paul's father considered her a local woman. No doubt he would give his approval to such a union. If Nora were out of the picture, Paul would get his ranch and his problems would be solved.

The baby kicked again, and Nora thought of Ed Russell. He would never acknowledge that the baby was his grandchild. Nora felt a sudden need to get away from the smoke-filled saloon. It was choking her. Gathering her jacket, she forced her way through the milling throng. Outside she inhaled a deep breath of fresh air and began to work her way through the swarming crowds.

Angrily she realized that Paul had the only key to the house where they were staying. Her anger slowly changed to apprehension as she hurried away from the noisy street. She glanced at her watch. The time was well past midnight. Fatigue weakened her, and she dropped onto a bench near the Stockmen's Bank where she used to work with Leslie—Leslie, whom she had thought was her friend and who was now dancing and making out with the man Nora loved. Paul had talked of Leslie's inability to be loyal to just one man. He'd certainly been the pot calling the kettle black on that.

Nora left the bench and slowly walked away from the center of town. After she'd gone a few blocks she realized she was near Leslie's apartment. The night air had cooled, and she felt the chill through her thin jacket. She mulled over her situation, then swallowed her pride and approached the duplex. Perhaps when Leslie came home, Nora could call Paul and give him a chance to explain his conduct at the Matador.

When she touched the doorknob, the door swung open as though she were expected. Hesitantly she entered the dark apartment and hurried to a small lamp near a chair in the corner. She touched the switch, and the room flooded with reassuring light.

Dropping into the chair, Nora stretched her long legs out in front of her. Her normally thin ankles were swollen. Going to the Matador had been an unwise thing to do for several reasons, not the least of which was her own physical well-being.

Second thoughts about her impulsive actions began to creep in as she flipped through several of Leslie's magazines. Some had articles about marriage and divorce. Nora grimaced. Could she find a how-to article about keeping an affair alive and well before marriage? Leslie had warned her that Paul had a reputation for dropping women left and right, and that his own track record was far from being admirable.

She started when footsteps sounded outside on the walkway approaching the apartment and she heard Leslie's melodious voice.

"Oh, I must have left a light on," Leslie cried. "Or maybe someone stopped by."

Nora heard another pair of heavier boot steps as Leslie's voice grew closer.

"Come inside. Let's talk," Leslie said.

"Where the hell could she have gone?" Paul's voice growled.

Nora pushed herself from the chair, alarmed that Leslie and Paul were still together.

"Come inside, Paulie. We'll find something to take your mind off your problems. Come on, darlin'," Leslie coaxed as she pushed the door open.

Paul's deep laughter came through the doorway. "You were always pretty good at making me forget my problems," he said, his large hand dropping to Leslie's shoulder as they entered the room.

Nora's ears roared as she confronted the startled man and woman.

"Nora!" Paul cried. "I've looked everywhere for you. Why did you leave?"

"You have to ask me a stupid question like that?" she shouted. "What were the two of you going to do to help you forget your problems, Paul?" She shook her clenched fist at him. "You talked about loyalty earlier, but you dropped me and turned to Leslie when I wasn't able to entertain you tonight. She's not fat and pregnant like I am. Damn you, Paul, you made promises to me and they were all lies, weren't they? Lies!" She brushed the hot tears from her cheeks. "Well, Paul Russell, you're free. I was doing fine before I met you and I'll make out fine without you. You don't really want me. You just feel obligated. Well, I'm no one's obligation!" She raced out the door and disappeared into the darkness.

"Nora, come back. I'm sorry!" Paul called after her, but Leslie pulled on his coat sleeve.

"We left her alone with George for too much of the evening," she said. "It's my fault for insisting you dance with me. . . and I shouldn't have kissed you, but I didn't think Nora would be unreasonable. I guess pregnant women can be emotional. Don't worry, Paul, we'll find her."

They hurried outside, but there was no trace of Nora. When they arrived at the house where Nora and Paul had been staying, Nora was not there, either. Paul shoved his fist into his jeans pocket and pulled out the set of keys to her small white car in the driveway.

"I borrowed her car yesterday and forgot to return her keys," he mumbled, slowly returning the keys to his pocket. "Leslie, I've got to find her. She's in no condition to be alone. She's been very emotional lately and I sure as hell haven't helped matters." He rubbed the side of his neck in frustration. "Damn it, she's right. I am stupid. I treated her terribly tonight." They cruised through the town in Paul's truck, looking for Nora in every business establishment still open, every saloon, the all-night gas station, but no one had seen her. They searched the small parks but found no trace of her. She had vanished in the darkness.

Paul called the hospital and talked to a nurse he knew who was on duty that night. He explained the situation to her and extracted a promise that she would notify him if Nora was brought into the emergency room.

His frantic search halted when the sun peeked over the mountains in the eastern sky. After dropping Leslie off at her door, he drove to his cousin's house, and dropped into the chair beside the phone to wait for it to ring.

Paul awoke a few hours later, vividly aware of the empty house and when he called Leslie and the hospital, neither had heard from Nora. He phoned the ranch and asked for help from his brothers.

The four Russell brothers scoured the town. A Labor

Day parade both helped and hindered their search, as thousands of people lined the two main streets in town. When they had covered all possible territory they met at the north end of town and compared notes. Paul's hand shook slightly as he thanked his brothers for helping in the fruitless search.

"Why don't you come home with us, Paul?" Steven suggested. "Mom misses you and dad said he would sure like to have you back."

"I can't. Nora might come back to the house."

"I'll go there and watch for her," Russ, Jr., volunteered. He squeezed his brother's hand as he took the truck keys from him.

"Let's get some coffee," Steven said, guiding him to the family Wagoneer. "Nora couldn't just disappear. Maybe she left town. The bus! Let's check the bus depot. Fanny Joslin will know if anyone bought a ticket going north or south." They drove as close to the bus depot as the parade crowd would allow, parked and ran through the crowd to the depot and caught Mrs. Joslin as she locked the door.

Paul described Nora to the woman, but she shook her head.

"Sorry, guys, but no pregnant woman took the bus."

"My God, what's happened to her?" Paul asked, but his brothers could only shake their heads in bewilderment.

Steven again suggested that Paul go with them to the ranch, and reluctantly he agreed.

"But I'm coming back this afternoon," he insisted, as he grabbed his brother's arm in a steely grip.

"Sure," Steven said. "Hey, easc up, Paul. We'll stop at the police station and talk to the dispatcher. He'll cooperate."

They parked in the back of the courthouse while

Steven went inside. A few minutes later he returned. "It was John Anson. I explained the situation and he promised to call the ranch and the house if he hears of her. Take it easy, old man." He patted Paul's shoulder. "We'll find her."

"WHAT ARE YOU GOING TO DO, PAUL?" his mother asked as she cleared away the luncheon dishes.

Paul slumped deeper into his chair and ran his hand through his dark hair. "I don't know. I have her car keys. The key to her storage space is on the same ring. All her clothes are at Carrie's house in town, where we're staying. She's stranded without money or clothing or food. Surely she'll come back."

Julie frowned and shook her head. Steven stood up.

"I've got to get back to the cabin," he said. "I'd stay if I thought it would do any good."

Paul shook his head. "I doubt it. Thanks anyway, little brother."

After Steven left, Julie poured Paul a fresh cup of coffee. "I'm sure she wouldn't leave without her car and clothing. She must still be in town. Perhaps someone has taken her in. She has to get in touch with you sooner or later, Paul."

"Maybe." He gulped the coffee and left his chair. "I'm going back to town and look some more. Russ, Jr., plans to stay the night in town with me. He'll bring the Wagoneer back tomorrow. Damn it all, I miss her. She's the first woman I've ever really loved." He looked at his mother's warm, smiling face. "Except for you, of course," he declared, giving her a hug and a kiss on the cheek before sailing from the room.

He scoured the town again, stopped at Leslie's for a quick beer and an encouraging word, then returned to his cousin's house, where Russ, Jr., told him that no attempt had been made by Nora to contact him.

Paul thought of her physical condition and the occasional bouts of depression that still haunted her from her past. She had told him that once, when she had felt as though she were going insane, she had thought about suicide.

He knew so little about her life with her first husband. They must have been very much in love and her first child had been conceived in that love. Perhaps she still felt their own relationship was built on physical desire rather than commitment and love. Was it possible she resented the baby now that there was no turning back? She was wrong if she thought he didn't love her. Hadn't he reassured her often? He had thought so, but obviously something was wrong.

Quick calls to the police department and hospital proved fruitless, and after the calls he couldn't decide if he was relieved or more anxious than ever. Nora needed his protection, his care, but most of all he wanted to give her his love. He had to find her, for her sake as well as his own.

CHAPTER ELEVEN

NORA RAN THROUGH THE DARKNESS, enraged by Paul's betrayal and determined to escape from the sound of his shouting.

Hiding in the shadows of a store entrance, she saw his truck turn the corner and slowly drive by. Frantically she tried to think of a place to spend the night. She knew all the motels would be filled because of the holiday. The neon light of a grocery store shone a few blocks away, and she could see newspaper racks near the entrance.

Perhaps she could find a room for a few days until she made a decision about what to do. Her back ached. The baby kicked against her ribs. Quickly she walked to the store, dropped some coins into the slot on the rack and withdrew a paper.

She turned to the classified section and found two room rentals listed. One advertisement listed only a phone number, but the other also carried a street address. The location was just a few blocks away from the store. She checked the dark street for Paul's headlights before hurrying to her destination, but her heart sank when she found the darkened house. Her watch showed the time to be past two in the morning, and she didn't dare waken the owner.

She pulled her light jacket snugly around her for protection against the cold night air. Cautiously she opened the gate and entered the yard. A soft growl came from the darkened porch as a small white dog jumped from a wooden swing and approached the top of the stairs.

"Come here, doggie," she whispered, praying the dog wouldn't bark. To her surprise, the dog wagged its tail and scampered down to her.

Nora tiptoed up the steps and dropped into the swing. A granny-square afghan had been neatly folded and laid over the back of the swing. She pulled the afghan around her shoulders and found a comfortable position as the tiny white dog jumped onto the swing and curled into a fluffy ball beside her. It whined once and laid its nose on Nora's lap, then closed its eyes.

"Good night, little dog," Nora whispered. "You seem to be my only friend tonight."

When Nora awoke, the sun was above the eastern horizon. She glimpsed an older woman moving from the interior of the house toward the front door. Quickly she refolded the afghan and tossed it on the porch swing, tugged at her wrinkled clothes and knocked on the door, hoping the woman inside had not seen her.

The door was opened by a plump, white-haired woman several inches shorter than Nora. An orange apron was tied around her ample waist. "Yes?" the woman asked, surprised by her early-morning visitor.

"I...I saw...your ad in the paper...about a room," Nora stammered.

"Yes," the woman replied, holding the door open. "Well, hello, Bridget," she cried, swooping the little dog up in her arms. Her hazel eyes sparkled as the dog barked excitedly. "You were out all night, you bad little girl. I was afraid you had run away."

She turned back to Nora. "Yes, the room is still

available. Oh, my! I didn't notice your condition. You look exhausted, my dear. Do come in."

She led Nora through the living room into a cozy yellow kitchen and insisted she join her for breakfast. She refused to discuss the room until Nora had eaten every bite of food set before her.

"Now, my dear, about the room." She described the room and advised Nora of the rent and the privileges that went with the room. "I've never rented a room in my house before, but I'm all alone and it gets very quiet, so I thought I would give it a try. My daughter cautioned me to be very selective about who I let into my house, but you look pretty harmless to me. What's your name?"

"Nora...Nora Lane," Nora replied. "And yours?"

"Ida Belle Innes. Call me Ida or Mrs. Innes," the woman said.

"The rent is fine," Nora said, "but I can't pay you until I go to the bank tomorrow." She was on the verge of tears and knew she would break down if Ida Innes began asking probing questions.

The older woman came to her and put her plump arm around Nora's shoulders. "Of course, that will be just fine. Now come with me and I'll show you the room. The bath is just down the hall. You can freshen up." She scanned the room, then frowned at Nora. "Don't you have any luggage?"

"It's...it's at the bus depot," Nora lied. "I'll get it later today. I'm very tired. I would like to lie down for a while." She forced herself from the chair, her swollen ankles throbbing as she followed Ida Belle Innes down the short hallway and into the room.

Ida breezed around the room, explaining its features, then hurried to the door. "You rest," she said, then was gone.

For a few minutes after her friendly landlady closed the door, Nora remained in the middle of the small bedroom. The numbness that had enabled her to maintain her composure during the morning began to ebb away. Paul's handsome face pushed its way into her thoughts, undermining her self-control. She knew she could care for her child and eventually find employment. She would withdraw funds from her ample savings account and begin to rebuild a stable life for herself and her baby.

She could handle everything, except Paul Russell. Her child would be a constant reminder of its father, the man she both loved and hated. She wished she could rage at him and show him she didn't need or want him in her life, but she would be lying. Yet his conduct with Leslie proved to her he had no sense of faithfulness. He had probably spent the night with cute, bubbly Leslie.

She needed a change of clothing but had none, so she pulled the hand-appliqued Rose of Sharon quilt to the foot of the twin bed, then slipped between the clean sheets and tried to relax. A subtle trembling began in the pit of her stomach and quickly consumed her aching body. As sobs that had choked her raw throat grew stronger, she buried her face in the soft pillow and hoped Mrs. Ida Belle Innes was far away in some other part of the tidy house.

LATE IN THE AFTERNOON Nora awoke to pangs of hunger. She left the room, freshened up in the nearby bathroom and made her way to the kitchen.

Ida Innes clapped her hands when Nora appeared in the doorway. "Oh, good!" she cried. "I've been holding dinner until you woke up, my dear." Immediately she spread a small feast of fried chicken, mashed potatoes, broccoli, fresh-brewed coffee and blackberry pie before a surprised Nora.

"Good nutrition is important when you're expecting, dear," she said with a firmness not to be challenged.

Nora began to eat the delicious food and, in spite of her own problems, found Ida Innes a delightful conversationalist. The older woman had lived in the area all her life, and her parents had homesteaded in the Sweetwater country east of town.

"Two of my sisters and a brother still live in town. My daughter lives here, too, and one son ranches in the Big Hole. My other son is a banker in Billings." She tossed her white head back in lighthearted laughter. "I was a Schroeder before I married Teddy Innes, God rest his soul. He was such a fine man, but the last two months of his life were filled with pain. He died of cancer five years ago. We Innes and Schroeder descendants just can't get out of Montana for long. When we do leave, we come back." Suddenly she became very serious. "I went to the bus depot this afternoon, but they said there were no suitcases to be claimed." She stared at Nora's pale face and waited for a reply.

Nora's appetite vanished as memories of Paul returned. She had managed to keep him out of her thoughts for almost an hour. "I lied to you, Mrs. Innes. I don't have a suitcase. I've left my. . .husband. He was with another woman. . .and I just couldn't take it anymore." She stopped speaking as the weight of her new lie compounded her problem.

While Ida Innes waited for Nora to explain, she brought the coffeepot to the table and refilled Nora's cup, then served them each a piece of blackberry pie. "I just love blackberry pie," she said with a soft laugh. "I'm so glad these teeth of mine aren't store bought like most of my friends'. I don't have to worry about seeds under my plate. It's great!"

Nora glanced at the older woman. She was acting as though they were long-time friends, and Nora suddenly felt the need of a sympathetic ear. "He said he loved me," she began, "but his actions certainly didn't show it. He fooled around with a friend, so I left. I don't know if I did the right thing."

"To leave him?" Ida asked.

Nora nodded.

"What is your young man like?"

"He's very handsome and other women like him... and he's very nice when he wants to be. He's tall..." Nora's voice softened as she recalled the summer she'd spent with Paul in the mountains. "He has dark curly hair and the darkest brown eyes. Sometimes they shimmer like coffee."

"He sounds rather nice," Ida said. "Go on."

"We spent the summer in a cabin in the Blacktail Mountains. It was perfect until...he doesn't get along very well with his father, but his mother is very nice. I like her. But it's too late now. I don't expect to ever see him again. He's probably still with that woman, and all along I thought she was a friend. I'm sure he's relieved to be free of me." She glanced down at her body. "None of this was planned by either of us. As soon as I can arrange it, I plan to leave here," she said, her voice filled with determination.

"What about the baby? Aren't you due anytime?"

"The end of the month," Nora admitted.

"Won't your husband want to know about his child?"

"He didn't act like a father-to-be last night," Nora replied. "I think he would rather be free." But in her heart she was under no delusion about Paul's feelings for the baby. "Mrs. Innes, I lied to you," Nora said, her blue eyes troubled. "I'm not married at all. I did spend the summer with this man, but he's not my husband...oh, Mrs. Innes, how could this make any sense to a nice woman like you when it hardly makes sense to me?"

"It is a little confusing, my dear," Ida said, a tiny smile tugging at the corner of her mouth.

"I won't try to explain why Paul...I mean... Oh, it's all so crazy and stupid on my part for...he was a stranger when... I'm getting just what I deserve for being so careless and reckless and...and..." She pressed the heels of her hands tightly against her eyelids until her emotions were once again under control.

"What's your young man's name, Nora?"

"Paul Russell."

Ida Innes gasped, then quickly covered her mouth.

"What is it? Do you know him?" Nora asked.

"Possible," Ida said, slowly nodding her head. "The name sounds familiar. Oh, well, your problems will work themselves out, I'm sure. Time puts them in their proper perspective."

"Not this one," Nora replied sadly.

After dinner Nora helped Ida wash the dishes and tidy the kitchen, then they spent a few hours watching television. Nora was aware that Ida was watching her closely, but brushed it off as simple curiosity.

The living room in which they were sitting was furnished with nineteenth-century pieces. The dark finish of the tables and chests contrasted sharply with the white and ecru doilies placed on them, giving the room a cozy warmth. Numerous photographs cluttered every available surface and most of the walls. Children's school photos in vivid color were mixed with older black-and-white snapshots.

"Who are all the children?" Nora asked.

"The black-and-white ones are my own children and my nieces and nephews," Ida said. "The colored ones are my grandchildren here and in Billings. I'm partial, but aren't they all lovely?"

Separate photos of two young boys caught Nora's eye. The boys in the pictures were perhaps six and eight, their dark eyes and hair identical. They could have passed for twins except for their age difference. The younger boy had lost both his front teeth, and the older boy had a beautiful shiner on his left eye. Nora could imagine his mother's chagrin when she saw her handsome young son with one brown eye and the other rimmed with green-and-purple bruises.

"Yes," Nora agreed, "especially these two." She rose from her chair and touched the two photos of the dark-eyed boys. "Are they brothers?"

"No," Ida replied, laughing as she picked up the photos and dusted them with her fingertips before carefully replacing them on the table. "They're one and the same. That's my oldest grandson when he was six and eight. His mother had a fit when he fell off a fence and blackened his eye the weekend before school pictures were to be taken. Now it's her favorite photo. You should recognize him, my dear."

"I doubt it," Nora replied. "There's no reason why I. . .should." She glanced at Mrs. Innes and was surprised to see her smiling. "What is his name?"

"Paul. He's much older now."

Nora turned pale as she reached for the photograph again. "Russell? No, it can't be."

Mrs. Innes nodded. "I recognized my grandson when you described your young man."

"But your name is Innes," Nora protested, trying desperately to deny the obvious.

"Julie Russell is my daughter," replied Mrs. Innes. "It's really quite simple. I don't see them as much as I would like to. They live out in the country, but they stop in occasionally, especially the younger ones still in school."

"Then I must leave!" Nora cried. "I don't want Paul to know..." A sharp pain twisted through her body, taking her breath away. She doubled over to relieve the lingering cramp.

Ida rushed to her side. "Are you all right, my dear? Is it the baby?"

"Yes...no," Nora replied, still gasping for breath. "I'll be okay." Slowly she straightened and took a step toward a chair. "Mrs. Innes, I can't stay here if there's even a remote chance that Paul will come to see you." She rubbed her temples. "I feel so confused. I need time to think and make plans." She grabbed Ida Innes's hand. "You must promise me you won't tell him about me."

"Nora, I think you're making a mistake," the older woman said, "but I respect your wishes...for now. But if problems arise or you get sick, I would have to notify someone, and Paul would want to know. He has always been an impulsive, temperamental boy, but loyal to a fault where family is concerned." She patted Nora's hand reassuringly.

"But family loyalties are part of our problems."

"Perhaps that's because he has two families now."

"How can you have a family without a marriage?" Nora asked.

"A family is an emotional tie as much as legal, my dear."

"I thought so, too, but emotions change. They don't bind a couple the way a marriage license does." Nora stood up. "I think I'll go to bed again. I'm still very tired. Thank you so much for being understanding about everything. I don't know what I would have done if you had turned me away."

Ida nodded her white head. "I have something for you, Nora. You'll be more comfortable tonight. You're a bit taller than I am, but we're about the same distance around the middle." She laughed. "Come with me." She led the way to her own bedroom, carefully removed a flannel nightgown and quilted robe from her closet and handed them to Nora. "You can wear these. When you've changed, give me your clothes. I'll wash them and you'll feel fresh and clean tomorrow morning. Now, no disagreements," she said, wagging a finger at Nora. "At least one grandchild gives me a flannel gown each Christmas. I guess they think that's all a grandmother ever wears to bed at night." She cocked a finely arched brow at Nora and smiled. "Frankly, I still prefer silky things."

She gently steered Nora to her own room. "Go now, my dear. To bed with you. I'll wait out here for your clothes."

Nora quickly changed into the flannel gown and carried her soiled clothing to the door.

"Aha!" Ida exclaimed when she saw Nora in her gown. "Just as I thought." She pointed to Nora's long legs, which showed beneath the hem of the blue flannel gown. "Good night, Nora," Ida called as she took the clothing and disappeared into the darkened hallway.

"Good night, Mrs. Innes," Nora whispered. "You're a wonderful woman and a lifesaver to me just now." She turned to the bed and crawled between the sheets, but as she curled into a comfortable position the baby kicked, and Paul's handsome face filled her mind, staying there as she fell asleep.

Life seemed a little brighter the next morning. Nora awoke to find her clothes laundered and folded on the nearby dresser. As she dressed, she peeked through the lace curtains and out the window at the clear blue sky.

Perhaps today she could think more rationally about the alternatives available to her. Her first order of business would have to be a trip to the bank.

When she entered the kitchen she found Ida Innes engrossed in an early-morning news program on the small color television set perched on the kitchen counter.

"Shh," Ida cautioned as she offered Nora a plate of scrambled eggs and bacon bits. She watched attentively as a television star was being interviewed. When the interview ended she turned to Nora and smiled. "That man is so handsome, I just love him. My granddaughters say he's a hunk! I think I agree. I never miss his series." She offered Nora a plate of warm blueberry muffins.

Nora smiled in spite of her worries about the upcoming visit to the bank. She buttered a muffin and took a bite. "Mmm, delicious. You're spoiling me, Mrs. Innes."

"My pleasure," Ida replied. "You're carrying another of my great-grandchildren, and I intend to keep spoiling you. And please stop calling me Mrs. Innes. It reminds me of my schoolteaching days before I met Teddy and got married. Call me Grandma Innes, if you like."

When they had finished washing the breakfast dishes, Nora collected her purse and jacket and left the house. She missed her car, but Paul had the only set of keys, and she hadn't decided what to do about that. She hurried on to the bank. When she walked in, Leslie was nowhere in sight. She ignored the curious stares of her former co-workers, and after closing out her accounts, she took the cash and a cashier's check and hurried out the door.

"Nora!" a voice called from behind her when she was a block away from the bank.

Nora hastened her steps, but a hand caught her arm and tugged hard. She turned to find Leslie Coleman gasping and breathless.

"Go away," she cried, trying to free her sleeve.

"No, we've got to talk," Leslie said.

"*We* have nothing to talk about," Nora replied tersely.

"We have something very important to talk about and you know it," Leslie insisted. "Paul."

"You can have him. You two deserve each other."

"Nora, don't be stubborn. And don't be silly, either. Paul and I spent that entire night—"

"I don't want to hear how you and Paul spent the night together," Nora said, cutting her off. "I don't want to know what you did or what you said or anything. I can just imagine, knowing how you are with men. Well, if Paul wants a woman like you, he can have you. And don't you dare tell him you saw me!" She ducked through the doors of a busy department store and headed for the back. A tall display of canning supplies blocked her from the view of anyone in the front of the store. She caught her breath, then slipped out the rear entrance and hurried to Ida Innes's house and safety.

The next two weeks were spent in the privacy of the Innes house, reading and thinking, trying to decide what to do. Twice she picked up the telephone and dialed the first two digits of the Russell ranch number before coming to her senses and hanging up. She went to the second bank in town and opened two new accounts. Mrs. Innes had suggested Nora stay with her until the baby was born and she was well enough to make plans about her future, and Nora had agreed.

When she visited the hospital, Nora was surprised to find herself preregistered, though some of the information was missing on the form. She asked who had initiated the paperwork, but the hospital had no record. "I want to pay the bill in advance," she told the woman in admitting. "How much will it be?"

"You've already paid five hundred dollars, so the balance will be... just a moment."

"No, that can't be," Nora protested. "I..."

The woman turned away to her calculator and soon returned with the balance due.

Paul Russell had to be the culprit! Nora's pride bristled at the thought of his arrogance. "I'll cover the total amount, please. Whoever paid this wasted his money. He can receive a refund."

"But..."

"I insist," Nora replied. She wrote the check for the total anticipated bill, accepted her receipt from the puzzled clerk and left the hospital.

A similar situation greeted her at the clinic, and she wrote another check for the total fee, leaving the frustrated bookkeeper mumbling about the unnecessary credit balance on her account.

As she made her way back to Mrs. Innes's house, her anger grew by leaps and bounds. Paul didn't want her, yet he insisted on paying her way, undermining her right to take care of herself. She was perfectly capable of managing without him. How could he have spent the night with Leslie and still feel obligated to her? Obligated... that was the word that cut so deeply. She had never wanted to be his obligation, just the woman he loved.

When she entered the quiet house, Nora found Ida Innes asleep on the sofa while her favorite soap opera plodded through its complicated plots. She had promised to take Mrs. Innes out to dinner that evening to thank her for being so kind. She had treated Nora as though she were her own granddaughter, and Nora had grown to love her like the grandmother she had never known.

She changed into the new maternity pantsuit she had bought. The top was lavender with tiny bouquets of blue and mauve straw flowers scattered across the fabric, and the pastel shades brought out the delicate tones in her complexion and hair. She felt a renewed sense of self-esteem. She had her life under her own control again. She could make it without Paul Russell. She stretched, pressed her hands on the small of her back and took a deep breath. Except for a nagging discomfort that had surged and receded all day, she felt better than she had in ages.

As she left the room, she felt a contraction and wondered if her time was near. When Jeremy was born, Jerry had been with her. Thinking about going through the birth process alone unsettled her, but she had no choice. Husbands and wives should share such an experience, but Paul was not her husband. Leslie was the only person with whom she had been close, but that friendship had come to an unhappy ending.

Nora had expected she would have to wake Mrs. Innes, but instead found her ready and waiting, wearing a sprightly green two-piece suit and matching pillbox hat that accented her white hair.

"Shall we go?" Nora asked, offering her arm.

"To dine," Mrs. Innes said with a laugh. "We'd have a night on the town, but my daughter is coming by this evening for a visit."

"Paul's mother?" Nora exclaimed. "You promised you wouldn't."

"She called me," Mrs. Innes explained. "I haven't seen her for over a month. You can stay in your room if you wish, but I can't avoid my own family. Frankly, my dear, I think you should talk to her. She wants her son to be happy, and if you love him as I think you do, you should—"

"No!" Nora replied sharply.

"As you wish," Mrs. Innes said gently.

"I'm sorry, Grandma Innes," Nora apologized. "My back has been bothering me. I'll go to bed early and stay out of sight."

"This would be a golden opportunity for you to..." She stopped, seeing the determined expression in Nora's blue eyes. "Now shall we go eat? I'm starved. I'll tell you a few more stories about Teddy and me when we were newlyweds on the Sweetwater and roughed it."

Dinner was delightful and Mrs. Innes an enjoyable companion, but Nora's discomfort had grown steadily as the meal progressed. Twice on the way home she had to stop and catch her breath. Mrs. Innes frowned and offered Nora her arm in support, and when they arrived at the house, Nora went directly to her room.

She heard the doorbell ring, and soft muffled voices floated through the hallway into her room as she drifted to sleep. Sometime later she was awakened by a hard contraction that doubled her over when she sat up, and she had to bite her lower lip to keep from groaning aloud. She needed help, and she knew she couldn't go through the next several hours alone.

Perspiration dampened her forehead as she made her way to the living room.

"Help me," she cried, reaching out to the two women, who immediately jumped up from their chairs.

Julie caught Nora's hand and led her to the nearest chair. "Nora, I knew it had to be you when my mother described her new roomer. There just couldn't be two young women with the same set of problems, and all caused by my own son."

Nora's gaze swung to Mrs. Innes. "She promised to not tell you."

"Shh, now," Mrs. Innes said. "I kept my promise. I can't be responsible for my intuitive daughter."

"Are you in labor?" Julie asked.

Nora nodded, then pleaded, "Don't tell Paul. He doesn't care and I don't want him there."

"I'll take you to the hospital, but I have to call home and let them know I'm being detained in town. Trust me to do what's right, Nora."

Julie hurried into the kitchen, and Nora could hear murmuring into the phone, then there was silence. When she returned from the kitchen, she was carrying her jacket and purse.

"This is your second birth," Julie said.

Nora nodded.

"Then your labor will probably be shorter and easier." She turned to her mother. "Mom, thanks for everything." Mrs. Innes gave Nora a hug as Julie ushered her out the door, and within minutes the two younger women were in the car and on the way to the hospital.

A few blocks from the hospital Nora turned to Julie. "Did you tell him?"

"No," Julie replied, "but I think you're wrong to

shut out my son. He has a right to share in this birth. If you insist on going through this alone, you'll never be able to fill this void." She pulled over to the curb. "He's been miserable since you left him."

"But you don't understand," Nora began.

"You're wrong. I do understand. One morning he told Steven and me about last New Year's Eve, and—"

"Oh, no, how could he!"

Julie patted Nora's hand. "Not everything, but he did tell us about the memory of you staying with him, haunting his every waking hour."

"He went to Leslie and..."

"He's been faithful to you, Nora."

"I know he went to Leslie and they..."

"Yes, he went to Leslie, but to ask for her help in finding you. They've known each other since grade school. In high school she was a cheerleader and he played varsity football and basketball. They were homecoming king and queen their senior year. They dated quite a lot, but they had a spat and broke off when he went away to college." Julie rested her forehead on her hands as she gripped the steering wheel. "To state it quite bluntly, I think they may have slept together since his return, but I'm sure it was just physical attraction. Nothing like the love I know he has for you."

"A man can't love one woman and sleep with another."

"His involvement with Leslie was before he met you," Julie insisted. She turned to Nora. "He's been working twice as hard as necessary since he returned to the ranch. He takes the dirtiest, smelliest and hardest jobs that need to be done. It's as though he's doing penance for his sins against you. He's had everyone in the family looking for you when they come to town. I wonder what he would do if he knew you'd been staying with his own grandmother." A smile warmed her hazel eyes. "I guess that proves he should visit her more often."

"Paul told me once that his relatives were everywhere," Nora replied. "If only he...he...if only..." Hot tears spilled down her flushed cheeks.

Julie pulled back into the light traffic and headed for the hospital. "Do you love my son?"

Nora wiped her cheeks and nose with a tissue and whispered, "Yes."

"We're here," Julie said, and she got out of the car and hastened to the emergency entrance. A nurse pushing a wheelchair approached the car and helped Nora out. Nora looked questioningly at Julie as she slid back into the driver's seat. "I'll try to come back later. Lisa is home sick, and I have a prescription I must take to her. I'm sorry I can't stay now, but you'll be all right, Nora. Remember we love you. That includes my son."

"You promised not to tell him," Nora said.

"I keep my word," Julie replied but a grim determination tightened her features as she shifted the car into reverse and sped away in the darkness.

THE BLACK HAND on the wall clock jumped to the next minute as Nora lay alone in the labor room. Dr. Peters had come in and examined her, patted her hand, then left to check on another patient. Two nurses had stayed with her when her distraught emotions had threatened to overpower the relaxation exercises she'd tried to practice.

"Don't you have anyone we can call?" asked the petite nurse with the lilting British accent. "You shouldn't be alone."

"No," Nora insisted. She glanced at the clock again. Two hours had passed since her arrival. Julie had promised to return but had not arrived. Leslie was her only friend in town, but knowing that Leslie and Paul had... She forced thoughts of Paul from her mind.

Dr. Peters returned. Nora knew from her discomfort that time was running out. "Let's get her ready for the delivery room," the doctor said to the two nurses. "I think we'll have ourselves a new baby before midnight." She left to change into surgical gear, while the two nurses pushed the gurney into the delivery room and helped Nora onto the table.

"What's the matter?" Nora asked, disturbed by a commotion in the hallway outside but unable to see anyone.

"Nothing," a nurse said. "Someone wants to speak to Dr. Peters. She'll be back in a moment."

Nora could still hear the muffled sounds of raised voices, but no words were distinguishable. Dr. Peters reappeared and motioned to the nurses, and another whispered conversation took place. Suddenly they all left the room. Nora covered her eyes with her hands, trying to remain calm, but her confidence had evaporated with the medical team. Every muscle in her body cried out for relief.

A door swished open, then swung shut.

"Nora." Strong hands pulled hers away from her red, tear-stained eyes.

"Nora," the voice called again, and she looked up into Paul Russell's troubled eyes.

She froze for only a moment, trying to make sense out of his presence, then frantically glanced around the green-and-white room.

"Dr. Peters gave me three minutes to talk to you."

He gripped her shoulders. "I want to stay with you. I won't leave."

She tried to push his hands away. *"No."*

"Yes," he whispered.

His insistence broke through her resolve, and as her tears began to flow, she clung to him.

"I love you, pretty lady," he murmured. His hand slid beneath her damp hair and massaged her neck, calming her, then his lips grazed hers. "Try to relax, sweetheart. We have work to do." He kissed her again as the doctor and two nurses returned, and the room suddenly became a flurry of activity.

At some point, Paul had changed into a green gown and cap, but Nora couldn't remember his leaving her. The bearing-down sensations became overpowering, and she lost track of time as the baby was born. Paul left her for a moment, then returned wearing a grin, and she heard a faint whimper that quickly changed into an indignant wail.

"We have a son," Paul whispered.

CHAPTER TWELVE

THE HOSPITAL ROOM was quiet now that Nora's visitors had left. Mrs. Innes and Julie had spent an hour with her, carrying on about the baby.

Nora lay quietly, mulling over Paul's unexpected appearance the night before. He had said nothing about a reconciliation, and she refused to be the one to ask for a commitment. She eased onto her side and stared out the window. Suddenly the door flew open, and before she could roll over, Paul's hands gripped her shoulders.

"Why the hell did you pay the hospital bill?" he demanded, his voice angry.

"I had to... it was my responsibility," she said, turning to look at him. "You were gone."

"You were the one who ran away. We were going to get married in a few days."

"But you and Leslie..."

"To hell with Leslie," he seethed.

"I don't have to justify my actions to you!" she declared, her chin jutting sharply.

They stared at each other for several seconds.

"Why are you asking about the hospital bill, anyway?" she queried. "It's paid in full and it's no concern of yours."

"You're wrong, Nora. I finished paying the full amount again, and now the accounting people are complaining about the credit balance." He ran his fingers through his dark hair.

"Well, I won't take my payment back," Nora insisted.

"Neither will I," he said, his mouth tight.

She lay staring at him, admiring the brown of his eyes in spite of her anger. She'd always thought his eyes were much darker, but today he wore a green polo shirt instead of his customary Western-cut clothing, and his eyes shimmered like hot coffee. She suppressed an impulse to smile.

"Did you do the same thing about Dr. Peters's fee?" he asked, frowning.

"Yes," she replied, determined to win this argument.

A smile softened his rugged features as he sat down on the edge of her bed. "Then, my darling Nora, we'll just let them both stay on the books until we have our second child."

"Second?"

"Of course," he said. "Our son will need a little brother or sister to play with someday." His hand slowly reached out and touched her cheek. "I still want to marry you."

"Why?"

"I love you... and God knows how I missed you."

"But you and Leslie. You can't just expect me to forget what happened that night."

"And just what do you think happened, Nora? Have you let your own jealous imagination run wild?"

She bristled at the insinuation.

"Nora," he said, taking her hand, "life lost all meaning for me when you disappeared. It's hard to explain, but I've never had another human being become so important to me. I want the three of us together. I know I made a complete fool of myself that last night, but believe me, I've paid for it a thousand times over. Leslie told me she saw you." He held up a hand to silence her. "She knew how anxious I was to find you. She's still your friend, Nora. She was hurt that you'd think she would betray your friendship by messing around with me.

"She's my friend, too, remember. She helped me hunt for you, and she tried to help me understand what you were going through. I don't get frightened very often, sweetheart, but I was scared when you ran out that door and disappeared." He leaned down and kissed her lightly on the cheek. "You must trust me. I would never get involved with another woman. I admit that once I had an affair with Leslie, but that was long ago and I can't do anything to erase it. As God is my witness, I love you, only you."

She sighed deeply and took his hand. "And I love you, Paul."

He beamed. "We can get our blood tests done here at the hospital and get the license on our way out of here."

"Out of here? Where are we going?"

"Not to the Rocking R," Paul said. "I tried to talk to my father, but it was like talking to a brick wall. He brags that he's a stubborn old goat and I'm afraid he's right... at least for now. We can only hope that he comes around when he gets to know you better and sees his grandson. Someday he'll accept you."

"No, he won't," Nora replied. "Paul, you didn't see him that afternoon at the cabin. He hated me then, and he'll hate me more now that I have the baby. He insists it's not yours. He...he thinks I'm a tramp who's duped his oldest son into taking on my illegitimate son. He still thinks of me as Nellie!" She eased herself upright, pulling away from his touch.

"We'll stay in town with my grandmother for a while. She's already asked me to ask you, and she's anxious to get her hands on that little boy whose picture she's been showing to all her friends. I can drive out to the ranch every day. Fall roundup is starting in a few weeks."

"It won't work," she said skeptically.

"Let's give it a try before we knock it," he said. "If it fails, we can do something else."

Nora wondered if she was letting him talk her into another fantasy doomed to failure, but the blissful memories of the cabin overlaid the memories of his father's intrusion and the fire. If things didn't work out, she would still have enough money to tide her over until she could return to work. "Perhaps we could try again," she agreed.

The door opened and a nurse entered carrying a squirming blue bundle. Paul took the baby from her.

He stood away from the bed, and Nora watched as he examined the newborn infant. A tiny fist appeared and Paul touched it. His soft smile brought a tightening to Nora's breast. He was enjoying all the pleasure and pride of a man in his first-born son. The baby cried, and Paul started. He handed the baby to Nora.

He frowned as he watched Nora give the baby a small bottle of formula. "You're not nursing?"

"No."

"Why not?"

"I thought I would have to go to work right away," she explained, unable to break away from his solemn gaze. "I didn't think I would ever see you again." Her love welled up anew, smothering her lingering doubts about the wisdom of his proposed reconciliation.

"How did you know I was here?" she asked. "Did your mother tell you? She promised me she wouldn't."

"No, she said nothing, but I knew something was wrong the moment she walked in the door. I asked her what the problem was and she just stared at me as though she felt sorry for me. She hurried to Lisa's bedroom, then to her own and wouldn't come out. Later my grandmother called. I answered the phone and grandmother asked if you had had the baby yet. Needless to say, I was stunned by her question. She thought I was Steven and was very upset when she realized it was me. She almost hung up. You had quite a conspiracy going on, Nora. I did a lot of fast talking, and we had a very interesting discussion about her new boarder. I confronted mom, but she still wouldn't say anything that made sense. She kept mumbling that she had promised. Her silence was the confirmation I needed. I don't think I ever drove that dirt road any faster or crazier."

They sat quietly as the baby drank more than an ounce of formula. Nora put him to her shoulder, patted his tiny bottom and rubbed his back through his shirt until he burped twice. The baby was asleep when she glanced at Paul and caught him staring intently at her again. She laid the sleeping infant on the bed.

"He's almost a day old and he's listed as baby Lane," Paul said. "The nurses are calling him Lane. He needs more than just one name."

"Would you mind if I named him Paul?" Nora asked.

"Then we'll call him Paul Lane Russell. I like the ring of that." He smiled at the sleeping baby.

"Are you sure?" she asked.

"Yes."

"What's your middle name?"

"Innes. Paul Innes Russell," he said, grinning.

She groaned. "I would have known right away about your grandmother. Oh, Paul, how did I happen to choose your grandmother's house out of all the homes in town?" Her rising voice woke the baby, and he started to cry. They laughed as she calmed the baby, picking him up again and holding him snugly in the crook of her arm.

"You make a beautiful mother," Paul said.

"Thank you," was all she could say. "I'll return the baby to the nursery." She began to ease herself off the bed, but Paul stopped her when she made a grimace.

"Let me," he said, taking the sleeping baby from her arms and leaving the room.

A few moments later he returned. Nora lay in bed, the white sheets bringing an unnatural paleness to her complexion.

"You're tired," he said.

"Yes," she admitted. "I'm glad we paid for an extra day. I need it to think about...the future. So much has happened."

"Nora," he began, taking her hand, "I want to ask you a question, and I hope you take it the right way."

"Go ahead," she replied.

"Does having this baby make you think of Jerry and your other son?"

Her blue eyes took on a distant expression, and when she spoke her voice was soft. "There's a lingering desire to compare, I suppose, but that part of my life is over, Paul. I would rather leave it that way." She changed the subject. "You have a handsome son. He looks like his father."

"Thank you." He grinned and bowed from the waist. "And now what are we going to call this handsome son of ours? Paul or Lane?"

"I don't know. I like them both, but..." She hesitated. "Lane was my married name, you know."

Paul looked at her, understanding in his dark eyes. "It's a good name, Nora, and the one I first knew you by.

Besides, he's already baby Lane. Let's make it Lane and that'll cut any confusion with me down the road. He really is a cute little guy," he bragged. "Better looking than the other baby in the nursery."

Nora sagged against the soft pillow. "I'm glad you came. I was so frightened, but too proud to call you." She touched his bare forearm and felt a warm glow encircle them as she traced the muscles to his wrist. A drowsiness surged through her, and she closed her eyes.

"Sleep, honey," he whispered. "I'll be back tomorrow morning to take you and Lane home. He kissed her parted lips and straightened, but continued to study her. A frown troubled his forehead as he watched her deep, steady breathing.

He stopped at the nursery window and admired the sleeping baby in his bassinet near the window. Was this baby boy as handsome as Nora's first son? Did he himself look like her first husband? He pushed the disturbing thoughts from his mind as he glanced at the other baby and reaffirmed his opinion regarding his own child's beauty.

Tomorrow he would begin a new life with Nora. He had been given a third chance with the woman he loved. He would work out the problems with his father later.

"I FEEL LIKE A VAGABOND with no real home to call my own," Nora said as Paul helped her into his truck.

"Home is where the heart is, not a building or location," Paul replied. He drove to the courthouse and parked. Several minutes later they returned to the truck, Nora carrying the baby and Paul tucking an official marriage license into his shirt pocket. "I spoke to the justice of the peace again. He's agreed to perform the ceremony in three days at my grandmother's house.

He's an old friend of the family." As they drove away he added, "I bought the rings last summer before I came to take you to the cabin. Mom will be at the wedding. I don't know about my father. That's his decision. Steven and Mary will be there. I don't know about the rest of the family. They would all like to, but there's work to do at the places. You understand, don't you? You can ask Leslie if you want..."

"Paul, you're rambling and acting very high-handed about this wedding," Nora said. "It's becoming a shotgun wedding, and you're holding the gun. Don't I have a say in all this?"

"No."

"Paul!"

"I'm joking," he said, but a muscle twitched near the corner of one of his eyes.

"I've never seen you so tense before," Nora remarked. "What's the matter? Having second thoughts?"

Paul touched the baby's dark hair as he lay asleep in his safety seat. "You got away from me twice. I don't want it to happen again. I won't let it happen again, damn it."

The fierceness in his voice alarmed her. "Paul, I'm not your property," she cautioned. "You don't own me and you never will. I will be your wife, but never your chattel. Don't carry this Old West philosophy to extremes. It makes you sound like your father."

His dark eyes flew to hers. "Sorry," he murmured. "It's just that...I love you." He put the truck in gear and pulled away from the curb.

"Arc we still going to Grandma Innes's house?" Nora asked.

"Yes. I thought it would be best until we make more definite plans. Okay?"

Nora sighed. "Thank you." She sensed a tension between them, as though both were afraid to speak honestly to each other.

Paul seemed to have read her mind. He parked the truck in front of his grandmother's house but didn't get out. He reached for her hand. "Let's start all over again, Nora."

"What do you mean?"

"Let me court you the way I wanted to the first time I met you. I want to take you places, buy you gifts, do those corny things a love-struck man needs to do. . . and get to know you without the pregnancy in our way."

"We certainly know the mistakes, don't we?" she said. "But this time we must be honest with each other. I'll do my best to make our marriage work, but if we fail, what then? Are you willing to call it quits if it becomes hopeless, Paul?"

"It won't!" he thundered.

The baby woke up and began to wail. His fists flailed the air and his body grew rigid with fear and rage.

Nora released him from his carrier and cuddled him against her breast, trying to calm him. She looked pleadingly at Paul.

"My God, I'm sorry, Nora," Paul apologized. His face had become pale. "I'm sorry." The baby started to hiccup as he gradually stopped crying. Paul yanked the infant restraint seat out of the way and slid across the cab. Hesitantly he took Nora and the baby in his arms.

She glanced up at his face and was surprised to find his brown eyes misty. His tears were all she needed to lose her own control. She began to sob, and he tightened his hold on her as the three of them shed a few tears together.

Slowly he released her, took a tissue and wiped her eyes and cheeks, then touched her mouth with his. "Let's go. Grandmother will wonder why we're just sitting out here instead of going inside. Is the baby all right?"

Lane had fallen asleep again. Paul helped Nora from the cab and they soon found themselves engulfed in hugs from Mrs. Innes, who had been waiting on the porch.

"Hi, grandmother," Paul said, grabbing her around her ample waist and hugging her. He playfully lifted her off the floor and held her up to his eye level, his muscles bulging. "Love you, grandma," he said, kissing her rosy cheek before putting her down again. He laughed as he took the baby from Nora's arms, carefully tucked the blanket around him, and turned to his grandmother. "And this cute little guy is Paul Lane Russell, another addition to your growing number of great-grandchildren. Do you want to hold him?"

"Of course," Mrs. Innes said. As she cuddled the baby he woke up, and two dark brownish-blue eyes stared back at her. After cooing and clucking to him, she finally glanced at Paul and Nora and motioned for them to follow her into the house.

She led them into a small bedroom that had been magically converted into a nursery. A white wicker bassinet had been placed to one side of the room. Nearby two comfortable-looking overstuffed chairs sat on either side of a small end table. A chest of drawers decorated with colorful clowns and balloons had been placed next to a chiffonier with matching clowns and balloons. A gentle breeze stirred the blue-and-white gingham curtains at the window. An area rug in swirls of blue, green and white sprawled across the middle of the nursery.

Nora stepped closer to the chest of drawers and pulled one open. "You've filled it with the baby clothes I bought. Oh, thank you, Grandma Innes. You're so thoughtful." She examined the designs on the furniture. The clowns and balloons were hand painted on maple, not the decals she'd expected. She turned to Mrs. Innes, who was still holding the baby. "Where did this furniture come from?"

"My husband, Teddy, bought it when I had our first child. He was quite artistic, and he painted the clowns one weekend when we were snowed in at our ranch east of town. When our second son was born, he added the balloons. Julie was the first to have her own children so I gave the set to her. She used it with her six children, and we agreed that whoever had the first grandchild would get the furniture. Technically it belongs to my granddaughter in the Big Hole, but she wanted brand-new pieces with all that fancy plastic trim. So it's yours if you want it. I hope you'll accept it as my gift to this fine boy here." Mrs. Innes looked down at Lane. "May he bring you two as much happiness as our own children brought to Teddy and me."

Paul looked at Nora. "Do you want to accept it?"

"Of course," she murmured. "I think it's very thoughtful."

"There's a full-size crib, but I didn't think there was any need for that now," Mrs. Innes added. "When you find a place of your own, you can have it, too. I know the furniture is old and scarred from all those babies, but the slats on the crib are close together and its' all sturdy and very safe. I know how concerned I was as a new mother and I know you are, too." She bustled about the room, touching a crooked picture frame on the wall, adjusting the curtains, checking the chairs. "We'll move in a rocker, too, if you want. Shall I put him down? Then I can show you to your room."

Nora nodded, and Mrs. Innes laid Lane in the bassinet, then left to see the other room. It was the one in which Nora had stayed, but the twin bed had been replaced with a sturdy maple double bed and covered with a handmade quilt in a lone-star design with a multitude of blue-and-brown prints.

"If this is suitable, I'll leave you two alone. Lunch will be ready at noon. I'll try not to disturb you," Mrs. Innes said as she tactfully slipped from the room.

Nora moved to the window and nervously fingered the lacy blue-and-white curtain, aware of how many unsolved problems they still had. The promised property north of town, jeopardized by their imminent marriage. His father's opinion of her, in spite of Paul's optimism that everything would work out.

"Nora?" Paul's voice sounded deep and husky from behind her.

Her heart thudded. She was just two days past giving birth to his child, yet his voice aroused her. She had wondered, during the time with his grandmother, how she would react if he came back into her life. Had she stayed with his grandmother in the hope he would learn of her whereabouts and seek her out?

He touched her shoulders. She remained motionless as his hands slid down her arms. Without thinking, she leaned her head against his shoulder. Neither spoke. He nuzzled her hair and she tilted her head, allowing him access to her neck. The warmth of his breath caressed her sensitive skin, and she knew he would be aware of the pulsating vein in her neck. His lips nibbled at her skin, sending a tremor through her.

She didn't want to be vulnerable to his touch so soon, and she turned in his arms. "Please don't," she whispered.

"Why not?"

"It's not right. . . the baby. . ."

"I just want to hold you," he assured her. "You've changed."

"How?"

"You're more reserved...cautious? I'm not sure. Does this all seem like a repeat of your first marriage?"

"It couldn't be...we're not married," she said. "Maybe it will seem more right when..." She paused. "Maybe I'm a prude, Paul. I always thought I would be married when I had children." She tried to pull away, but he refused to release her. "I don't want to talk about my first marriage."

"All right," he replied, and slid his arms around her waist.

She tensed. "I look dumpy in this loose dress. My body is still thick."

"It's only temporary, love. I think you're more beautiful than before. I didn't think that could be possible, but you are." He turned her face toward him.

"Nora," he murmured, just before his lips covered hers. His kiss was warm and soft, never hardening in desire. "Come lie beside me. We have a half hour before lunch. The baby is asleep and you need your rest." Releasing her, he moved to the bed. Pulling off his boots, he stretched out on the quilted spread and reached for her hand.

His arm went around her shoulders as she came to him, her head against his chest and broad shoulder. She listened to the rhythmic beat of his heart, and her hand slid to his chest as she succumbed to the security and warmth he offered, languishing in the haven of his arms.

THE DAY OF THEIR WEDDING began with a blustery wind and gray clouds, but soon the sun burst forth in a bright promise.

"This hardly seems like a wedding," Nora said with a

laugh as she slid the long slip over her head and smoothed it down past her hips.

"Why not?" Paul asked, adjusting the knot of his black tie. He reached for the charcoal gray dress jacket.

"Here we are, the bride and groom, dressing in the same room."

"Pretty good idea, if you ask me," he said, grinning.

She turned her back to him. "Then come help me. I can't reach the zipper." His hands stilled her fumbling one, and he quickly zipped the long opening of the ankle-length, cream-colored chiffon dress. The dress was styled with tiny accordion pleats flowing from its high neckline down to its hem. It had no waist and came with three belts: a gold chain; a stiff, wide vinyl belt she had set aside for later use when her waist was small again; and a cloth tie of the same soft chiffon material. She draped the chiffon tie loosely around her middle and grimaced at herself in the mirror. "Maybe we should postpone this wedding until I look better."

"You look fine," he assured her. "Now stop fussing and let's get married." He put on his jacket and turned to her. "Ready to get hitched, pretty lady?"

"I reckon so, cowboy," she replied, and they both laughed.

When they entered the living room of Mrs. Innes's house, most of the invited guests were present. Julie Russell, Mary and Lisa, Tim and Russ, Jr., D. A. McCormack and his daughter, Annie, David and Sammy McCormack, whom Nora had not met before. Steven Russell and Leslie Coleman had agreed to be witnesses, although Nora still had some reservations about Leslie. At the last minute George Holman slipped sheepishly through the door.

Paul and Nora exchanged glances, aware that one important guest was missing.

"He didn't come," she murmured.

"Damn him," Paul cursed.

"It's for the best," Nora said, taking his arm. "I think the justice of the peace is getting restless. We'd better hurry and join him before he decides to leave."

Within minutes the ceremony was completed. Matching gold bands were placed on ring fingers, and the kiss exchanged drew sighs from the women and girls and chuckles from the men. Ida Innes invited everyone to stay for a small reception.

"We have punch for the teetotalers, champagne for the classier members of this gathering and beer for you red-neck cowboys who don't know any better," she announced, pointing a finger at her grandsons.

Lane woke from his nap and was content to be passed from one aunt to another, finally ending up in Sammy McCormack's arms. Mary spent much of her time with Annie and D.A., and Leslie divided her attention between George and Russ, Jr., apparently determined to get Russ, Jr., to talk to her. Paul, Steven and David McCormack were soon talking cattle, until Ida Innes insisted they not discuss business on such a joyful occasion.

When Paul sought out his bride and found her sitting alone and pale, he suggested the party end and thanked them all for coming. Instead of a honeymoon night alone, they slept in their room in Paul's grandmother's house, content to lie in each other's arms and talk of their future.

THE NEXT SEVERAL WEEKS passed in a peaceful blur. Paul left each morning before daybreak for the ranch, where he was involved in moving the herds down from their summer pastures and attending the fall livestock sales. Occasionally he had to spend the night, but Nora didn't worry. A trust was slowly building between them.

Four weeks after Lane's birth Nora was back into fitted jeans. The baby quickly adapted to a reasonable schedule of eating, napping and good-natured periods of wakefulness. One evening Paul was holding him, talking nonsense mixed with cowboy jargon, when suddenly Lane's small pink mouth twisted into a lopsided grin, snaring father and son together in an unbreakable bond of love. As Nora watched Paul holding his son, she knew any lingering doubts about his feelings for his family were firmly put to rest.

The morning of Nora and Lane's six weeks' medical examination brought heavily overcast skies and snow predicted for later in the day.

"Don't worry, honey, I'll make it home," Paul assured her as he kissed her goodbye and headed for the truck.

When Nora and Lane left the clinic later that morning the snow had begun. By midafternoon the storm had grown into a full-blown blizzard. Nora called the ranch as soon as she reached Mrs. Innes's house, but Julie told her that all the men were out moving some cattle and later planned to deliver hay to a few isolated herds several miles from the home ranch.

"I'll tell him you called," she promised.

"Thanks," Nora said, sighing as she replaced the receiver. She had planned a special dinner, and as she began the preparations she thought about the evening ahead. Tonight she and Paul could resume their sex life. Sex. It had been an unmentionable part of their new life together. Paul held her each night but never touched her intimately. Even her breasts had become off limits in his self-imposed celibacy.

Darkness fell early as the heavy cloud cover blocked out the sun, and the snowfall quickly buried the streets and sidewalks. When the streetlights came on, they shone like soft shimmering balls of diffused light through the blowing snow.

Mrs. Innes and Nora sat down to dinner, and Nora glanced wistfully at Paul's empty chair.

Mrs. Innes patted her hand. "He'll be here. Paul won't let a little snowstorm keep him away."

After dinner was finished, Nora bathed and fed the baby, and put him down for the night. Mrs. Innes wished her good-night and retired to her room.

Nora decided to call the ranch again, and this time Paul's father answered. Her heart tightened as she asked for Paul.

"Is this Nellie or Leslie?" he asked, chuckling as though he had told a joke.

"Please, Mr. Russell, may I speak to Paul? Is he there?" she persisted, determined not to let him goad her.

"He's not here. Left hours ago. Maybe he stopped off on the way home."

She heard a scuffle and mumbling voices rising in pitch.

"Paul left about an hour ago, but the snow is very heavy out here," Julie said. "His father tried to talk him into staying, but he was adamant. I'm sure it will take him a while to drive in. I said a prayer for his safety when he left. Forgive my husband. He forgot his manners. Be patient, my dear. Paul will be there soon."

Another hour passed as Nora kept her vigil near the window in the darkened living room with only the dim porch light sending out a beacon to him. She went to check on the baby and found him sleeping soundly. She had just left his room when she heard the kitchen door open. Running to the back of the house, she flipped on the overhead light.

"Paul!" she cried.

He was covered with snow. His broad shoulders in the leather coat were hunched over as he knocked clumps of the melting snow from his boots, then removed them and set them aside. His hat lay on the kitchen counter near the sink.

"Hi, sweetheart." He smiled at her. "It's nasty out there."

"I didn't hear the truck," she said.

"I left it at the corner. I couldn't see through the windshield. I've never seen it snow so heavy so fast. I walked the rest of the way." He removed the heavy coat and hung it on a hook near the door, then turned to her. "Well? Are you going to just stand there staring at me?"

Her feet seemed glued to the floor, a sudden shyness holding her immobile as she continued to stare at him.

"Well?" he asked again.

"You still have snow on your face," she said, tossing him a kitchen towel.

He wiped the flakes from his lean cheeks. "Anything else?"

Her hand shook. To stop the shaking she pressed both palms against her flaming cheeks. She took a step back into the hallway, but he strode toward her and swooped her up in his arms. She clung to him, pressing against his powerful chest.

"Oh, Paul, I was so afraid you wouldn't make it... and I wanted this night to be special. Dr. Peters says I'm fine."

"I would have made it home no matter how deep the snow became. This is the night I've been waiting for, the night I'm going to make love to my beautiful wife," he murmured against her hair as he carried her down the hall into their room.

He nudged the door shut with his stocking foot, then sat her down on the edge of the bed and knelt before her. Slowly he unbuttoned her blouse, his fingers burning her skin as they worked their way down to her waist. His hands slid back up her soft smooth skin, until they met the barrier of her bra.

"Can I help?" she asked, slightly amused by his intense concentration.

"No," he replied, his voice hoarse with need.

In spite of his insistence she slid her hands behind her back and under the cotton blouse, unhooking the confining bra. As both her blouse and bra fell away, she heard him groan, but instead of touching her he leaned back on his heels, and her skin seemed to glow beneath the warmth of his gaze.

"I think I've developed a fetish," he said.

"What are you talking about?"

"You have the most beautiful breasts I've ever seen." He put the palms of both hands on her knees. "Your breasts are fuller than most. They're the color of cream and the texture of satin." He slid his hands to her thighs.

"I want to touch them, but if I do, you might disappear. If I ever lost you again, life wouldn't be worth living. I would like to go to bed with you and stay there forever." His hands moved to her hips and he drew closer. Her own hands went to the sides of his dark head and caressed the fine curls behind his ears.

At his words her nipples hardened and were tingling. "Please touch me, Paul," she whispered, drawing his head closer.

His hot breath singed her skin as he complied, his lips

caressing the full outside curve of one breast, then the other, as pangs of longing shot through her. His hands inched their way to her slim waist, lingered awhile, then explored each rib.

She held her breath as his mouth finally covered one nipple. His tongue played with it, teased it, until she pushed herself suggestively against him.

"Please," she moaned. She was desperate to temper the fire raging in her, but when his lips moved to cover the other breast, she found no satisfaction as new fuel was thrown on the raging flames.

She resented the clothing covering their bodies. Pushing him away, she reached for the snaps on his shirt and ripped them apart. He laughed at her impatience and teasingly began to resnap the shirt.

"No!" she moaned, stopping his hands.

The pleading tone of her sultry voice swept away any lingering playfulness and he pulled her hard against him, his arms bands of steel.

"Love me, Paul," she murmured, turning her face up to his. "Make love to me."

His mouth claimed her parted lips, returning her heated passion, but her starving body craved more.

He undressed her, then quickly shed his own clothing and joined her on the bed.

"Nora, Nora," he groaned as he pulled her against him. She felt his hardened desire and drew him between her thighs, teasing him as he had teased her breasts.

"That's not enough, love," his gravelly voice whispered against her throat.

She offered herself to him, moaning softly as they became one, and in their shared passion she met his plunging thrusts until their taut bodies shuddered in mutual fulfillment.

When she lay spent in his arms, she thought of a book she'd read once. The author had insisted any good session of lovemaking should take at least two hours. They had made a shambles of that philosophy, yet the satisfaction she now languished in told her that such time limits were silly. How could any boundary of time be applied to what they had experienced?

In their impatience they had made love on top of the quilted spread. A tremor raced through her as Paul eased away, then swept the quilt over them, forming a cocoon.

He nuzzled her ear. "Do you like large families, Nora?"

"Why do you ask, darling?"

"I was just thinking about Lane. We shouldn't raise him as an only child."

"What do you suggest?" she asked, propping herself up and studying his features in the dim lamplight.

"I want several little blond girls who look just like their mother and enough brown-haired boys to help me with the work." Suddenly he laughed. "Good Lord, I sound like my father."

"But they would be *our* children, Paul, our children. That makes it different. Our children would be special and loved. But we should wait awhile."

"Maybe in a few months," he suggested.

"Or a year," she countered.

"Want to argue?"

"I don't have enough energy," she replied, snuggling deeper in his arms. "I feel renewed but so weak, like a butterfly must feel after going through metamorphosis."

"You're as lovely as a butterfly," he whispered, adjusting the edge of the quilt under her chin. "My Southern California butterfly, so surprisingly full of fire." And his lips met hers in a tender kiss.

CHAPTER THIRTEEN

A LIGHT KNOCK awakened them. Nora shot up to a sitting position, still wrapped in the lone-star quilt.

"Lunch is ready," Mrs. Innes called. "Lane and I have had a lovely morning, but I think he would like to see his parents sometime today."

Embarrassment brought a self-conscious stammer to Nora's voice. "We'll be there shortly, Grandma Innes. We were late. . . getting to sleep."

"Go away, grandmother," Paul's booming voice called.

"Paul," Nora chided, brushing away his inquisitive hand from her waist. "Grandma Innes, we'll dress and be out in a few minutes," Nora called, then giggled as his fingers traced circles around her navel.

"Take your time, my dears," Mrs. Innes's voice sounded through the closed door. "Lane and I will set the table, but we're not holding the meal. We're both hungry." Her footsteps tapped a retreat down the hall.

Paul pulled Nora down into the warm folds of the quilt and nuzzled her forehead. "Good morning," he said, giving her a light kiss.

"Good morning, yourself, my impetuous husband," she murmured, smiling as she recalled their lovemaking the night before.

"We set a speed record, didn't we?" he chuckled. "Tonight we'll try again with a little finesse."

"Oh, you had plenty of finesse last night," she assured him.

"Then perhaps more patience." He raised himself on one elbow and gazed down at her. "You're sexy in the morning. Your lips are still swollen from my kisses, and your eyes...your eyes are turquoise. Not really blue and not green, either. I've never seen a woman with eyes quite like yours."

He ran his fingers through her hair, fanning it out onto the quilt. "Your hair is like honey...no, more like corn silk. You know, the part you get when you shuck the ear of corn and find that stuff beneath the husk." He smiled, obviously pleased with his appraisal of her features.

"You sound like a farmer bragging about his crop," she teased.

"Dad's the rancher, but mom's great-grandfather was a Missouri farmer and it's in her genes. She always plants a garden and babies it to maturity. Sometimes the frost gets it first, but usually we have a few dinners with fresh corn on the cob. I remember shucking the ears when I was a boy."

"Sometimes I think you're still a boy at heart. You're still playing cowboys, aren't you, with your brothers?"

She must have struck a sensitive nerve, because he drew away a little, putting an end to the intimacy they'd shared. "I'm sorry, Paul. I was just teasing."

"No, it's not that." He stared out the window, a thoughtful expression masking his emotions. "I have to go to the ranch today. Dad's selling that ill-tempered bull I've told you about. The buyer is coming to get him this afternoon and I promised to help them load him. He's a mean hombre, the meanest dad has ever had. Dad should have sold him years ago. I'll call and make sure the deal is still on, but a little snow never stopped the sale of a bull around the country." He turned to look at Nora. "Come with me, honey."

She shook her head.

"Please," he insisted. "Bring the baby and grandmother, too. Grandma loves to visit the ranch. She spent most of her married life on the Innes Sweetwater place east of town."

Still she declined.

"You have to face dad sooner or later. Mom wants to see Lane, and dad has never seen him. You two are my family now, and he might as well accept the fact. I don't know how one man can remain so belligerent. He has this narrow-minded idea that only someone who has lived here most of his or her life can be counted on to do his share, to understand the hardships involved in raising cattle and fighting the elements. Because he has never had to change his ways, he assumes no one else can." He slid out from under the quilt, wrapped a huge towel around his trim waist and left the room.

When he returned, his hair was damp from his shower and a few drops of moisture glistened on his chest. His eyes lingered on her as he began to dress.

Nora knew she was hopelessly in love with him. He had become the light of her life and the center of her universe, the very things she'd vowed she didn't want to happen. She had become vulnerable again.

"We'll go with you," she said.

PAUL, NORA, the sleeping baby and Ida Innes were all crowded into the cab of Paul's truck.

"It's Saturday and no school buses are out, and the auto patrol goes only to the end of the pavement this early in the season," Paul remarked.

Nora had been thinking about the imminent confrontation with Paul's father and had missed part of his comment. "What's an auto patrol?"

He laughed. "Sorry, hon. Make that snowplow. Auto patrol is one of those phrases we natives use."

"I'll never be a native to your father."

Ida Innes turned to Nora, her face flushed as she shook her fist. "Darn that pigheaded son-in-law of mine. Don't you let him get to you, darling. Those Russell men always did have a habit of making asses of themselves, and Ed Russell's no exception. I remember when Ed's father told me to my face that my daughter wasn't good enough for his son. Well, let me tell you, I told him a thing or two about the Inneses, Schroeders, Russells and Morbishes. They all have skeletons in their closets. My son-in-law has a very poor memory, and I suppose it's high time I reminded him of a few things." She patted Nora's arm. "Ed Russell had an uncle who was charged with murdering two rustlers years ago. In fact, the two men were merely reclaiming some of their strays. The brands were partly covered with long winter coats, but by the time the law found that out, the men were dead, killed by Peter Morbish's impulsive gun. No one ever explained how the steers got into Pete's herd in the first place. His family's money got him committed to Warm Springs instead of the prison at Deer Lodge."

"What's Warm Springs?" Nora asked.

"The state psychiatric hospital. He was there for ten years and then released. He was killed in a car accident a few years later, driving drunk on a snow-packed county road. He left a wife and three children to fend for themselves because of his recklessness."

"How awful," Nora said. "What happened to the family?"

"They left the state. The Morbishes refused to provide for them. It was years ago, but Ed doesn't like to be reminded of it. I could tell you a few stories about the Russell men, too. Morbish and Russell men can be real jerks at times."

"Grandmother, I'm a Russell," Paul said with a sidelong glance.

"But you're trying to overcome those inherited weaknesses and concentrate on the Innes strengths, I hope." Ida Innes tossed her white head and laughed. "I talk too much, Nora. Don't worry, dear. I have more tact than to embarrass you, but that thickheaded son-in-law of mine needs to straighten out, and I'm the one who can make him see the light." A pleased smile lit her face.

Nora lowered her head and tried to hide her own smile. She almost wished she could see Ed Russell's reaction when Grandma Innes let him have it with both barrels of her well-aimed verbal shotgun.

Paul motioned to the snow-covered road ahead. The plows had stopped at the end of the pavement several miles from town, but tracks of trucks with heavy tires and high underchassis had beaten the snow down into two wide trails. The wind had blown the snow against the jackleg fences, and now only the top rail and anchor posts peeked out from beneath the drifts. The white countryside glistened under the bright sun, the peaceful landscape contrasting with the tension Nora felt inside.

Several miles up the road they passed under the cross beams of the entrance to the Rocking R Ranch. The sprawling white house was nearly invisible beneath its snow-covered roof, and the yard was covered with a thick blanket of white.

The stables and corrals presented a different picture. Horses in a small pasture nearby had trampled the snow into slushy mud. A large maroon truck and stock trailer were backed up to a loading chute, and several yards from the wooden chute, isolated in a separate corral from the other cattle, stood an Angus Saler cross-bred bull, his black head swinging from side to side and his nostrils flaring as he snorted at the men outside the fence. The bull continually pawed at the ground with his front hoof, gradually turning the dirt and snow into mud.

"We should have stayed in town," she whispered to Paul as she looked at the fearsome bull.

"Don't worry," he reassured her. "We do this all the time, except usually the bulls are easier to work with. We'll be back in town tonight. Remember my promise." He grinned at her provocatively.

As they left the truck, Paul's father came stomping from the corrals. "Where the hell have you been, Paul? We needed you hours ago." He frowned at Nora, and she clutched the bundled baby closer.

"It doesn't matter, dad," Paul replied. "We're here now and I'm ready to help you. Nora, you and grandmother go on into the house." He smiled encouragingly. "I think mom's set up a crib for the baby."

"Sure as hell has," Ed Russell grumbled. "Cluttering up the whole living room."

"Good for her," Ida Innes said with obvious relish. She glared at her son-in-law. "Hello, *Edwin*. Still the same, I see." Before he could respond, she took Nora by the arm and led her to the house.

"Let's go, dad," Paul said. "We want to be home by dark."

Inside the warm house the women had gathered around the harvest table in the kitchen. Julie poured coffee for the buyer's wife and slid a platter of coffee cake toward Nora once she had sat down.

Nora glanced around the table. "Where's Mary?"

Lisa giggled. "She's stuck in town."

"Yesterday's storm caught her in town," Julie explained. "She and D.A. McCormack couldn't make it home after their college classes let out and had to take rooms at the Montana Inn. She should be home soon."

"The drifts were quite deep when we came out," Nora said. "If we had been in my car we would never have made it." She took two bites of the coffee cake. "This is delicious," she said as she finished it. "May I have another piece?" As she reached for the platter, a blood-curdling scream shook the room. Shouts and snorts rose from the corral.

Nora's hand froze in midair. "That's Paul!" she cried. "Something has happened to Paul!" She dropped the piece of cake onto the table, spilled her cup of coffee and knocked over her chair as she ran frantically from the room.

In the corral across the yard the men were fighting to get the raging bull away from a body lying in the urine-stained snow.

In a slow-motion haze, she saw Ed Russell shoving at the massive head of the bull, but the bull continued to trample the victim on the ground. Steven jabbed the bull's flank several times with an electric prod until finally the bull took a few awkward steps away.

Ed Russell, the bull's buyer, Russ, Jr., and Tim hurriedly moved the bull through the chute, up the ramp and into the stock trailer. When Steven dropped to his knees by the fallen man, Nora could make out the muddy leather coat, its fleece lining stained with excrement. It was her Paul, lying unconscious in a pool of blood.

Nora raced through the snow and muck and dropped to her knees beside Steven. He tried to shield her, but she pulled free and turned to Paul. The left side of his face had been savagely torn, his cheek split from cheekbone to jaw. She suppressed a wave of nausea as she stared at the gaping wound. When Paul moved his head slightly and groaned, white bone was visible.

"He'll get dirt in it," she cried, and scooting to his side, she carefully lifted his head onto her lap. "Paul, oh, my darling." She turned to Steven. "What happened?"

"The bull knocked him down," Steven explained, his face somber. "He's had a grudge match with Paul for years. I don't know why. The bull stepped on his arm and face. Damn it all, not once but twice." He jerked his flannel shirttails out of his jeans, flipped open his pocket knife and began to cut a large ragged square from his thermal undershirt. "Press this against the wound, Nora."

She put the pad of material against the gaping wound. "We have to get him to the hospital."

"I'll get the Wagoneer," Steven replied, jumping to his feet. An eternity passed before he backed the station wagon through the corral gate and the men lifted Paul into the back of the car. "Get in, Nora," he said. She crawled in and sat cross-legged beside Paul's inert body, and Steven slammed the tailgate behind her.

Paul's lashes fluttered and his eyes opened. "Nora," he whispered.

She squeezed his hand with her free one, still maintaining a tight hold on the compress.

"Keep it pressed to the wound," Steven said, glancing at her in the rearview mirror.

Paul coughed and spat up blood.

"Steven," Nora cried. "Does he have internal injuries? Did the bull step on his stomach or abdomen?"

"I don't think so," Steven replied. "He's probably swallowed his own blood. His cheek is ripped through to the inside of his mouth. He's going to have a hard time eating for a while."

They drove for several miles at breakneck speed, sliding dangerously around the curve in the snow-packed road.

"Please slow down, Steven. We don't want to have a wreck ourselves," she cautioned. "Did anyone call the hospital?"

"Dad will. He has his faults, but he's good in an emergency."

The car bumped onto the pavement, and Nora knew they would soon be in town.

The compress was blood soaked as they squealed to a stop at the emergency entrance of the hospital. Immediately the car was surrounded with medical personnel.

"My God!" the on-call physician muttered when he removed the compress from Paul's face and examined the wound. "Quick, Joyce," he called to the nurse nearest him. "Call Roger Thorson's house. I think his brother is visiting for the week. He's an oral surgeon from Billings and this man needs his expertise. I can do the facial repair, but I need him for the broken jaw." He turned to Steven and Nora. "Come with me. We need information. His injuries don't appear to be life threatening, but infection could complicate matters. When did he have his last tetanus shot?"

As Nora followed the doctor into a small office, she turned and watched the stretcher bearing her husband disappear down the long barren corridor.

BACK AT THE ROCKING R, Julie Russell tried to present a composed face for the rest of the family. "We'll all just wait here," she said.

The truck and stock trailer had pulled away shortly after the Wagoneer had left for the hospital. The others had made their way back into the warm house, cleaned up from the messy job of loading the bull and regrouped in the family room.

Ed Russell had called the hospital to alert the staff about Paul's accident and his impending arrival. Now he paced restlessly about the room.

"Russ, why don't you tend to the fireplace," Julie suggested.

He grunted as he stirred the coals and added a few logs, then dropped into his favorite chair.

Lane awoke from his nap and cried. Julie changed him, gave him a few ounces of formula and carried him into the family room.

Ed frowned at the wriggling infant. "Why did *she* go with him? One of us should have gone." He gave Julie a stern look of disapproval as she cooed and clucked at the grinning baby boy.

"She's his wife, Russ. She's part of the family now."

"Like hell she is," he snarled. He motioned to the baby. "And that brat. He's a bastard kid fathered by some drunken cowboy. Paul's a fool for taking on that kid's care. Nellie is bad enough, but why the kid?"

Ida Innes left her chair and planted herself directly in front of her son-in-law.

"Her name is Nora. N-o-r-a. Nora, you thickheaded, ignorant man. If there was a drunken cowboy involved, it was your own son! And that little boy is your first grandchild. I've always hoped for some sign that you inherited some smarts from your nice mother, but maybe I've wasted my time. You're as stubborn and imbecilic as your own father."

She returned to her chair, grabbed her purse and

stomped back to the same spot she'd left. "Hold this," she demanded, dumping her bulky purse onto his lap. She fumbled for a small photo album buried deep within.

When she found it she flipped to a picture of Paul taken when he was three months old. "Julie, give that so-called 'bastard' child to Ed," she said, and she grabbed her purse from his lap and dropped it on the floor.

Before he could react, Ed Russell found himself holding a wriggling, brown-haired baby whose cherub face broke into a lopsided grin in spite of Ed's surly frown.

"Here," Ida announced as she laid the picture on the baby's chest. "How can any man run three successful places like you do and be so stupid about his own children? Can't you see the resemblance?"

The picture began to slide off Lane's round stomach. Ed put one steadying hand on the baby and caught the falling picture with the other. The baby made a gurgling sound when the large hand gripped him.

Ed glanced at the picture, then frowned again at the baby. "I don't see it," he declared, flipping the photograph down on the end table near his chair. "All brown-haired babies look alike."

"Good grief, man, have you become senile? I have an excuse at my age, but not you." In frustration she drew herself up to her full five feet and kicked his shin.

"Hey, cut that out, Ida Belle, you're hurting me," Ed grumbled. Then he turned to Julie. "Doesn't he look just like that Swanson kid . . . and the Morrisons' grandkid?"

"No," Julie replied.

"Saying all brown-haired children look alike is just like saying all American Indians or Englishmen or Norwegians look alike, and it just isn't so," Ida said. "Look at his eyes and his hair and the shape of his face. He's the spitting image of your oldest son when he was a baby."

"My son wouldn't. . ."

"Paul *did*, and he was man enough to own up to it," Ida said.

Ed continued to shake his head. "Maybe he gets his looks from his mother's family. We don't know her family."

Ida Innes huffed and stomped her small foot. "His mother has blond hair, blue eyes and a lovely oval face, you ninny. This child has brown hair, eyes that are turning dark just like your son's, and a face that will someday be angular and very handsome. His name is Paul Lane Russell, but he gets his good looks from the Innes side of his family, just like your son did. Only their coloring is yours." She laughed aloud as Ed began to study the baby on his lap.

"You wouldn't be half bad-looking yourself if you wouldn't be so nasty tempered all the time," she remarked.

Ed glanced at the photograph, then back at the baby on his lap. "Maybe it's a coincidence. How do you all know he's Paul's son?"

Russ, Jr., spoke up from his position near the fire. "Because Paul said so."

"Yeah," Tim agreed. "He told us."

"That's right, dear," Julie added. "He told me. So—" she leaned down to give him a light kiss on his ruddy cheek "—you might as well say hello to your firstborn grandchild."

Ed stared down at the baby, who stared back at him. When he finally looked up again, he found himself alone. He returned his attention to the baby on his lap.

"What do you think, kid? Are they right?"

The baby cooed and grinned at Ed, waving his chubby arms and kicking his legs excitedly.

"Could they be right and me wrong?" Ed asked, his stern mouth softening. Lane squealed again. Ed touched his little fist, and the baby closed his tiny fingers around Ed's forefinger and clung tightly.

"Hey, you're a strong little guy. My own boys were strong at your age, too. Maybe. . .maybe I owe your mother an apology. Maybe. We'll see."

DARKNESS HAD SETTLED by the time Nora returned to Paul's private room at the hospital. Steven had stayed with her during the surgery.

"Are you sure you'll be all right, sis?" he asked, obviously reluctant to leave her alone.

"I'm fine," she assured him. "You go back. The others will want to know all the details. I'll call them and let them know he's okay and that you're on your way home."

"Well, if you're sure." He gave her a quick hug.

"Steven, thanks for. . .everything."

"That's what families are for," he told her, then was gone.

She phoned his parents, and much to her surprise Ed Russell answered and called her Nora. He had little to say to her, other than to tell her the baby was sleeping and to ask about his own son.

She told him the details of the corrective surgery on Paul's face and jaw, then repeated the information to Julie. "Steven is on his way home. He'll tell you everything."

"Don't worry about Lane," Julie said. "My mother is going to stay here for a few days with him, and Mary or one of the boys will pick up some formula and extra diapers. We'll all be in to see Paul in a few days. He must be in a great deal of pain, and you're the one he needs with him now. Take care, Nora, and give him our love."

"Goodbye, Julie...and thanks. Tell Grandma Innes we couldn't do without her." Slowly Nora returned the receiver to its cradle.

When she went back to see Paul he was still asleep from the anesthetic. The left side of his face was heavily bandaged, and gingerly she touched his uninjured right cheek. Miraculously his limbs had sustained no broken bones.

He shifted his bruised body under the covers and groaned.

"What happened?" he asked, his words slightly slurred. "I can't remember..." He lay quietly for a few minutes. "The bull...I was trampled." He frowned, trying to recall the afternoon's events. "What's the matter with my face? God, it hurts. I can't open my mouth!" He tried to fight the wires holding his lower face immobile, and panic filled his eyes.

"Be still, Paul," Nora soothed him. "Don't talk." She laid a reassuring hand on his chest as she tried to calm him, and his breathing gradually settled. "Your cheek was torn by the bull's hoof. The blow knocked out some teeth and broke your jaw. It's wired to keep it immobile."

His eyes were glued to her face as she told him the extent of his injuries. The full impact of the accident suddenly hit her, and she was unable to think of anything comforting to say to him. "What if the bull had stepped on your head? Oh, Paul, you could have been killed!"

Tears filled her eyes as she touched his bare cheek

with the open palm of her hand. "I love you, Paul. I'll stay here with you for a while. Lane is with your mother and she wants to keep him for a few days. Steven stayed with me through the surgery, but he's gone home now to tell the others. Now rest. The physician says you're going to hurt a little tomorrow." She held his hand, talking quitely, until he fell asleep again.

Nora spent the night alone in Mrs. Innes's house, finally succumbing to the tension that had threatened to overcome her at the hospital. She cried until her eyes burned and her throat ached, knowing how close Paul had come to a serious brain injury or even death.

The silence of the house awakened her from a restless sleep. She rolled over to touch Paul, then jerked her hand away from the cold sheets. For an instant she had forgotten the accident.

Last night was to have been a night of loving, a night of leisurely exploration, whispered words in the dim lamplight, rediscovering what pleased and satisfied each other. She had planned to buy a bottle of pink Chablis, and they would sip the chilled wine from the long-stemmed glasses she'd found in his grandmother's kitchen cupboard.

She pushed herself from the bed, thinking ironically that sipping was all Paul could do now.

When she entered his hospital room a few hours later he was asleep. Her heart ached for him. Purple bruises darkened his eyes, and his left eye was swollen shut from his injury. The swelling covered most of his nose and mouth as well, hiding his handsome face under a grotesque distortion of bruised flesh.

He stirred. One brown eye opened and stared at her as he raised his hand and groaned a greeting.

"Hello, darling," she said, her voice shaky. "I want

to kiss you, but I don't know where." She frowned as she surveyed his battered face. "I've seen you looking better." Finally she kissed him lightly on his forehead.

He stared at her with his one good eye. "Help me," he mumbled. "I want to sit up." He rested his hand on her shoulder as he swung his long legs off the side of the bed. "My mouth tastes like some varmint crawled in it and died. Can you get me a drink, honey?" he asked, his words still slightly slurred. After several sips through a flexible straw, he seemed refreshed. "Dr. Morrison says I can go home in a few days if the swelling goes down."

"I was frightened when I first saw you this morning," she said. "What caused the swelling?"

"I picked up an infection from all that muck I was lying in. It started during the night and they've been giving me antibiotics. It could have been worse if I hadn't kept my tetanus shots up to date. It should be a lot better by tomorrow."

"Good," she said, squeezing his hand. "What about your jaw and mouth? Have you seen the doctor this morning?"

"I'll need a bridge once my face heals, and the dentist who put on these wires says they have to stay on for a month or more." He reached for a small case on the nearby nightstand. "Check this out," he mumbled, handing it to her.

The package contained a small pair of cutting pliers. "What are they for?" Nora asked.

"In case I choke or strangle. Someone can cut the wires and save my life." He glanced at her. "Would you save my life, Nora?"

"Of course," she murmured, wanting to hold him. "I wish I could hug you."

"Don't try it," he mumbled. "I think I've bruised every muscle in my body." He swung his legs back onto the bed and dropped to the pillow. He was silent for a few minutes before turning to her. "You have the advantage over me now, Nora. What are you going to do with yourself and the baby. . . and me?"

The sadness and doubt she saw in his face tore at her.

"Without us you could meet your father's terms for the property," she said, giving him a chance to express himself.

"No piece of land is as important to me as my wife and child," he replied.

She leaned over the bed and gently kissed his lopsided mouth. "I love you, Paul Russell. The moment you laid your hand on mine in the Matador and insisted I dance with you was the moment I became ensnared in your trap."

"Is that what it is?" he asked. "A trap?"

"It was a trap of desire at first, but now it has become a haven of love. There was a time when I wanted never to see you again, but now your hold on me is right here—" she touched her breast "—in my heart. I could never leave you. They would have to carry me away kicking and screaming." She smiled as she watched the fear and uncertainty leave his face.

It was two hours before she rose from her chair. "I'm going now," she said. "I need to see our son and tell him his father is going to be just fine."

She put on her coat. "Your father has changed."

"What do you mean?"

"He called me Nora instead of Nellie."

"He did?" Paul looked thoughtful. "I wonder what he's up to?" He watched as she took a brush from her purse and ran it through her hair. "Be careful. I don't think he would do anything crazy, but I don't completely trust him, either. Just be careful."

She reached for her purse. "I will, darling. Rest now," she said and kissed him. "I'll see you this evening."

DURING THE NEXT FEW DAYS Paul continued to improve. The Levin tube through which he received his nourishment while the inside of his mouth healed was removed, and the swelling in his face responded to the antibiotics.

When Nora entered his room just before lunch she was pleased to see him smiling more naturally. "You're in a good mood today," she remarked, kissing him lightly on his lips.

"I get my first food today," he said, giving her a twisted smile. "And tomorrow the sutures come out."

"Just how do you expect to eat, Mr. Russell?"

He shrugged his broad shoulders. "I'm not sure. But I'm about to find out." He cocked his head, listening to the sounds in the hallway.

The door to the room swung open and a nurse entered, followed by an aide carrying a glass.

"Here's your steak and baked potato," the aide said.

"What is it really?" Paul mumbled through his wired jaw.

"It looks like a chocolate milk shake, but it's actually a high-protein drink," the nurse explained. "It's not really good, but it's not too bad, either."

"It's better than nothing. You might as well get used to it," the nurse's aide advised before she sailed out of the room.

"Let me help," Nora said. She cranked the head of his bed up as far as it would go, rolled the bedside tray close to his chest, and tried to insert the flexible straw through his lips, but without success.

"Do it like this," the nurse said as she worked the straw along the inside of his uninjured cheek and through the natural opening behind his molars. "Sip very slowly so you don't choke. Easy now," she coaxed. "You'll get the hang of it."

He drank half the liquid and pulled the straw from his mouth. "That aide was right—not good...not bad." He tried to smile, but the pain from the injured muscles turned the attempt into a lopsided comic grin. "It tastes a little like mud."

"Now that you're doing so well here, I'll be leaving," Nora said. "I'm going to the Rocking R to get Lane. It's time he came home where he belongs. I'll bring him to see you later."

CHAPTER FOURTEEN

NORA'S ADRENALINE WAS RUNNING high as she drove along the snow-covered dirt road. There was no reason to leave Lane with his grandparents any longer. She missed him terribly. It was bad enough to have Paul away for a few more days. Bringing Lane home to Mrs. Innes's house would help keep the loneliness away.

As she turned into the entrance to the ranch, she looked ahead to the rambling white house in the distance. The grounds were deserted. She glanced at her watch. It was almost dinnertime. Perhaps she would be invited to stay for dinner now that Paul's father had accepted her into the family.

After parking her white compact car near the front porch, she raced up the steps. She tilted her head to catch any sounds coming from the interior of the house but heard nothing. She tapped lightly on the door, and when it opened immediately, she drew back in surprise.

Ed Russell stepped out on the porch, closing the door behind him. "What do you want?"

"I came for Lane," she said. "I came to take him home."

"He's where he belongs," Ed replied. "He's my grandson and he's home. You'd best leave now." He turned away, dismissing her.

"But he's my son," she insisted, a rising suspicion

putting her on guard. "Mr. Russell, please let me in to get Lane. Where's your wife?"

"She's not part of this," he replied.

"Mr. Russell, I want my son. You have no right to—"

"Paul made a big mistake when he married you, probably the biggest of his life," Ed ranted. "He gave up a place of his own for a woman like you who hangs around the bars and lets any man who comes along have what you're offering for the night. The nice girls around here don't do those kind of—"

"Mr. Russell!" Nora broke in, outraged.

"I'm just sorry he was foolish enough to take up with you."

"That's not true."

"Can you deny you met him in a bar in town?"

"No."

"Do you deny you enticed him into your bed the very first night you met him?"

"I didn't entice him at all!"

"You slept with him," Ed declared emphatically. "Same thing."

She stared at him, trying to think of a proper response.

"Well, didn't you?" he demanded, taking a step closer.

"Yes," she wavered.

"When Paul gets well, he'll come to his senses and see the error of his ways," Ed announced confidently. "He belongs here at the place with his family."

"But I'm his family now," Nora insisted.

"You're not fit to be part of the Russell family," Ed sneered. "Your actions proved that."

"I want my baby. He's inside and—"

"Lady, you don't deserve that boy. He's a fine boy. He looks just like his father. There's no trace of his mother in him. Just look at him and you can tell that."

"I want my son," Nora repeated, taking a step toward him.

"He's staying here. When Paul divorces you he'll need someone to care for his son. My wife will do that."

"Julie? Does she know what you're up to?" Nora asked.

"My wife supports me in everything I do."

"Mr. Russell, this has gone far enough," Nora reasoned. "I want Lane. I want my son."

"You're not a fit mother. You're not the kind of woman to raise a boy proper. You'd probably pamper him and make him a sissy. I know what happens to boys who get pampered by their mothers. They become—"

"You're crazy!" Nora cried.

"I'll make him into a real boy," Ed went on. "Go on back to town now like a good girl." He turned again toward the door.

"Mr. Russell," Nora said, her anger rising, "I want my son. I won't leave without him."

"Lady, either you leave peaceable-like or I'll call the sheriff and tell him what you've done. Come Monday I intend to go to the courthouse and file a complaint." His chest puffed with confidence.

"What kind of complaint?"

"A complaint," he said, poking at her upper arm, "charging you...as an...unfit...mother." With each pause in his words he pushed Nora harder, forcing her to back down the steps of the porch.

"You can't do this," she gasped.

"Get out of here."

"He's my son."

"He's Paul's boy and that makes him mine. You get out of here and don't ever come back. I know all about you. You got your first old man shot and your own son killed. Anyone who would do a stupid thing like that doesn't deserve another kid. You're plain dangerous. Now get!" He swaggered back to the door, closing it quietly behind him.

Nora remained on the bottom step for several minutes. In a daze she began to move toward her car. Automatically her hand slid the key into the ignition, and the sound of the engine turning over startled her. She blinked several times, shifted the car into drive and returned the same route she had come, her heart aching.

She drove to Mrs. Innes's house and let herself into the quiet living room. Dusk descended, but she failed to notice. Ed Russell's threatening words filled her mind. This was a confrontation between her and Ed, and only as a last resort would she involve Paul, particularly in his present condition.

Her thoughts drifted back to San Diego and Jerry and Jeremy. She recalled the pleasant memories of a trip they had taken to Balboa Park and the zoo, but as they walked down the lush paths pushing the baby's stroller, she glanced at her husband. He was Paul Russell. She looked down at the stroller. It was empty. Jeremy was gone. . . Lane was gone.

She was jolted awake by a loud knock on the door. The room was in total darkness. The knock sounded again, like nails being pounded into a coffin. She screamed and the door flew open.

Light flooded the room as Mrs. Innes flicked the wall switch, and Julie Russell ran to Nora's side.

"Where have you been?" Julie cried. "We waited in Paul's room for you to return. He said you had gone to our place to get Lane, but when? Why didn't you come to the ranch, Nora?''

Nora looked into Julie's warm hazel eyes.

''I did,'' she sobbed. ''I did, but he wouldn't let me in.''

''Who wouldn't?'' Julie asked.

''Your... your husband,'' Nora choked. ''He said he was keeping Lane and that I couldn't have him again.''

''Oh, my God! Nora, when were you there?''

''This afternoon about four.''

''I never knew you came,'' Julie told her. ''It's almost impossible to hear the front door when I'm in the kitchen. I've told Russ so many times we need a doorbell, but he...'' Her hazel eyes blazed. ''That man! I knew he was up to something, but never this! Kidnapping his own grandchild?'' She jumped up from the sofa and began to pace the room.

''I want my baby back,'' Nora cried. ''He has no right! What made him change? He didn't even acknowledge Lane as his grandchild until a few days ago.''

''After you and Paul left with Steven the day of the accident, we had an argument and Ed was in the center of it,'' Julie explained. ''We finally convinced him that Lane was Paul's child. By last night he was talking about all the plans he had for Lane, giving him a horse, teaching him to work alongside his grandpa, all the things he had overdone with Paul when he was just a boy. It made me so sad to see him determined to make the same mistakes with Lane that he had made with Paul.

''This morning he picked up where he had left off last night. I reminded him that the baby would be leaving us any day, but he refused to listen. I had no idea he would try anything as desperate as this.''

"He accused me of being an unfit mother because I let my first husband and son be killed, and said he was going to the sheriff about me. He called me a bar tramp and said I had seduced Paul."

"Oh, damn him!" Julie cried. "Mother and I told him a little about how you and Paul first met and about the deaths of your first husband and baby. He's twisted it all around and made it fit his own purposes. He's wrong. You and Paul are perfect for each other, and I know what a good mother you are. Mom will certainly attest to that."

"How can I get Lane back?" Nora asked. "I need your help."

Julie returned to the sofa and took Nora's hand. "Don't worry, my dear. I'll bring the baby to you tomorrow morning."

"He has an appointment with Dr. Peters at ten tomorrow," Nora said. "First immunization shots and a checkup."

"That's it," Julie said, squeezing her hands together. "I'll bring him to you then. If Russ asks questions, I'll tell him about the baby's appointment with Dr. Peters. Please don't worry anymore. You'll have your son back. I would hate to have to call the sheriff on my own husband, but this time he's gone too far!"

Nora's gaze swung from one woman to the other. "I haven't told Paul. I didn't want to burden him."

Julie patted her shoulder. "Everything will turn out all right," she assured Nora.

"What if he refuses to let you leave with Lane?"

"He'll be delivering hay tomorrow to the outlying pastures," Julie said. "It takes him most of the day. I'll leave after he's gone."

"Will you be in any danger?" Nora asked. "Will he hurt you?"

"I don't think so. I suspect he doesn't want me to know what he did and he'll keep quiet, assuming that you'll be frightened enough to stay away." Julie smiled as she hugged Nora, then rose from her seat. "He has no idea what he's taking on when he pits himself against three women over the welfare of a sweet little baby boy."

Ida Innes went to the kitchen and soon called them to join her for coffee. She told them she had phoned the hospital to let Paul know that Nora was fine. "Don't worry, Nora," she said. "This isn't the first time Julie and I have had to put our heads together to solve a problem with Ed, but I'll admit it's by far the most serious. I just don't understand that man." She shook her head. "We've beat him before and we'll do it again. Don't you worry your pretty head. My suitcase is in Julie's car. I can only take so long being under that man's roof. You won't be alone tonight and tomorrow you'll have Lane. We promise."

"I hope so," Nora said. "If you're not successful, I'll have to tell Paul. It's a good thing he's in the hospital. I don't know what he might do if he were well." She stood up. "I'm going to bed. I'm very tired. Thank you both for all your help." She kissed each woman and left the room.

That night was the longest Nora had ever spent. Occasionally she dozed, then would wake with a start, immediately thinking of Lane. What if Julie's plan failed? Then what would she do? The local law enforcement knew Ed Russell as a respected citizen of the community. Would they listen to her side of the story?

When the doorbell rang midmorning, Nora ran to answer it. "Thank God," she sighed as Julie deposited a wriggling bundle into her aching arms. She clutched the baby to her breast, trying to choke down her emotions.

"Oh, thank you, Julie, thank you," she cried. "I'll never forget this. I love you." She hesitated. "Does your husband know?"

"No," Julie replied. "He left very early, without saying a word about your visit. I gave him a chance. I asked him if he didn't think it was strange you hadn't bothered to visit last night." She smiled wryly as she recalled the conversation. "He said he doubted you had very strong maternal instinct."

As Mrs. Innes and Nora ate lunch, Nora continued to hold Lane, even though he had fallen asleep long ago. She wanted to bring Paul home from the hospital, gather her family around her and lock them all away together in a safe place. She would be more alert to the possible dangers surrounding them in the future. She had never expected one of those dangers to be Paul's father.

As the hospital's visiting hours approached, Nora grew increasingly anxious to see Paul again. When she arrived with a wakeful Lane in her arms, she was trembling with relief.

Paul's facial swelling had all but disappeared, the darkness under his eyes had faded to a jaundiced yellow-green, and a smaller bandage covered his injury.

"Hi, hon," he said through his wired jaws. "What did you bring me?"

"Your son," she replied, and she placed Lane on the bed.

Paul made a funny face at the baby, then grimaced when the muscles of his cheek rebelled.

"I get to leave tomorrow, Nora," he said.

"I'm so glad."

"While we were loading the bull, just before the accident, dad asked me to come home."

Nora's face blanched. "Would you?"

"He meant us, not just me. I told him I would have to discuss it with you. Nora, what's the matter? You're pale as a ghost! Come here, sweetheart."

He pulled her closer, and the warmth of his arm relaxed her.

"Yesterday when I went to get Lane and bring him home, your father tried to keep him."

"He what?"

"He refused to let me have him."

"But he's right here. What happened to make him change his mind? Good Lord, Nora, he couldn't do that. That's kidnapping!"

"Your mother brought Lane in this morning. Your father may have been bluffing this time, but he scares me to death. I could never feel safe under his roof."

Before Paul could reply, the door to his room flew open. A flushed Ed Russell entered, bringing with him the smell of livestock. His ruddy complexion lost its color when he saw Nora and Lane.

"How the hell did my grandson get here?" he sputtered.

"Where else would he be, dad?" Paul asked.

Nora's eyes flew to Paul's face. The throbbing pulse in his temple belied his outward calm. She had expected a violent explosion and accusations, but instead Paul was calling his father's bluff.

"What's the matter, dad?" he asked. "You're green around the gills. What have you been up to since I've been in here?"

"Nothing much," Ed muttered.

"Did you get the pairs stranded at Pinto's Meadow down to the home pastures?"

"I... I... sure..." Ed stammered, but his attention remained glued on Nora and Lane.

Nora stepped closer to Paul's bed, touching the baby before laying her hand on Paul's shoulder.

Paul reached for Nora's hand and held it while he discussed the work schedule at the ranch for the next few weeks. Ed stayed only a few minutes. Finally he asked Paul, "Are you coming home, boy?"

"Doubtful," Paul replied.

"You're all welcome... even Nora," Ed said, darting a glance at her.

"Considering what has happened, I don't think now is the time to make plans, dad," Paul remarked.

"But I didn't..." Ed began, then caught himself.

"I won't be much good for a few weeks. I can't ride or do anything that would injure my jaw. The wires stay on for another month. We'll see. We'll be staying in town with grandmother for a while. I've already given her money for food and rent, and she seems to enjoy us."

Ed snorted. "That woman doesn't know when to keep her nose out of other people's business."

Nora remained silent until Ed Russell left.

Paul went to use the bathroom, and when he returned he stopped behind Nora and slid his arms around her waist. He nuzzled the side of her neck, then kissed her cheek.

Nora felt her pulse quicken. She leaned against his hard lean body, then turned in his arms. "I'm so glad you're better."

"I see nothing but a clear road ahead of us, pretty lady," Paul whispered, then his lips descended to hers, a light caress that quickly hardened into passion. Seconds later he pulled away, groaning. "My mouth...my face...my jaws. Damn it all, I can't even kiss you the way I want."

"Then let me," Nora said. "You're very handsome, cowboy, even with that roguish scar you'll have on your cheek." Stretched on tiptoes, she massaged his pliant lips with hers, telling him in her own way how she felt. "I love you, Paul," she whispered, then dropped her head against his chest, enjoying the sound of his heart thudding beneath her ear. His arms tightened around her, leaving her light-headed and gasping for air when at last he released her.

They chatted about various things—the town, Leslie, their past difficulties and, finally, the night they had met.

"I remember very little after you picked me up in your arms. I must have been thoroughly intoxicated to allow you to take such liberties," Nora said.

"You were," Paul agreed, "but by then I wanted to make love to you so badly I ignored the fact that your willingness was caused by the drinks. I asked you if I could stay, and you rubbed against me and whispered in my ear that I could."

"Oh, no, was I really so brazen?"

"You started to unsnap that turquoise-and gold shirt and your fingers were all thumbs. I took over, and you let me finish."

"You're only the second man I've ever been with," she told him. "I was a virgin when I married Jerry."

"We satisfied each other, Nora. There was nothing one-sided about that first time. Then you started to cry. I don't know what to do when women cry. You pleaded for me to hold you, so I did. You talked about San Diego, about us, about loneliness. I thought about leaving then, but you asked me to kiss you again." He laughed and kissed her cheek lightly. "How could I turn down a beautiful lady who lay naked in my arms." He grew thoughtful. "During the second time we made love, you called me Jerry, and I knew it wasn't me you were loving. Even though I hardly knew you, that hurt."

He paused. "I know you'll never forget your first husband and son, but I hope you let me have a permanent place in your life, too. I want to make up for all the misery I've brought you and all the pain in your past."

"You have already," Nora replied.

"Sometimes I wonder if..." He stared at her intently, then quickly shifted his gaze to the windows. "Forget it." He slid back into the bed and Nora picked up Lane, who was sleeping.

"I'll be here tomorrow to take you home," she said. "Call me when you're ready to leave." She leaned over his bed and teasingly kissed his forehead and eyes, the tip of his nose and finally his lips, savoring their sensuous fullness until he pulled away.

"Good grief, Nora, I won't be able to sleep if you keep this up," he laughed.

When Nora arrived at the hospital the following morning, Paul looked well on the way to recovery. The bandage protecting his cheek was even smaller than before.

"I'm all checked out," he said, "Let's go home."

"Good." She grinned. "Your grandmother has lunch all ready for us—something special."

"Oh?" he asked.

"I bought a blender with ten speeds...just for you, darling."

AFTER A WEEK of inactivity, Paul and Nora packed Lane's diaper bag and took an all-day drive to Bozeman. They spent the day shopping, visiting a few of Paul's former university professors and enjoying a leisurely tour of the Museum of the Rockies located on a hill behind the university campus.

They arrived back in Dillon late that evening. Ida Innes was still awake when they returned. "Oh, I'm so glad you're back. I have an urgent message for you from Leslie. She said under no circumstances are you to retire without calling her."

Nora hurried to the kitchen phone. When Leslie answered, Nora heard a man's voice laughing in the background. "Sorry to call so late, Leslie," she said. "You have a message for us?"

"Just you, Nora. It's from your sister."

"Oh, my goodness. My sister? How did she...where is...oh, dear," Nora stuttered, trying to recover from the shocking news.

"She called the bank just before closing time today," Leslie explained. "She returned to San Diego on a month's leave and went to your house and found out about everything from your former next-door neighbor. She said your neighbor knew the town you'd moved to, but that was all. She said she tried both banks in town, knowing that you were a teller. The receptionist gave the call to the manager, who gave it to me, and I promised to give you her number."

"That's fantastic, Leslie," Nora exclaimed. "It's been years since we've been in touch."

"She seemed very nice and quite concerned about you," Leslie added. "I told her you had remarried and had a baby."

"Thanks, Leslie," Nora said after she wrote down the long-distance telephone number.

When she dialed the number and heard her sister's voice, memories came rushing back, childhood memories of times before her father had died and her mother had remarried, before the time when pain and tragedy had rocked her life. "Nancy, is this really you?" she cried. "Oh, Nancy, I didn't think I would ever hear from you again."

They talked for several moments until Paul interrupted Nora with a waving motion of his hand. "Nancy, my husband wants to tell me something." She covered the mouthpiece and turned to him.

"Let's go see her," he suggested. "I can't work, and this killing time is getting to me. Besides, you deserve it, honey." He pointed to the phone. "Tell her we'll fly and be there tomorrow. We can rent a car at the airport."

Nora quickly made arrangements for the reunion. She wrote down the address of the motel where her sister was staying, asked her to reserve another room for them, then said goodbye.

Late the next afternoon they arrived at the motel in San Diego. Nora and her sister embraced and cried, laughed and hugged. Finally Nora turned to Paul, who was holding Lane.

"Paul, this is my sister, Nancy. She's twenty-eight and is a lieutenant in the United States Air Force..." She raised her brow questioningly. "And never married?"

"Not yet," Nancy said with a laugh. She had short strawberry blond hair and was a few inches taller than Nora, shapely yet slender, and dressed casually in a matching knit top and slacks.

"Nancy Browning," Nora continued, "this is my husband, Paul." Nora held the baby as Paul shook her sister's hand and accepted a light kiss on his scarred cheek.

"You Browning women have a definite family resemblance," Paul remarked. "You're both very beautiful." He smiled and put his arms around the two of them.

Lane wriggled and squirmed, beaming at them. "Our son, Paul Lane Russell," Nora said as Nancy reached for the baby.

"Lane?" Nancy asked curiously.

"I know," Nora said. "It just seemed the right name."

Nancy glanced toward Paul, who shrugged. "We both liked it," he confirmed.

"Well, Lane's a doll, anyway," Nancy said. "Looks just like his father. Hey, let's eat. I've been waiting for you to get here. Oh, Nora, we have so much to talk about. I've been on Guam for two years, and suddenly this summer I got this irresistible desire to see you. I'm so glad I did."

The two sisters spent the next few days catching up on the years they had been out of touch. Nora told Paul and Nancy about the anguish and grief she'd experienced when her first husband and son had been killed, her depression, the numbness she had felt when she relocated to the north. She breezed over the way she had met Paul, but did mention her refusal to marry him.

"But I don't understand," Nancy said. "If a gorgeous man like Paul wanted to marry me, I would certainly let him have his way. How *did* you two meet?"

"Just take my word for it," Nora advised her. "Our meeting was unusual and we'll never be able to tell our children."

"Nora's right," Paul agreed. "Just call our meeting fate."

Later in the afternoon Paul asked Nora to show him where she had lived.

"I'll take care of Lane," Nancy offered. "Take as long as you want. I think Lane needs to get to know his Aunt Nancy."

Paul and Nora visited the home where Nora had grown up and walked the grounds of the grade school she had attended.

"Did you ever have a nickname?" Nora asked Paul.

"Just Paul. You can't do much to change a name like that. What about you?"

She nodded. "Angel."

"Angel? It's perfect," he said, laughing as they walked back to the rental car.

Before sliding the key into the ignition, Paul turned to her, all trace of humor erased from his features. "Now show me where you lived. . . with Jerry."

"Why?" Nora asked.

"I need to settle something."

"But. . ."

"Please, Nora. Humor me."

She gave him directions to an older part of San Diego near Balboa Park. They turned down a tree-lined residential street with neatly groomed lawns surrounding medium-size brick houses, many with tricycles and bicycles cluttering the carports and driveways.

"The white one with yellow trim," she said, pointing. "About the middle of the block." The car rolled to a stop in front of the house, and the two of them sat quietly for several moments, looking at it. Nora was unaware she was crying until Paul's finger brushed a tear from her cheek.

"Come here, sweetheart," he said, and his arms encircled her. "I had to see where you lived before you met me. It's always bothered me to think of some other guy loving you. You came to me with your past cut off, yet I knew there were good memories hidden somewhere, even though you wouldn't talk about them. You've never shown me a picture of Jerry or Jeremy. I want to know them."

"You never really asked," Nora said.

"I'm asking now."

"I'm sorry, Paul. I didn't know it was important to you."

"Everything about you is important."

She reached for her purse, retrieved her wallet and removed a small photograph of a young man and woman and a toddler wearing a San Diego Padres baseball outfit. She handed the picture to Paul.

He studied it for several moments. "How old is... Jeremy?"

"Ten months."

"And Jerry?"

"Twenty-four."

Paul nodded. "My age," he said softly. "I was afraid he might look like me, but he doesn't, does he?" He glanced at Nora. "I've wondered at times if you used me to replace him emotionally."

"No," she assured him, "and you don't act like him, either, silly. He was an ensign in the navy. You're the only cowboy I know. His hair was dark but straight. He was tall, but shorter than you and much thinner. I loved him, Paul, but I love you more. I can't erase his memories. We spent two wonderful years together."

Paul stared out the windshield for a long time. "Some

things can't be undone, can they?" He returned the photograph to her.

"Paul," she asked, "why did you need to see them?"

He reached for her hand. "You know all about me and my family. They've surrounded us ever since we met. But you were like an orphan. I didn't want you to always be my little orphan Nora. Your sister's call and this visit have solved that problem."

He stroked the back of her hand, then gave it a squeeze. "I'll admit I was more than a little jealous of the man who made love to you before me. I felt at times he was a ghostly rival in our bed."

"Oh, no, Paul, how could you think such a thing?"

"The first night I was with you, you called me Jerry."

"Jerry will always have a special place in my life, but he's only a memory. You're the man I love now, you're the only one with me at night, the man I long for, the one who will father my children. No one...not your father or Leslie or my dead husband or anyone will ever come between us again."

He kissed her fingertips. "Let's go back. I think I've seen enough."

"I want to go back home," Nora said as they pulled into the motel parking lot. "Thanksgiving is only a week away, and I promised your grandmother I would help her with a turkey."

"I agree," he said. "I just wish I could chew the dark meat of a turkey drumstick."

She elbowed his ribs. "If you keep lying around you're going to become as chubby as your father, you lazy cowboy."

"Be nice," he chided. "I'm an invalid recovering from a painful accident."

"I'll remember that the next time you want to make love. I wouldn't want to hurt the poor sick invalid," she teased.

"Well," he said, smiling, "I'm well on the way to recovery. Some exercise is therapeutic, and besides, it's my mouth that's recovering. The rest of me is fine. Want me to prove it?"

"Not here in the motel parking lot, cowboy."

"Then let's go home," he said, kissing her soundly.

Two days later they said goodbye to Nancy. When they arrived back in Dillon, they were greeted by Grandma Innes.

"I missed you all so much," she said, giving them each a hug as she welcomed them home.

They settled into an easy routine in Mrs. Innes's house. Julie invited them to Thanksgiving dinner, but Paul declined.

"I would have to drink my dinner, anyway, mom," he said. "Grandmother and Nora have made plans and the turkey is already thawing. I don't think the time is right yet."

"I understand," Julie said. "Kiss my grandson for me. We'll miss you all."

Mrs. Innes and Nora spent the morning of the holiday bustling around the kitchen, refusing to let Paul help.

"Can't I at least set the table?" he pleaded. The women relented, and he joined them in the kitchen. "It was lonely out there in the living room. Lane is no company when he's asleep, and I can only take so much football on television."

Nora looked at all the food being prepared. "Why don't we invite Leslie to join us? She's alone. Her folks left town and I know she must be lonely."

Mrs. Innes nodded her head and smiled. "Tell her to

bring a friend if she wants. We'll make our own family."

Leslie accepted and promised to be there in half an hour. When she arrived she had smiling George Holman in tow.

As the group gathered around the table, Paul spotted a tall glass sitting on a plate at the head of the table. It was filled with a thick liquid in shades of brown and beige. "What's that?" he asked suspiciously.

"That's your dinner," his grandmother said. "I put a little of everything together. Turkey—I know you like the dark meat—dressing, a big spoon of sweet potato salad, baked zucchini and a big chunk of hot roll. I dumped it into the blender and presto! Your dinner! I left the pumpkin pie and ice cream out and put it in a separate glass. It's in the refrigerator."

Paul looked longingly at the juicy turkey as he carved and served generous slabs of meat. "This is cruel," he grumbled.

Paul drank his dinner quickly and waited for the others to finish. When Lane woke from his nap and cried, he motioned for Nora to stay in her chair and left the room, returning a few minutes later with Lane in his arms.

"Oh, he's precious," Leslie cried, and she reached for Lane. She cuddled him for several moments and looked wistfully at Nora. "Sometimes I wish I had a baby." She glanced at George, who frowned at her. "But they must be a lot of work," she added, sighing as she returned the baby to Paul.

George and Leslie left in the early evening to have a few drinks at the Matador.

"Want to join us?" Leslie asked.

"No, thanks," Paul replied. "Nora and I have other

plans." Paul dropped his arm around Nora's shoulders and she nodded, though she had no idea what he was talking about.

Later that night when everyone had retired, Paul left their bedroom and returned with two long-stemmed glasses and a bottle of pink Chablis.

Nora dropped the book she'd been reading and sat up in the bed, one tiny strap of her nightgown slipping off her shoulder. "Oh, Paul, how did you know?"

He smiled, giving her a promise of things to come, then opened the bottle and filled their glasses.

CHAPTER FIFTEEN

"I'll get it," Nora said, when the phone rang. "I'm closest." She had just settled into the living room with Paul and his grandmother after dinner, but now she hurried to the kitchen and caught the call on the third ring. "Hello?"

"Is my boy there?" Ed Russell asked.

"Yes, I'll call him," Nora replied tersely.

"No," he said. "You're the one I want to talk to. Are you alone?"

"Yes, I'm alone in the kitchen, but we have nothing to discuss."

"Listen, girlie, we have a lot to discuss," he insisted. "My boy and I got along fine before you snared him, and I've been giving this serious thought. I'm willing to be reasonable. By the way, how was your Thanksgiving dinner?"

Nora was thrown off guard by the question.

"Fine. We invited Leslie Coleman and her friend George Holman. I believe you know them both."

"Sure do. George is a good worker and Leslie... Leslie is the girl Paul should have married. She's a local girl, fine and decent."

"Mr. Russell, why did you call?" Nora asked.

"I want my boy back."

"And what are you going to do about it? You can't dictate what your children do. You treat them like property! Most of them are adults now and free to decide for themselves who they want to be with and what they want to do in their lives. They're free to choose—"

"I hold the purse strings, Nellie. That gives me the right. You'll see. But that's not why I called. I want to extend my offer to you again."

"You never made me an offer, Mr. Russell. You held my baby hostage and demanded that I stay away."

"I want to sweeten the deal. It means a lot to me to have my boy back home where he belongs, so I'm willing to pay. You can keep the little boy. When Paul remarries he'll have more sons and they'll be brought up proper. I'll give you money for a plane ticket to anywhere you want to go, plus, oh...let's see now... two thousand dollars to tide you over and get you settled."

"Mr. Russell, how could you?" Nora snapped into the receiver. "Paul can't be bought."

"We'll see, Nellie. That place up north of town is pretty important to my boy, and I haven't sold it yet. We'll see. I know you'll keep this little transaction just between you and me. I wouldn't want others to get the wrong impression. They might not see the picture the way you and I do, right?" He laughed. "See, I told you we had a lot to discuss. You think on my offer. You could do a lot with two thousand dollars."

"Two thousand dollars is nothing," Nora cried.

"Not enough? Maybe I could add a little more to the kitty. It would be worth it to have my boy back. I'll double it to four thousand. That's probably more than you've ever had at one time, missy, so you think about it for a few days. You keep your mouth shut about this deal, especially to my boy. He's got a temper like his old man and he might not understand. So you think about it and I'll call you say. . . Wednesday. Don't forget." The dial tone sounded.

Nora's legs felt rubbery as she walked out of the kitchen. How could Paul's father possibly think she would sell her husband for a few thousand dollars? She wondered what Paul would say if she told him. She bypassed the living room and went directly to their room.

Minutes later as she slid beneath the bed covers, Paul entered and sat down on her side of the bed.

"Who was it, honey?" he asked.

"Just a. . . an acquaintance."

"Does the acquaintance have a name?"

"You wouldn't believe it if I told you."

"It's early to be going to bed," he remarked.

"I'm tired," she said. "Lane is already down for the night and I thought I would read for a while."

"Okay." He looked at her thoughtfully, then left the room.

She lay in bed, her face composed but her body rigid underneath the covers. Her hands twisted the material of her nightgown into a wrinkled wad at her waist. She started when Paul reappeared, undressed and joined her. Immediately his hand slid to her waist and stopped the wringing motion of her fingers.

"Who was that on the phone?" he asked.

She turned her head away. "I told you, no one special."

"No one special wouldn't have you this upset, Nora. Was it a local call or long distance?"

"Local."

"Man or woman?" he persisted.

"Man," she replied without thinking.

"A man?" A frown marred his features. "An old boyfriend?" he asked, half teasing.

She turned to him and he saw the agony in her eyes. "I can't tell you, Paul," she whispered. "Please don't make me."

"You told me you didn't have any boyfriends in town, and I believe you. Who was it? Did he threaten you?"

"Yes," she whispered against his chest. "Yes!"

"Who was it, Nora?" He sat up, pulling her with him. "Who?"

"Your father."

He released her instantly and she fell back on the bed. "Dad? Why would dad threaten you? You're lying."

She refused to elaborate.

"I frightened you," he said. "I'm sorry. Tell me, Nora, what did he say?"

She gazed into his brown eyes. "I don't know if he was serious or crazy, Paul. He offered me four thousand dollars and a plane ticket if I would take Lane and leave you."

Paul began to laugh. "He must have been joking."

"He said that if I left, he would give you the property north of town. Does it mean that much to you, Paul?"

"I certainly wouldn't trade my family for a piece of ground, Nora. What kind of a man do you take me for?" The warmth in his voice convinced her of his sincerity.

"The property north of town would give us a chance to make a start on our own," he said, "but mom says he's already had two nibbles. I doubt he would be so generous at this late date. Money talks with my father. You must have misunderstood him."

"I'm sorry, Paul. Perhaps I overreacted. You know

how he scares me. If you're so sure I mistook his offer to leave, why don't you call him? It will clear the air. I don't think I could sleep until this is settled."

He jumped from the bed and into his robe. "I'll call him right now, honey."

When he had left, Nora lay in bed, searching for all possible interpretations of her call from Ed Russell. It had seemed so clear at the time. Her thoughts were interrupted by Paul's return.

"What did he say?" she asked.

"He didn't want to discuss it over the phone." He grinned. "He said he wants me to meet him tomorrow morning to talk about the place north of town. Our attorney will be there, too. He said it may take most of the morning. Will you miss me?"

"Of course," she replied. "But what about the money he offered me?"

"At first he denied it, then he said you misunderstood. So, pretty lady, you can sleep soundly tonight. Tomorrow you may find yourself married to an independently wealthy rancher instead of a wealthy rancher's son waiting for his inheritance."

"But Paul..."

"Kiss me, sweet. It hurts a little when I try too hard."

"Paul, listen to me," she began. "He offered me a bribe. I didn't misunderstand him. He's up to something and now he's lied to you to cover up. He never thought I would tell you about it."

He turned off the light. "Tomorrow will prove what's really going on, Nora. Now kiss me good-night and don't worry about a thing. Tomorrow is a new day with unbelievable prospects looming."

"Oh, Paul," she whispered, "you're so excited.

There's no reasoning with you tonight.'' She kissed him gently on his wired mouth.

''You're probably right,'' he murmured, drawing her into the curve of his body. He was asleep in minutes.

Nora lay awake, staring into the darkness, wondering what trouble Ed Russell was brewing now.

''I DON'T UNDERSTAND why dad has had such a change of heart,'' Paul said between sips of blended ham and eggs.

Nora poured him a refill of coffee, then slid into her seat. Her plate of food was untouched. ''I'm sure he has your best interests at heart.''

''When I called him again this morning, he said he had the legal papers ready for signature,'' Paul told her. ''I was really surprised. He said he had them drawn up while I was in the hospital, that he had dangled the property in front of me long enough and that no matter what happens in the future the land is mine. He wants to give me my part of his estate to enjoy while he is still alive, and he said that you and Lane were the major factors in making him change his mind about keeping title for another five years. Now that I'm twenty-five, the trust fund is legally mine, but I'd rather not cash it in, and Dad hasn't actually said so, but his stipulation about my bride seems to be forgotten. I'll relinquish any rights to the home ranch and Pinto's Meadow and leave them for the rest of the guys. My sisters get money instead of property. It's our father's chauvinistic way.'' Paul shook his head. ''I still can't believe he's doing this. He also said I should thank you, that without your cooperation none of this would be happening and that you would understand.'' He smiled, his brown eyes sparkling, ''Have you two been plotting behind my back, honey?''

''Definitely not,'' Nora replied, recalling every word

of her telephone conversation with Ed Russell the previous night and marveling at the way he had managed to squirm out of a tight spot.

Paul got up, kissed Lane, who was sitting on the table in an infant seat and grabbed his heavy coat. He reached for Nora's hand and she followed him to the door. "Thanks again, honey, even if you insist you had no part in this." He pulled her closer and gave her a rib-bruising hug and as deep a kiss as his wired jaws would allow. He left the house taking the steps two at a time and whistling as he jogged to the truck, his boots crunching on the ice.

An hour later the phone rang.

Nora answered it. "Hello?"

"You're a smart lady, Nellie." Ed Russell laughed. "My son signed the papers this morning. The place is his with no strings. The money is waiting for you at the Stockmen's Bank. Take it and leave town this morning. Do I make myself clear? We're going to have breakfast and I expect you gone when he gets back there."

"I don't want your tainted money, Mr. Russell. I have no secrets from Paul. I told him everything. He didn't believe you would do such a thing, but we know differently, don't we? I know how important this matter is to him, but I also know how important Lane and I are to him. You're an evil, hateful tyrannical man, but I would never leave Paul because of you and your bribes."

"You'll wise up when you think about what that money can buy you, Nellic. I know women and their wants. You'll be gone by the time my boy returns for his belongings." He chuckled. "Why he's so excited, he won't even notice you're not there."

"You don't know your son at all," Nora said.

"You just be gone," he ordered. "I went through with this because you and me made a deal."

"The deal was never on, Mr. Russell. You just thought I'd take the money and run, but you're in for a surprise. You gave away that property free and clear." She laughed. "You did something nice for a change in spite of your nasty plans."

Mrs. Innes returned to the kitchen with Lane as Nora hung up the receiver. As she mulled over Ed Russell's words, she grew steadily more curious about the money. Was it really set aside for her at the bank? If it was, she had to tell the manager to send it back. If there was no trace of the funds, she would try to accept the fact that she had misunderstood and misjudged Paul's father.

"Grandma Innes," Nora said, "I have to go to the Stockmen's Bank on some personal business. Will you watch Lane? I'll only be gone for twenty or thirty minutes."

"But Paul said he would be back soon," Mrs. Innes said.

"I know, but it takes a while to drive to the ranch and back. I'll be back before he gets here," Nora promised.

"But he told me this morning he's not going. . ."

Nora glanced at her watch. "I've got to hurry. Thanks." She rushed to the bedroom. Paul wouldn't return from the ranch for a few hours. She could see the manager and be back long before he returned. Frantically she searched for a piece of paper, found a rose-embossed sheet of pink stationery and quickly wrote him a note. If she got back to the house before him, she would destroy the note and he would never have to know she had felt compelled to check upon his father.

She slid the folded piece of paper under the lamp on his side of the bed and raced out of the house to her car.

She pulled into the bank's customer lot and parked next to Leslie's new bronze four-wheel drive pickup truck. During Thanksgiving dinner Leslie had announced she'd decided to join the cowboy crowd all the way.

Inside the manager was busy with a customer, and his secretary asked if she could help Nora.

"It's about some money Ed Russell says he left here for me," Nora said, hoping the secretary would know nothing about it.

"Oh, yes," the woman replied. "It's in Mr. Stone's office. I believe you're supposed to sign for it. Please wait, Nora. He'll only be a few more minutes."

"But I don't want the money," Nora insisted. "Tell Mr. Stone to give it back to Mr. Russell. His money is tainted."

"Goodness," the secretary murmured. "You'd better explain it to him. I'm all confused."

"I'll be glad to wait," Nora said, glancing around the spacious lobby. A teller waved, and Nora went to the window to say hello.

Suddenly the teller's eyes darted past Nora's head. "Oh, no!" she gasped.

Nora turned. Two men stood near the customer entrance. The taller one was moving in long loping steps toward the manager's office. The other man darted to the row of teller windows and pulled a long black revolver from the back of his belt.

Oh, God! Not again!

The manager walked out of his office, his face pale and drawn. "Give them everything," he said as he approached the line of terrified tellers. "Everything!"

The tellers began handing over their cash, and Nora felt herself reliving a scene from her past. She glanced toward the customer entrance again. Someone was pushing through the door. A man in a rust leather coat appeared, a smiling infant in an orange snowsuit pulled snugly against his waist. Paul Russell took two angry steps into the room, and Lane's dark curly head bobbed with the movement. Mrs. Innes followed on Paul's heels, and the three of them seemed to fill the room.

"Nora," Paul called hoarsely. "You can't do this!"

"What thc hell?" swore one of the robbers, whirling toward the door.

"No!" Nora screamed. "No, go back," she cried, lunging at the man who was waving his revolver at Paul and the baby. "No!"

The man turned to her as she charged him. He caught her by one arm, twirled her around and captured her waist, pulling her hard against his wiry body.

He pressed the barrel against her temple. "Be still," he snarled, "or I'll blow your brains out. All of you, away from the door," he ordered, waving the gun in the air. "We're leaving, and if any of you get a smart idea to follow, you'll find this pretty thing splattered all over the road. Do you hear?" he shouted. "If any macho guy tries to follow, this little chick is *dead*."

He tightened his hold on Nora and dragged her with him while his partner held the door open. When they left the building, the partner pointed his revolver at the bank's front door and fired.

CAUTIOUSLY PAUL LIFTED HIS HEAD and surveyed the scene. He had pulled his grandmother down and used his own body to shield her and his son when the robber had raised the gun and pointed it at the glass. The bullet had exploded seconds later.

Lane was crying hysterically, his body rigid with fear and his arms and legs kicking angrily.

Paul picked him up. "It's okay, little guy, don't cry. Everyone's safe...except your mother. Why the hell was she here anyway? Everything was going so fine." He helped his grandmother to her feet and handed Lane to her as he looked around the bank's lobby.

The manager sat propped against a teller's window, holding a handkerchief to his forehead. Two tellers were crying, and Leslie was trying to comfort them. A male customer was helping people to their feet and checking for injuries, but other than minor cuts from the exploding glass door no one seemed hurt.

"Call the sheriff," the manager yelled. "Anyone!"

Paul ran to a desk and dialed the sheriff's office just as the Dillon chief of police and two officers stepped through the damaged doorway.

Paul listened to the dispatcher on the other end of the phone.

"There was an accident south of town, Paul," the dispatcher said. "The getaway car sideswiped a cattle truck, and the truck rolled. There are dead cattle everywhere and the semi is blocking the roadway, but there are conflicting reports on the car. Some witnesses said it was a yellow sedan and others insist it's a blue foreign make—"

Paul cut him off. "They've taken a hostage—my wife!"

"My God," the dispatcher said. "I'll tell the sheriff. This changes things, Paul. I'm so sorry. We'll find her. If the police chief is there, let me talk to him."

"Thanks, Ben," Paul said. He motioned the police chief to the phone and rejoined his grandmother and son. Lane smiled as Paul approached him.

"We'll find her, Lane. We need her and she needs us." Paul frowned as the officials began to question the witnesses. "If they can't find her, I will. If those creeps have harmed her. . ."

The police chief motioned Paul and his grandmother to follow him into the manager's office.

"Paul, these two aren't amateurs," the chief began, choosing his words carefully. "They robbed a bank in Kalispell and took a teller hostage. The Flathead County sheriff's department found her body a week later. She'd been raped and tortured."

Paul's knuckles whitened as he pushed himself from the chair. "If they lay a hand on Nora. . . Either you get those two or I'll find them myself, and I promise you the courts won't have to waste money on a trial."

Mrs. Innes laid her hand on Paul's sleeve. "Paul, the police know how to track these evil men. Cooperate with them."

He turned to her, his features distorted by pain and frustration.

"Please, Paul, sit down and listen." She turned to the chief again. "What else do you know about them?"

"Your grandmother is right, Paul," the chief advised. "Stay out of this for a while. I know how you must feel, but—"

"How could you?" Paul cut in. "She's my wife."

"I know, I know, but listen. Give us a chance. Come with me to the station and I'll show you the pictures the Flathead County people sent us. They're from the bank's surveillance cameras and aren't too clear, but they're better than nothing. They match the wanted posters from the RCMP in Lethbridge, Alberta. I'll tell you everything we know about them."

Paul handed Lane to his grandmother, along with his keys.

She shook her head. "I can't drive your truck... never could handle those big things."

The bank manager entered carrying Nora's abandoned purse and car keys and gave them to Paul with his condolences.

Paul handed the key ring to Ida Innes. "I saw her car in the parking lot not far from my truck. Take Lane to your place. I'll be there as soon as I finish this business with the police. Oh, God! I feel so helpless. Call the ranch and tell them. I know mom would want to know."

As he drove to the station with the chief, Paul could think of nothing to say. He couldn't put into words the way he felt. When he had left Nora a few hours earlier, everything had seemed perfect. His father had called to change the meeting place from the ranch to the attorney's office in town, eliminating two hours of travel time. The review of the legal documents had taken only a few moments and he had signed the deed and various other papers, then waited impatiently while his father made a private phone call in the outer office. He wanted to get back to see Nora, and when his father walked back into the room, Paul rose from his chair.

"I have to go now, dad, I want to get home. Thanks again for everything. When Nora told me about your offer last night, I knew she had misunderstood your terms and that if you offered her money it was for all of us. We'll pick it up at the bank this afternoon. That spread will become one of the most profitable ranches in the valley in a few years, and thanks also for the loan. That gives us enough working capital to carry us over until next fall." He shook his father's hand warmly.

"But I—" his father sputtered.

"That's okay, dad. I won't tell a soul about your generosity. It might spoil your tough image."

Paul had hurried home, rushed inside the house and found Nora gone. He asked his grandmother where she was.

"She had some banking to do, Paul," Mrs. Innes had said, "but she *was* acting a little strange. She promised to come right back."

Puzzled, Paul had sauntered to their bedroom, and as he looked around the room, he noticed the folded piece of pink stationery on the nightstand.

Dear Paul,

I am going to see the bank manager about your father and the money. I love you.

Nora

"Grandmother," he called as Mrs. Innes came out of Lane's room. "What happened this morning? Think carefully. Did Nora receive any mail or phone calls or messages. Think!"

"Just a telephone call, but I don't know who it was," she replied. "What's happened?"

"She says dad offered her a bribe to leave town. This note says she's going to the bank to get the money." He waved the piece of paper. "Surely she wouldn't take him up on his outlandish offer. When did she leave? How long ago?"

"Not more than fifteen minutes, I'm sure. Maybe not that long. I tried to tell her your father had called and you didn't have to go to the ranch, but she ran out of the room like the devil himself was after her." She pressed her hands against her cheeks. "There must be a terrible mistake, Paul. Maybe she's still at the bank."

"Get the baby. Come with me and hurry." He ran out of the house, and minutes later was pulling the truck into the bank's parking lot. "She can't tear our lives apart like this. Give Lane to me, grandmother. If anyone can make her come to her senses it's him."

He had taken his son in his arms and strode into the bank, his grandmother running to keep up. Then all hell had broken loose.

As Paul rode to the police station with the chief, he relived the horror of the robbery. The police car pulled into the parking area behind the courthouse and the two men hurried into the station. An officer waving a piece of paper greeted the chief.

"A deputy found the car abandoned on Blacktail Road about twelve miles from town...and Chief, the car was a white station wagon, older model." He shook his head. "It looks like they switched vehicles and went on up the Blacktail."

"How do they know it's the robbers' car?" Paul demanded.

"They found some money and a woman's left shoe. A black suede loafer, size seven and a half. Does your wife have a pair of shoes like that, Paul?" he asked.

"Yes...she had them on this morning."

"The bank called," the officer added. "The robbers took more than twenty thousand. The Lima sheriff's substation has moved its road blocks to the Centennial Valley. The deputies are working their way north. The sheriff has taken his men and they're searching the roads leading off the Blacktail from our end. Technically the Dillon police are out of it, but the sheriff has asked for help if we can spare the personnel. He's called in the Search and Rescue volunteers. What should I tell him?"

"Give him all our men who aren't on active duty this shift," the chief ordered. "Have the dispatcher call them at home and call the Women's Crisis Center advocates. We may need them. Good grief, that's rugged country. There are dozens of dirt roads and cattle trails. If they have a four-wheel-drive vehicle they could take any one of them, and the trails all switch back across each other. The area is littered with old homesteaders' cabins and line shacks. Any one would make a good hiding place. You know what I mean, Paul. That's your country."

Paul nodded, his mind picturing the countryside, cataloging each log building and trail. "I want to help," he said, jumping from the chair.

"No," the chief replied, laying his hand on Paul's arm. "You're too close to the problem. Give us a chance first." He opened a folder on his desk. "Here, let me show you what I have on the two men we suspect."

He gave Paul two separate bulletins, each showing a frontal shot and profile of a man in his forties. He pointed to the thinner of the two men. "That's Oscar Piper. He's six feet, one hundred and sixty pounds and as mean as they come. He's been in prison more than once.

"The other fellow is Gerald Wheeler. He's from Chicago, got his start in the Chicago crime scene and worked his way west. These two met in the state prison at Florence, Arizona, a few years ago, both in on short sentences. They were released six months ago and went north to Fort Macleod, Alberta, where Piper has family. They've left a trail of crimes behind them ever since. They hanged themselves when they killed that young teller in Kalispell."

A female officer approached the chief and handed him another bulletin. A huddled conference took place.

Paul grew restless. "What now?"

"Snow," the chief said, handing the bulletin to Paul. "Heavy snow possible in the mountains tonight. You know what that will do to any tracks. Let's pray we find your wife before dark. Those fellows aren't known for their chivalry."

Paul stoop up. "Can I have a copy of these two pictures? I want to show them around, in case they've doubled back or something."

"Sure," the chief said. He went to the copy machine and returned with extra copies for Paul.

"I have to go," Paul said. "Thanks. I know you're doing the best you can. Just don't give up. I haven't." He would give them until daybreak, then he would find her himself.

His grandmother had lunch ready when he returned to the house, but he drank only half of it before shoving the glass aside. An hour after lunch his mother arrived.

"I heard about the robbery on the radio just before mom called," she said. "When the reporter said a hostage had been taken and mom said it was Nora, I couldn't believe it. Your father was out at Pinto's Meadow so I wrote him a note and hurried in. Oh, Paul," she cried, hugging him, "isn't there anything we can do?"

"Not yet," he told her, explaining the organized police search and handing his mother the copies of the prison photographs.

Julie studied them. "Paul, this thin man looks familiar, but I can't place him. Maybe. . .no, it must be my imagination, yet. . ." She laid the pictures down but soon picked them up again. "I'm sure I've seen this man before."

The hours dragged by. Dusk fell and a light powdery snow began. As they sat down to dinner, a knock sounded at the door. Ed Russell and his daughters Lisa and Mary entered.

"What the hell's going on?" Ed demanded. "Your note said there was terrible trouble in town."

Julie rose from her chair. "It's Nora. She's gone!"

"Oh, I know that," her husband said with a shrug. "I saw her."

"You what?" they all cried.

"Where?" demanded Paul.

"On the Blacktail Road."

Paul's face flushed with anger. "When?"

"A little before noon. I passed them on my way to the McCormack place for coffee." Ed glanced around at all the anxious faces. "What's all the excitement about? She was in an old green Jeep. She was in the front seat between two guys. I figured they were her boyfriends. She finally showed her true colors and left town. I expected as much."

Paul's voice was husky. "She's been kidnapped."

"Nah," his father said. "She left of her own accord. I gave her some money. I left it at the bank for her yesterday. She was supposed to get it this morning and leave, but I thought she would go in her car, not be so brazen as to leave with her men." He laughed heartily.

Paul lunged at his father, grabbing him by the lapels. "She was taken hostage during a robbery this morning at the bank, damn you. Hostage, do you hear me? By two men who raped and killed a teller in Kalispell." He shook his father angrily. "She was there because of you, you son of a bitch. She told me all about your offer and I tried to convince her she was wrong. She went to the bank to— Damn you, she would never ask you for money." He released his father with a shove and turned away, trying to contain his rage.

"You're the one who called this morning, aren't you?" Ida accused her son-in-law, shaking her fist at him. "You tried to drive the most important person in your own son's life away from him. You must have been desperate to get her out of the picture to do that to Paul. You're so tight with your own money—just how much did you offer her?"

"Four thousand dollars," Ed replied, then laughed. "I offered her two thousand, but she wouldn't take it, so I doubled it. I guess everyone has a price they can't refuse. That's more money than she's ever had, I suppose."

"Nora has had over sixty thousand dollars in two savings accounts ever since she arrived in this town," Ida snapped. "It was from the sale of her house and insurance from the death of her first husband. He was in the navy. She told me she felt guilty spending it, and other than paying for Lane's medical expenses, she's never touched it."

"She didn't need your filthy money," Paul muttered, running his fingers through his curly dark hair.

"You come with me, Paul, and I'll prove I'm right," his father began. "She's no good for you. You've got your own place now and—"

"Good Lord, man, do you think some piece of ground is more important to me than she is?" Paul shouted.

His father took a step backward.

"Why do you hate her?" Paul demanded. "She's the only woman I've ever loved! She and Lane are the most important people in my life."

The ringing of the phone interrupted them. Lisa answered it. "It's for you, daddy," she said.

Muffled words came from the kitchen, and a few moments later a somber Ed Russell returned. He dropped into a chair and rubbed his forehead. "It was the bank manager. Nellie...I mean Nora, told his secretary that if he was holding any funds for her to give them back." He shifted his gaze from one family member to another. "She wouldn't take it."

"She loves him, that's why," Julie said in a low voice. "You're blind to love, Russ, even when it's all around you." She turned away. "You protect your own children because you think you own them, not because you love them."

"That's not true," he protested. "I love all of you."

"Well, you certainly don't act like it," his wife retorted.

"I don't think you know what real love is," Mary cried.

Paul looked at his father. "Dad, no piece of paper is worth my wife. Your narrow-mindedness has brought enough unhappiness to our family. If Nora dies, that money you left at the bank will be blood money. If those two killers harm her in any way, you'll be responsible and I'll never forgive you for what you've done."

Julie glanced again at the abandoned photos of the wanted men and picked them up. "Russ," she said, handing him the picture of the thin man identified as Oscar Piper. "I think I've seen this man before. Do you know him?"

Her husband studied the picture, shaking his head. He started to hand it back to Julie, then glanced at it again. "Yes, I think I do know him, but not as Oscar Piper. Sure! He looks just like Oscar Cheney who worked for the grazing association several years ago." He glanced at Paul. "The second summer you and Steven rode the rodeo circuit. That's why you didn't recognize him. Good Lord, he knows our Blacktail country like the back of his hand. He stayed in the McCormack cabin for a few weeks, then was moved on to the old Langley homestead." He turned to Paul. "Maybe that's why there's no trace of them. I'm sorry, Paul."

Paul jumped from his seat. "I'm going to get her." He hurried to his bedroom, and when he returned he was wearing his heavy leather coat and carrying insulated gloves, a woolen scarf and his hat. "I'll go to the ranch and hitch a trailer to my truck, then drive to the McCormack cabin. That will be my base. If they aren't there, I'll go on by horseback to the Langley place. That old wagon trail is too rugged for my truck." He glared at his father. "You said she was in a green Jeep?"

His father nodded.

"If I'm not back at the ranch by tomorrow morning, tell the sheriff where I've gone. I have a score to settle with those two scum." He turned to his father. "I'll settle matters with you later."

As Paul drove through the gently blowing snow, his thoughts were on Nora. Was she warm? Still safe? She must be terrified. His mouth tightened as he thought of what the two men might do to her.

When he arrived at the ranch, he hurried into the bathroom between his old bedroom and Steven's. The damned wires had been on long enough. Taking the small pair of pliers the oral surgeon had given him, he carefully clipped the tiny wires holding his jaws together. He opened his jaws, agonizing as the unused muscles rebelled, but gradually he worked the acrylic splint and the attached wires loose, freeing his mouth. Reaching for his toothbrush he cleaned his teeth and tongue, then gargled and repeated the brushing several times.

The oral surgeon had cautioned him about reinjuring his jaw, and he would be as careful as he could, but the frustration of having his mouth immobile was more than he could handle. He wanted to be able to concentrate on saving Nora.

He touched the red scar running down his cheek, and smiled. "I like it," Nora had said one night as he held her. "It makes you look. . .roguish."

Paul vowed he would hear her say those words again as he left the house and headed toward the horse barn. After hitching the horse trailer to his pickup truck, he saddled his two favorite mounts and led them up the ramp. Returning to the house, he found a rifle belonging to his father, grabbed a handful of shells and walked back to his truck. If Nora's safety was at stake, he wouldn't hesitate to use the weapon.

The snow was falling more heavily as he drove from the ranch toward the McCormack cabin, and he could feel a rush of adrenaline. The hunt was on, but this time his quarry was human.

CHAPTER SIXTEEN

THE THIN MAN removed the barrel of his revolver from Nora's temple and pushed it into the soft fleshy fullness of her breast.

"Do as we say or I'll blow it off," he threatened, forcing her into an old white station wagon.

As they drove along the narrow paved road, all Nora cared about was that Paul and Lane were safe. A few miles past the spot where the pavement ended, the two men abandoned the white car and pushed Nora toward a battered green Jeep. As the thin man opened the passenger door of the vehicle and shoved her inside, she felt his hand slide over her hip suggestively. She jerked away, and he laughed.

"Call me Oscar," he whispered into her ear as they settled onto the hard seat of the Jeep. "Let's get moving, Wheeler."

They rode for several miles in silence. Nora watched the overhead sign of the Rocking R Ranch flash by, and the seriousness of her predicament began to register. She would probably be left for dead somewhere in the remote countryside when they were through with her.

Fear of death was swept away by Oscar's dirty hand grazing the back of her neck as he slid his arm around her shoulders. She caught a strong whiff of body odor and tried to move away, but he trailed his fingers into the V of her blouse, and she shuddered in revolt. She concentrated on Paul and her baby. If she really tried, she told herself, she could ignore the man's filthy hands on her body.

She jumped when the driver spoke. "Leave her alone, Piper. Now where do I turn?"

Nora glanced toward him and found him leering at her. Until she figured out which man was the leader, she would consider both equally dangerous.

"About a half mile up the road," Piper said. "See that gate in the fence? Pull over and I'll open it." The Jeep stopped while Piper opened the wire and post gate, then drove through. After closing the gate, Piper climbed back into the Jeep.

They bounced over a narrow rutted trail, soon leaving the main road far behind. Snow began to fall lightly, and Nora knew that tracking the Jeep would soon be impossible for anyone searching for her. She was surprised when they stopped at the cabin where she and Paul had spent their idyllic summer. How did these men know where it was?

A wave of sadness swept over her as she was pushed through the front door. Looking around, she noticed that all traces of the fire were gone. Someone had cleared out the damaged blankets and replaced the charred boards in the wooden floor.

"We'll stay here for a while," said the man called Piper. "No one will think to look for us this far from the road." He laughed confidently, then shoved Nora into the tiny kitchen. "Find us some grub, sweetheart. I know there's always some canned goods around. . .and hurry up, I'm hungry."

Nora thought about escaping through the kitchen door, but Wheeler barged through the back entry with an armful of logs before she had a chance to act. After he dumped the logs onto the living-room floor he returned to the kitchen and kept his attention on her as she hunted for something to make a meal. The air was very cold in the cabin until the heat from the wood stove in the kitchen and the fireplace warmed the interior. Nora finally found a can of chili and half a stale loaf of unsliced bread, its crust covered with large patches of dried green mold. When she pulled the loaf apart, she found the center white and edible in spite of its hardness.

She pushed the pump handle at the sink several times, but the water refused to flow and she gave up. When the chili was ready, she set it on the table with the crumbled pieces of hard bread. For a moment she thought her two captors were going to fight over the food. They filled their bowls and dunked the pieces of bread into the hot chili, slurping as they ate.

When they had finished, Piper motioned Nora to the table. "What's left is yours, sweetheart." He turned to Wheeler. "You watch the broad. I'm going to catch a few. Wake me in an hour. We'll stay here until dark, then head to the Langley cabin up this trail."

Wheeler squinted at his partner. "Are you sure you aren't underestimating these country-bumpkin police? Maybe we should head out right now."

"Nah." Piper laughed. "We have plenty of time. They'll never find us in this storm." He waved his hand at Nora. "Don't fool with the dishes. The next saddle tramp who comes through can clean up."

Hunger gnawed at her stomach as she peered into the pan. She hadn't eaten since breakfast and then just a few bites. The men had left a spoon of scorched chili and two clumps of hard bread. She ate hungrily, wondering if she would be alive to eat again.

An hour after dusk they were back on the narrow dirt road, Wheeler complaining continually that they had stayed too long at the cabin. The snow was falling harder, and one headlight on the Jeep blinked on and off as they climbed steadily higher. She lost track of time until Piper's hand touched her breast and he leaned closer.

"You're mine when we get to the next shack," he whispered in her ear, then drew her against his dirty jacket. "It's only a few miles up this draw."

She tried to pull away, but he tightened his hold.

"I'm cold," she said, shivering.

"Where's your jacket?" Wheeler asked.

"I made her leave it at the cabin," Piper told him.

"You crazy, man?" Wheeler snarled. "She'll freeze."

"That was the idea," Piper replied, laughing. "She won't try to get away. I'll keep her warm."

Nora lost all sense of direction as they bounced over the rut-filled trail in the darkness. Visibility was limited as the falling snow reflected the single beam of light back at them. Finally they pulled up to a dilapidated homesteader's shanty. Piper jumped from the Jeep and ran to the door. Rusty hinges squeaked in protest as he pushed the door open.

"It's worse than I remembered," Piper said when he returned, "but we've got the sleeping bags in the back of the Jeep. We can build a fire inside on the dirt floor. Go get some firewood, Wheeler."

Wheeler grumbled as he reached for a small ax from behind the seat. He gathered some dead wood near the cabin and soon had it chopped into suitable pieces, using the headlight to work by.

They built a small fire in the center of the dirt floor

and the building soon filled with acrid smoke. Nora's eyes burned as she tried to rub warmth into her chilled arms, but her hands wouldn't respond.

The men huddled together and a muffled debate ensued. Occasionally one of them would glance at her. Piper's voice rose and she heard the word, "Mine!" She refused to think about her impending fate and instead looked around furtively for a weapon to defend herself, but there was nothing.

The outside temperature was well below freezing and the inside of the shack not much warmer. Nora's shoeless foot grew numb and she tried to rub it, making it tingle and burn. Listlessly she decided it was better numb.

Her heart stopped as Wheeler turned to her, a leering smile showing through the stubble on his face. His grotesque shadow danced on the walls as he approached her, carrying a bottle of whiskey in one hand. Where had they gotten the liquor, she wondered, panicking.

He squatted in front of her, his back to the fire, throwing his face into darkness.

For a few seconds she was sure she heard Paul's voice call her name. "No-o-r-r-a-a-a." She imagined the wings of a snowbird carrying the crisp sound through the night. *I must be going crazy,* she thought.

Wheeler touched her shoulder and she flinched.

"Drink this," he ordered. "It'll warm your insides." He held the bottle to her mouth and grabbed a handful of hair at the nape of her neck. "Drink," he commandcd, tipping the bottle.

The fiery amber liquor seared her throat, and she began to choke.

"Again," he insisted.

"No."

"Again," he growled, twisting his grimy fist in her tangled hair, determined to pour the liquor down her throat again.

Nora shoved him away and spit the whiskey in his face. His broad stubby hand came flying at her but she ducked. He lost his balance and fell on his elbow, cursing her as she crawled away. "Leave me alone," she muttered. "Just leave me alone." She rubbed her shoulders. "I'm so cold."

A dark shadow blocked her way. Oscar Piper's long legs covered in grimy jeans took a few steps toward her. He yanked on her arm and dragged her toward the two sleeping bags that had been dumped and opened near the fire.

"That's better, sweetheart," he said. "See, Wheeler, she's not fighting me."

"But I won her," Wheeler said.

The two men quarreled over Nora as she lay slumped on the sleeping bags, the strength draining from her limbs. *If they would just go away,* she thought, *I could sleep a little*. Images of her brown-eyed son came to her. She tried to recall his name. . .*Jeremy Lane. . . what?* She couldn't think of her own last name.

Stark terror struck as the men dropped down beside her, and Piper's hand touched her stomach. "Paul!" she screamed.

An explosion rocked the room as the door was kicked in and a shadowy giant filled the opening.

"Get your filthy hands off her!" Paul Russell shouted, waving his rifle at them. "Lay a hand on her and I'll blow your heads off."

"Paul," Nora whispered, sure she was hallucinating until she felt Piper's hand leave her belt buckle.

"The guns," Wheeler whispered. "Get the guns!"

"Step back," Paul ordered, his voice a low roar.

"My gun is in the Jeep," Piper whispered. "Where's yours?"

"Let's get the hell out of here," Wheeler muttered. He took a running dive through the window opening on the opposite of the room, and Paul pulled the trigger. The explosion shook the dilapidated log cabin. Clumps of snow and debris fell through the cracks in the dirt roof and a few rotten logs clattered to the floor, dousing the fire and plunging the room into darkness.

"Wait for me!" Piper yelled, and his booted feet scurried through the darkness.

"Nora," Paul called in a hushed whisper. "Where are you, honey?" Curses sounded from outside when the engine wouldn't respond, then a shout was heard and the Jeep roared away. Paul found Nora in the darkness and gathered her in his arms, alarmed about the coldness of her skin.

"Oh, baby, if they've hurt you..."

"Paul," her weak voice moaned, and she sagged in his arms.

Another log fell from the roof, sending a shower of snow down on them, as he carried her from the collapsing shack. His horse was ground reined several yards away, and it whinnied as Paul approached. Another horse was tethered nearby. Paul set Nora on the ground and ran to the other horse, quickly untied her coat, which he had found at the lower cabin, and a thick woolen blanket, then ran back to her crumpled body.

He slipped the coat around her cold shoulders, then propped her against his own saddled horse. "Nora, please wake up, sweetheart. Oh, God, Nora."

She stirred, her legs gradually regaining a little strength.

"Nora, can you stand?" he asked, and she nodded. "Good. Now hold on to the horn."

"The horn?"

"This," he said, putting her hand on the horn. "I want to wrap you up so you can begin to thaw out." He enfolded her in the heavy woolen blanket. The horse sidestepped as she leaned against him.

"Easy, Speckles," Paul soothed. "Easy." He lifted Nora onto the horse's back, then quickly swung up behind her and adjusted her against him, tucking her feet inside the blanket.

"I'm going to cover your face, honey, so don't be alarmed by the darkness...but first..." He tilted her face and gently kissed her bluish lips before covering her head completely with the blanket. He untied the reins of the horse he had brought for her use and slowly began to retrace the route he had traveled.

The light of a full moon above the cloud cover brought an eerie gray glow to the night. The falling snowflakes drifted like summer cottonwood tufts, but the freezing temperature held danger for Nora. She was dozing in his arms and already showed the first signs of hypothermia. She needed warmth and he had his own to give her, but first they had to reach the McCormack cabin and its fireplace. Perhaps he should have tried to drive the truck to the Langley cabin, but if he had become stranded in a deep rut, she would probably have been assaulted and possibly even dead by now.

Had the two bank robbers taken the trail over the top of the mountain, he wondered, as the gelding's steady gait covered the rock path. That mountain trail led to a winding dirt road a few miles on the other side of the range. He had traveled it several times while hunting deer and elk with his brothers, but always on horseback, never in a truck. He didn't know what he would do if the robbers had decided to turn back and were at the McCormack cabin. Nora's condition was critical. He had to get her to the cabin, and he didn't intend to let them stand in his way. He was sure he had missed his target when he had fired the rifle, but he didn't care. His rage had evaporated when he found Nora. She was all that mattered.

The ground leveled out and he urged the gelding into a canter. Another mile and he should be at the cabin, but it was a mile of rocky timber country that wound along the edge of a canyon. A narrow stream had carved its way through the canyon floor, and in the summer bubbling water usually bounced over the boulders in the shallow streambed, but now a foot of ice overlay either side of the stream, softening its melodious babbling to a hum. The stream was out of sight through the willows along the bank, but its faint sound reassured Paul that they would soon be inside the cabin, away from the snowfall and the freezing temperature. Inside he would build a roaring fire and revive Nora.

Thank God she was dry. If her clothing had become wet, she would probably be near death. He tightened his arm around her at the thought of losing her and pulled the woolen blanket from her face. He reined the gelding to a stop. "Nora," he whispered. "Nora, speak to me. I love you, sweetheart."

Her lashes lay still on her cheeks. He used his teeth to pull the insulated glove from his left hand and touched her lips. Her warm breath brushed against his fingers, and he slid his hand through her tangled blond hair and gripped the back of her neck, slowly rubbing the flesh to stimulate her circulation.

"Paul?" she whispered. Suddenly she tried to struggle out of his arms, but he tightened his hold. "Paul," she murmured as she settled against him again. "When did...where...are we? What happened to those terrible men?"

"I don't know. I hope they went over the pass. If they're ahead of us, there might be trouble." He shook his head. "Did I...was I in time? Did they harm you, honey?"

She shuddered. "You came in time. They were...so dirty. They smelled...and they kept touching me. It was awful." Her eyes shone through the darkness. "Where's Lane?"

He put his glove back on and adjusted her position. "Don't worry, Nora. Lane is safe. I left him with my mother, grandmother, Mary and Lisa, all wanting to spoil him."

He tightened his hold on her. "The important thing is getting you to the McCormack cabin. I know the best way to help a hypothermia victim."

"What is it?"

"Body heat. I've got it and you need it, and we'll both enjoy the treatment."

The gelding sidestepped restlessly under them, whinnying in protest at their lack of movement. Paul patted the horse's shoulder. "Okay, Speckles, let's go, fellow. Hold on, Nora," he warned. "We're moving out." He spurred the gelding, and horse and riders quickly covered the last quarter mile to the cabin.

When Paul helped her off the horse, Nora started to walk away, but her legs wobbled. "Oh," she cried, reaching for support.

"Easy, honey, you're not well yet," Paul said, lifting her into his arms and carrying her into the dark cabin. Within minutes he had a fire blazing, the two horses sheltered in the lean-to behind the cabin, the cabin door bolted, and Nora propped in a corner of the sofa. He went into the kitchen, and when he returned, he was carrying two mugs of hot steaming coffee.

Nora had nodded off, but his voice brought her back.

"Drink this. It will warm your insides. Fortunately the McCormacks keep this place stocked for just such emergencies."

When she had finished, he set the mugs aside. "Did you make the mess in the kitchen?"

She nodded.

"Three people and one can of chili?"

"That's all I found in the kitchen," she said. "The pantry! I was so frightened I forgot all about the pantry. And that darned pump! I couldn't get it primed." The room grew quiet and her eyelids began to droop. "I'm so sleepy. Is that good or bad?"

"I'm not sure yet. We'll stay here until daybreak, then head into town. I want you in the hospital," he said, frowning at her.

"I don't think I have the strength to get up," she murmured. "What about your treatment? You'd better give it to me before I fall asleep. What was it again?"

He knelt before her, removed the folds of blanket and began to unbutton her sweater and blouse. "What are you doing?" she asked, her hands fumbling to push his away.

"It's my treatment. Body heat is the best way for one person to help another person who's suffered from exposure to cold. I mean it. I'm going to give you my body heat. Clothes get in the way. Let me help you." He gently pushed her clumsy hands aside. "I brought sleeping bags along," he told her, pointing to two royal blue bags spread before the fireplace. He pushed her sweater and blouse from her shoulders, slid her jeans down her legs and quickly dispensed with her lone shoe and socks. "Get in, quickly," he directed, helping her into the bag, then he shed his own clothes and joined her.

"God, Nora, your feet are still icy cold." He began to massage her back and hips, his hands rubbing her skin and making it prickle. Turning her over he pulled her hips against his abdomen, encircling her shoulders with his muscular arms and bringing his hands to rest across her breasts.

"Oh, Paul, that feels so good," she moaned, rubbing against his warm body. Slowly his body transmitted its heat to hers. She turned in his arms and nuzzled his neck, kissing him near his ear. Suddenly she drew back. "Paul!"

"What?" he asked, frightened by her outcry.

"Your jaw. You're talking normally. Oh, Paul, what have you done? It's not time yet."

"I used that cute little pair of pliers." He laughed. "Felt great. I just couldn't take the chance of having trouble when I found you and still having those damned wires holding my jaws shut. I've been careful, lovely lady, and now I know it was all worth it." His hand traced the fine arch of her brow as she stared hypnotically at his dark features.

"Paul," she whispered as his mouth covered hers. Her lips parted, and she wondered if he intended to make love to her. The emotion she felt for him now had no sexual basis, yet she pressed closer against his hot body.

"Paul, I don't think..." She stopped as he smiled at her.

"I know, sweetheart. I just want to hold you close and keep warming you...and prove to both of us that you're safe and we're together again."

"Are you sure?" she asked, unable to hide her skepticism.

"Of course," he said, turning her over again and pulling her buttocks firmly against him.

"I feel like a hot dog being roasted," she said as she nestled against him in the cozy sleeping bags.

"Sleep," he whispered near her ear.

Her eyelids grew heavy, and her mind filled with images of summer wild flowers. Lane toddled from Paul to herself as she sat on a blanket in a meadow, the warm sun high overhead and fluffy clouds floating by. Paul dropped down beside her and laid his hand on her abdomen, and she realized she was pregnant again.

"We've got to use up those credits at the hospital."

His startling comment jolted her awake.

"Are you okay?" Paul asked, running his hand over her body.

"Oh, yes indeed, my darling, I'm perfectly fine," she murmured, and she relaxed against him again.

SOMEONE SHOOK NORA'S SHOULDER, lifting her from the depths of sleep. Her eyes flew open. Paul knelt over her, completely dressed, and he was holding two steaming mugs of coffee.

She brushed her hair from her face and yawned. "I must look terrible," she said, a blush burning her cheeks.

"You look charming," Paul assured her, offering her his hand and waiting patiently until she was sitting cross-legged in the warm sleeping bags before handing her one of the mugs.

"Where did you get water for the coffee?" she asked. "The pump—"

"Needs priming," he said. "It goes down naturally

from not being used, and that keeps the pipe from freezing and breaking. I put snow in the coffeepot and melted it."

"You're so resourceful."

The scar running down his cheek turned red as he smiled. "How do you feel, my lovely lady?"

"Almost normal. My feet still hurt a little, but other than needing a long hot shower, I think I'm going to make it...thanks to you." Her eyes unexpectedly brimmed with tears. "I didn't think I would ever see you again."

"When I read your note, I wondered if you were taking my father's bribe after all and leaving."

"Oh, no, I would never do that," she insisted fervently. "I just had to find out who was right...about your father and the money." The outcome of her actions weighed heavily on her. "My curiosity almost got us all... I shouldn't have been there. You and Lane were almost killed!"

She slid back into the sleeping bags, and only when Paul's strong arms encircled her, pulling her close to him, was she aware that she was crying.

Paul held her until her anguish was spent. "You're right, Nora. You should have left well enough alone, but you had nothing to do with our danger. You saved us, sweetheart. Don't you realize that? You saved us!" With his fingers he brushed her cheeks dry, then he kissed her. "All's well, my love. Now, can you dress yourself or do you need help?" Without waiting for her reply, be began to assist her.

Her legs were still weak, and he offered her his arm for support. "Ready?" he asked, helping her with her coat. "The horses are loaded, and the sun is just coming up. It's a new day."

After he walked Nora to the truck, Paul returned to the cabin to put out the fire. He had left the truck engine running, and the cab's heater was emitting delightful waves of warmth. Nora rubbed her hands together, savoring the heat.

The sounds of rumbling motors disturbed the quiet clearing. Nora whirled around in time to see two cars approaching the cabin. The sheriff's four-wheel-drive vehicle rolled to a stop in front of the cabin. The second was a late-model Wagoneer. Nora recognized Steven Russell and his younger brother Tim. When they spotted her in the cab they waved a victory signal.

Her heart froze when Ed Russell slid from the driver's seat and marched in the direction of the cabin. He stopped halfway to the door and turned toward the truck. His brow furrowed and his dark eyes locked with hers, making Nora flinch.

Minutes later Paul returned to the truck. "Let's get you to the hospital. I want them to check your feet for frostbite, just to be sure."

Nora's mind raced as she speculated on the reasons for Ed Russell's presence. "What did they want?"

He gave her a sidelong glance. "It will upset you."

"What will upset me?"

He exhaled slowly. "They found the two men."

"Where?" she cried. "Are they in custody?"

"One is," he hedged.

"One? Did the other escape?"

"No."

"I don't understand."

"One...is dead. The other is in custody," he explained.

"Oh, no," she cried, covering her mouth with her hand. "What happened?"

He turned to her. "Are you sure you're ready to handle this?"

"I've got to know," she replied.

"They had another truck waiting across the mountain, about five miles the other side, on the way to Lima and Dell. The storm was worse on that side and they didn't make it very far. They missed a curve and went over the side down a ten-foot ravine." He hesitated. "Nora, this isn't very pleasant."

"It can't be worse than what has already happened. Please go on, Paul. I have to know."

"The Lima deputies found them early this morning. The man named Piper had been thrown from the Jeep. He was dead, either from a broken neck or exposure. The coroner will determine the cause of death. The other one offered no resistance. The sheriff was on his way here with my father and brothers when he received the word on his radio."

He pulled over to the side of the road a few miles from town and embraced Nora. "Other than your testimony at the trial, you can try to forget them. Think about us and our son...and all those children we're going to have someday." He tilted her chin and grinned roguishly. "Won't we have fun making those babies?"

AT THE HOSPITAL Dr. Peters assured them Nora would be discharged the following day. She had narrowly escaped permanent damage to her feet and had picked up a respiratory infection. An antibiotic and lots of rest was the physician's prescription.

"I'll check in with grandmother and see how Lane is doing with all those women," Paul said as they finished lunch in Nora's hospital room. "Bye, sweetheart." He kissed her, then was gone.

Nora stared out the hospital window, thinking about the problems still surrounding her. Paul's father had said over the phone that Paul had signed the deed to the property north of town. But Ed had thought she had accepted his offer to leave, and Paul had refused to believe his father would make such an offer. Would Ed Russell now try to take back the property?

As she lay there, her head throbbing, she tried to think of her future with Paul, the man she loved, and all the children they would have. But somehow the image of surly Ed Russell kept coming back to haunt her, and she began to dread their inevitable encounter.

CHAPTER SEVENTEEN

NORA AWOKE WITH A START, wondering why her foot was being shaken. She tried to pull it free, but to no avail. The shaking grew stronger, and slowly she forced her eyes open. "Oh, no," she gasped.

Ed Russell stood at the end of her bed, shaking her foot with one hand and holding a large manila envelope in the other.

Nora glanced frantically around, looking for Julie or Paul—anyone to protect her from Ed's menacing presence.

"Get away, Mr. Russell, just get away," she ordered, shrinking back against the head of the bed.

"Please don't do that," Ed began, frowning.

"Leave me alone," Nora warned.

"Please don't," he repeated, lowering his eyes as he tossed the manila envelope onto the spread.

"Don't what?"

"Look at me like that. I'm not an animal."

She had thought he was angry, but now she realized he was nervous and ill at ease. He was clean shaven, and as she inhaled deeply, she caught a trace of the same citrus-and-spice after-shave Paul occasionally used.

"You're not an animal, Mr. Russell, but you've never treated me like another human being, either," she said.

He shrugged out of his heavy gray coat, and she was surprised to see he was wearing an attractive blue-and-beige Western shirt. He wasn't handsome, but for the first time she saw a strength of character in him that gave him a virile attractiveness. For a few seconds she recognized a bit of Paul in his father.

"Why are you here?" she asked.

"I want a truce. I want to. . . apologize."

Nora could see the words didn't come easily to him. "Apologize for what? What kind of truce? Frankly I have no desire to associate with you."

"I want to apologize for trying to bribe you to leave town. I shouldn't have done that." He ran his fingers through his thick dark hair, and again Nora thought of Paul. "My wife isn't speaking to me. Neither are any of my children." He mumbled an expletive in frustration. "I'm even beginning to miss Ida Belle's sharp tongue. Can you imagine?"

He chanced a glance at Nora, and the sincerity she saw in his pleading expression broke through her determination to be firm.

"What kind of truce are you looking for?" she asked.

"I. . . I want to be able to see my grandson. Paul says I don't deserve to know him, but listen, miss, I—"

"I'm not a miss," Nora interrupted. "I'm your son's wife, Mrs. Paul Innes Russell, or better yet, Mrs. Honora Louise Browning Lane Russell." She emphasized each name.

"Good God, woman, you were married twice before?" Ed burst out.

"No, Mr. Russell. My parents were Mr. and Mrs. Louis Browning. My Christian name is Honora Louise after my great-grandmother. She was Irish, and from the stories my father told me when I was a child, she would make Ida Belle Innes look gentle. My name is not miss or woman or girlie, and certainly not *Nellie*. Mr.

Russell—" she glared angrily at him "—don't you dare call me Nellie again. Ever! My name is *Nora*. N-o-r-a. Do you understand?"

He nodded.

"Then say it!"

"What?"

"Say it! My name. Nora."

"Nora."

"Now," she began, taking a moment to calm herself, "what is this truce you propose? I don't mind you seeing Lane as long as you never get another crazy idea about taking him away from me."

Ed pursed his thin lips and stared at her for several seconds, then picked up the manila envelope and handed it to her. "Take it, please. . . Nora."

She felt its thickness. Her fingers shook as she opened the clasp and emptied its contents onto the bed. Several dozen one-hundred-dollar bills fell into her lap, along with a folded piece of white paper.

"You are callous beyond belief, Mr. Russell," she seethed. "After all this truce talking, and still you try to bribe me? I don't believe it!" She brushed frantically at the money, trying to get it off the bed. Several bills floated to the floor.

At that moment the door opened.

"What the hell is going on here?" Paul asked, quickly taking in the scene. "Nora, is my father bothering you?" He spotted the scattered money. "What *is* going on here? Nora? Dad? One of you had better speak up. . . and damned quick."

"Your father tried to bribe me again," Nora said.

"Like hell I did," Ed countered.

"Wait, both of you," Paul intervened. "Nora, where did you get this money?"

"From your father."

"Dad, why did you give Nora this money?" Paul asked. "Didn't you learn the last time? Nora is here to stay. Why can't you accept that?"

"I do," Ed insisted.

"Then why did you give her the money?"

"Because...that's what I did...just gave her the money," Ed replied. "I gave her the money, but she won't let me explain."

Paul's gaze swung back to Nora.

She touched one of the pieces of currency. "I guess I didn't give him a chance to explain." She turned to Paul. "I jumped to conclusions. I'm sorry." She turned again to Ed. "Mr. Russell, why *did* you give me this money? I don't want it. Paul and I will make out just fine without it."

"I gave it to you because I'm sorry for the trouble I've caused, and I want to see my grandson. Can't you understand that? I...I love that little guy. I know he's only a few months old and I denied he was Paul's for a while, but..." He hung his head. "I just want to see my grandson grow up."

"Oh, dear," Nora sighed, sensing how difficult the apology had been for Ed. She turned to Paul. "I don't know what to say."

"I think I do," Paul said. "Dad, you're always welcome to spend time with Lane. It's not necessary to buy your visitation rights." He went to his father and put his arm around his shoulders, giving him an affectionate squeeze. Ed Russell seemed embarrassed by the emotional gesture from his son and eased away.

"There's five thousand there. Use it any way you want. I don't care. And here," he said, reaching for the folded piece of paper. "Paul, this is for you."

Paul opened it and his eyes widened.

"I know, I know." Ed waved his broad hand. "I must be getting senile."

"What is it?" Nora asked, craning her neck to see.

"I borrowed some money when I signed the deed, money to carry the operation for a year," Paul told her. "There was to be a lien against the property. This is it, but dad has marked it paid in full. I don't know what to say."

"I have to get back to the place," Ed announced. "Your mother doesn't know where I am or what I'm doing. I want to tell her myself. Maybe then she'll talk to me again. Good Lord, she wouldn't even sleep in the same bed last night." He pulled his coat on again and without another word left the room.

Paul helped her gather the money and put it back in the envelope. "Take it, please," Nora said. "You can have it. I don't want his money. I should forgive and forget, but it's all too soon. I need time to think."

Paul put his arm around her shoulders, and she nuzzled his neck and teasingly took a nip, wriggling away before he could retaliate. He ignored her, and just when she thought she was safe, he grabbed her and threw her down on the bed.

She giggled. "I'm supposed to be sick, remember? Be nice to me." His head came closer, and the expression in his eyes changed from lighthearted teasing to sensual desire. Nora lightly touched the scar on his cheek with her fingertips. "Paul," she murmured. His hands followed the curves of her body hidden beneath the high-necked flannel gown.

She jumped when she heard the door squeak and a timid voice exclaim, "Oh!" By the time she had the gown down past her knees and the covers drawn up to her waist, whoever had entered had disappeared again.

"You're blushing," Paul said as she tried to smooth her hair.

She slapped playfully at his hand. "It's all your fault."

They spent the next hour leisurely talking about their future.

"We can't stay with my grandmother forever," Paul said.

"But we can't go to your parent's place," Nora reminded him.

"True."

"What about the new place north of town?" she asked.

"There's a man living there with his wife and three children. His management contract runs for another year. He's doing a fine job, so I don't want to disturb that arrangement for now."

"It seems foolish to spend money on rent here in town. What shall we do? You're the head of the household. You can solve this problem."

"That doesn't sound like the liberated woman I knew several months ago," he said, grinning.

"Actually, it's nice to let you make the decisions for a while. Just don't leave me out completely. We'll discuss the options, but for now, Lane and I will go wherever you go."

"DON'T TURN OUT THE LIGHT," Paul said as they retired for the night a week later. "I want to discuss our housing options."

Nora's hand stopped in midair. "Yes?"

"David McCormack has offered me a job as foreman of his commercial Hereford operation. You met him at our wedding. The good-looking gray-haired man and his wife, Sammy? My father told him about the transfer of property, and he asked if I would be moving. When dad told him about the people already living there, he came over to my dad's place and offered me the job. It includes a two-bedroom house." He glanced at her. "Interested? It would buy us some time and give me good experience running a place without my father's heavy hand."

"Where is it?" she asked. "McCormack...McCormack? Isn't that what you called the cabin where we spent the summer?"

"Yes," he replied. "His home place is eight miles on up the Blacktail from the Rocking R. He raises purebred Simmental beef cattle and recently started dabbling in Arabians. I think he's overloaded himself and needs some relief."

"Didn't I meet his son? Of course! That absolutely gorgeous blond man with the little girl. The one you told me about and the one Mary..." She was surprised to see the beaming smile on Paul's face. "Did I say something funny?"

"No, but we've been so caught up in our own problems we've lost touch with the rest of the Russell family." He broke into light laughter.

"Are you just going to lie there and laugh or are you going to tell me about your family's goings on?"

"My little sister is getting married."

"Mary?"

He nodded. "It appears that D.A. and my little sister have been carrying on their own romance right under everyone's nose and no one noticed it. That's why the older house on the McCormack place is available. The timing is perfect. Mary's wedding will take place during the Christmas holidays and they'll be moving to town, where D.A. teaches. So the house is ours if you're willing to leave grandmother and the convenience of town living.

Do you want to be a full-time cowboy's wife and live on the range?"

"It sounds wonderful," Nora exclaimed. "When? Not before Christmas! We promised Grandma Innes to spend Christmas with her."

"I agree, and I have work to do before New Year's. I have some special plans for us that night, but they're secret, so you'll have to trust my judgment," he told her enigmatically, and nothing Nora could do would persuade him otherwise.

DURING CHRISTMAS dinner the phone rang. Paul answered it and spent several minutes chatting.

"Mom wished us all a Merry Christmas," he told them after he'd hung up. "She wanted to have us out but didn't think the time was right. I told her I agreed. I don't want you to have to deal with my father yet. He needs to think some more about what he did to all of us."

"Thank you," Nora said softly, appreciative of his thoughtfulness.

The phone rang again, and this time Paul beamed as he listened to the caller on the other end. "You've got a deal. Great! Tomorrow at eight? Fine. I'll meet you there." He listened again. "Yes, she's fine now...no lingering effects...yes...so am I. Goodbye."

When he returned to the table he immediately began to eat the piece of pumpkin pie his grandmother had set before him.

"Well," Nora said with a frown. "What was that all about?"

"It was David McCormack."

"Paul! Do we get to move in right away?" she asked excitedly.

He shook his dark head. "I have to do some remodeling first. We'll be in by the first of the year. Steven, Russ and Tim will move your belongings out of storage for you, so you don't have to worry about anything. You're not to go to the place until I say it's okay." He wagged his finger at her. "No exceptions, do you hear?"

She nodded her head in agreement, but her curiosity grew.

"Paul Russell, you're up to something," she accused him.

"Yup," he agreed, grinning.

Nora grew more curious with each passing day, fed by the mysterious comings and goings of her husband. Paul would set the alarm for five in the morning, bound out of bed and dress quietly in old clothing, then drop to the bed and kiss her goodbye.

"I'm eating with the McCormacks," he whispered. "David and I have been working out tentative plans for the spring."

"Can I come with you?" she finally asked on the third day.

"Definitely not. It's not ready yet."

"What's not ready?"

He merely raised a dark eyebrow, kissed her cheek and hurried from the room. She lay in the bed, listening for the sound of his truck's engine turning over and the crunching of the big snow tires on the icy driveway as he drove away.

Each evening he would return, his work clothes splattered with mortar and paint.

New Year's Eve arrived crisp and cold. Paul started to leave the room, then changed his mind and returned to the bed. He lifted Nora from the pillow and kissed her with such deep passion that she was left breathless.

"Oh, Paul," she murmured, pulling him closer to her. "Do that again." Her lips parted again as his mouth covered hers.

"You're tempting on a cold winter morning, pretty lady, but I have to go."

"Why, cowboy?" she asked as he laid her head back on the pillow. "I wish you didn't have to be gone all day."

"I'll be home early. Tonight we're going out. Dinner at the Eagle's Nest...prime rib...lobster...filet mignon...prawns...anything you desire, then dancing. The Eagle's Nest is a very classy place on New Year's, so no Western jeans. I want to see you in something clingy and sexy."

"Why?"

"Because we met one year ago tonight."

"You remembered," she said softly.

His expression grew tender. "How could I forget? You have the checkbook—now buy something new. Use *my* money. That's an order. I'll finish up at the house and be home by midafternoon." He kissed her again, yet still he didn't leave. A smile softened his dark features, and Nora wished she could read his thoughts.

"Be careful, darling," she said softly.

"I will." And he was gone.

The hours seemed to drag until Ida Innes learned of Paul and Nora's plans for the evening.

"Let's go out for lunch and shop afterward," she suggested. "I can watch Lane while you try on dresses." She smiled, rolling her hazel eyes heavenward. "If I were only slender and young like I was a hundred years ago."

The first dress shop they visited had just received a special shipment of evening wear, and the third dress

Nora tried on fitted as though it had been custom designed for her. Its icy blue-green color accented her eyes, and the bodice plunged down the front to the waistline, highlighting her full breasts, its panels held in place by a few strategically placed ties and tucks and two incredibly thin shoulder straps. The skirt was made of yards of frothy material and an underlayer of fabric a few shades darker.

The dress reminded Nora of a churning ocean, with frothy waves moving in a countercurrent over a sea of dark silk. When she modeled the dress for Mrs. Innes, the older woman's eyes grew as round as her bowed mouth.

"Oh, my," Ida cried. "If I were my grandson, I think I would like that. Now, you need a pair of high-heeled gold sandals and a matching evening bag, and you'll be the envy of the Eagle's Nest."

PAUL WAS AT A LOSS FOR WORDS when he saw Nora in the dress.

"Is it. . . too bold?" she asked hesitantly.

He came closer and trailed his forefinger around the exposed curve of her breast. "No," he said, "but I may have to fight off the other men at the restaurant."

As they collected their coats and Nora slipped into a pair of fur-lined snow boots, Paul pulled his grandmother aside and whispered in her ear.

"Of course," Mrs. Innes said, ushering them out the door.

Nora slid her hand through the arm of Paul's black dress jacket, feeling a strange sense of exhilaration. Something special and wonderful was going to happen tonight.

Their evening at the Eagle's Nest seemed to fly by, and Nora was surprised when Paul suggested they leave.

"But it's only eleven!" she protested.

"I know a more private place to usher in the new year," he announced, guiding her to the truck.

The countryside was hidden in darkness as they followed the road to the Russell ranch. Nora tried to read Paul's expression, but his attention was riveted to the icy patches on the gravel roadway.

They passed the entrance to the Rocking R, and after several more miles turned into a narrow lane on the opposite side of the road. They drove under a log archway with a suspended wooden sign showing the name, McCormack Simmental Cattle Company.

"Paul, is it our new home?" she asked excitedly.

He nodded. "I didn't want you to see it until it was all ready. David McCormack provided the materials, and my brothers and I have been working like crazy to get it ready." He chuckled. "Dad came over one afternoon and helped...without giving an order to anyone. Can you imagine?"

They drove past a sprawling house built from hewn logs and stone to an older, smaller log house, whose age had added to its character.

"It's charming," Nora said, trying to see more of the house in the headlight beams. "There's a light on." She turned to him curiously. "Could someone be waiting for us?"

"No," he replied, but he offered no other explanation as he helped her from the high cab.

"The boxes from your storage space are in the second bedroom. My things are there, too. Sammy McCormack stocked the kitchen with staples and some cooking basics until you get unpacked. Other than our personal items and the baby furniture at grandmother's it's all here. Even the baby crib grandma gave us. It's in the second bedroom, too, but you can't see it tonight. We can move tomorrow if you want. Hope you like it. You can rearrange it if you want—"

Nora laid her hand on his arm. "You're chattering like a magpie, Paul."

"I want you to be happy, Nora. You deserve it. Now come see your new home." He smiled and led her to the door.

She gasped as he swung the door open. Before she could move, he swept her up in his arms and carried her over the threshold and into the living room.

A fire blazed in the stone fireplace. Weathered boards taken from a mountain barn covered the walls on either side of the chimney, and antique pieces of farm implements were scattered across the boards, giving the room a feeling of living history. A singletree and a pair of hames, an old lantern, ice tongs and several old bicycle sprockets and numerous items from a pioneer kitchen were hung within reach.

The room was rustic, yet spacious and comfortable, with overstuffed chairs and a sofa positioned for conversation. The center of the floor was covered with a large blue braided rug, and a black fur rug lay near the fireplace hearth.

Paul returned from the kitchen with a bottle of wine plunged into a bucket of ice and knelt before the fireplace. He opened the bottle and poured the wine into two long-stemmed glasses, then motioned for Nora to come closer.

"Pink Chablis?" she asked, taking a sip.

"I know it's your favorite. I made myself a promise last summer." He reached for her hand, and she slid out of her coat and dropped her gold lamé purse on the floor, seeing and caring only for the man kneeling before her. "I promised I would make love to you on the bearskin rug."

"Oh, Paul," she sighed, dropping to her knees, her skirt billowing around her.

He kissed the tips of her fingers. "Tonight is different from a year ago. We were strangers then, who found each other in the darkness and made love without knowing why."

An inner heat began to burn in the pit of her stomach as Paul shed his coat and tie. She watched as he undid the buttons on his shirt, and as he exposed the matted dark hair on his chest, her heart leaped and she longed to touch him.

"Nora," he groaned, pressing her scantily covered breasts against him. His mouth seared hers, then lowered to her throat, each kiss bringing a shudder from her.

He released her and refilled their glasses. As Nora drank the wine, she caressed the bearskin rug with the flat of her palm.

"It feels as if it might tickle," she said.

"We'll see."

He threaded his fingers through her hair, allowing it to flow like spun gold. "This dress," he said, fingering the fabric over her nipple, "is the most provocative piece of clothing I've ever seen."

Without realizing Paul had moved, Nora felt the shoulder straps slip to her waist, leaving her bare.

"No," she cried, before he could touch her body again. "You must be the same." Slowly she slid his white dress shirt off his broad shoulders. "Your body...did anyone ever tell you you have a very handsome body, Paul?" She realized the wine was loosening her tongue, and she glanced toward the windows. "Can anyone see us?"

"No, love." His fingers caressed her cheek. "Have I told you how important you are to me? You're the woman who let me into her house, the woman who bore my first son, the woman whose eyes light up when I come home and who makes me feel the day has been worth all the effort. I want to make love to you. Every time I laid another piece of stone in this fireplace I knew I would soon be lying beside it with you."

She shivered at his words, but he mistook her reaction. Pulling her to her feet, he quickly dispensed with her clothing and wrapped her in a soft fleecy blanket.

"Sit down," he said, as he shed his own clothing.

He refilled the glasses then joined her beneath the warm blanket. When her glass was empty, he set it aside and eased her back on the rug. Her hair fanned out across the jet black fur, arousing his own passions.

His hands outlined the gentle curves of her hips while his lips rained tender kisses on the soft skin of her throat. The vein in her neck told him of her own desires, and her hands found the sensitive areas of his body, sending him close to the breaking point.

"I've been wanting to touch this spot all evening," he whispered as his lips sought out the rounded swell of her breast.

The sensation of moist heat from his tongue was almost unbearable. "Please," she moaned, drawing him closer until at last he filled her. Their bodies moved together rhythmically, their mutual desire merging in an explosive release.

"I wish we could stay here tonight," she murmured, tracing a path across his chest to his collarbone, as their racing heartbeats subsided.

He covered her hand, stilling its movement. "We can. I told grandmother we would be staying here tonight. I'm going to miss her, but this is our home for a while. We'll just have to be sure to visit her often." He leaned down to kiss her, then drew back in surprise.

Her eyes were moist with tears of joy as she was filled with a happiness beyond her wildest dreams.

"Did I do something wrong?" he asked.

"Oh, no, Paul, I'm just so happy because I love you and you love me and this all seems much too wonderful to be true."

He tightened his embrace. "We believed in our dreams, and they're coming true at last."

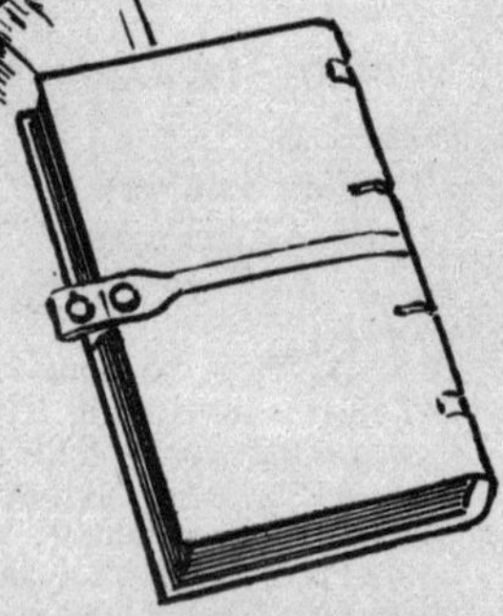